Elizabeth had to be good at it, Aidan thought as they reached her cottage. The woman he was getting to know didn't jive with what he knew her to be—a ruthless killer.

"Although I didn't ask you to, thanks for walking me home, Aidan."

He shrugged. "It's the least I could do."

She arched one eyebrow. "Really? And you expected nothing in return?"

Aidan chuckled. "Well, maybe one thing."

"And what would that be?" She tossed down the gauntlet.

One side of his mouth quirked as he slowly leaned toward her until he was barely an inch away. "Last chance."

His breath was warm against her lips. She imagined just how much warmer his mouth would be on hers. And so she closed that last little distance and covered his mouth with hers....

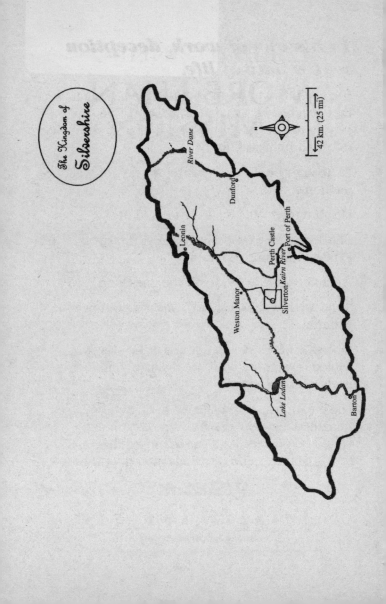

The Kingdom of Silvershire

River Dane

Dunford

Leonia

Weston Manor

Perth Castle

Silverton *Kairn River*

Port of Perth

Lake Lodam

Barton

42 km. (25 mi)

CARIDAD PIÑEIRO
MORE THAN A MISSION

Silhouette

INTIMATE MOMENTS™

Published by Silhouette Books

America's Publisher of Contemporary Romance

If you purchased this book without a cover you should be aware that this book is stolen property. It was reported as "unsold and destroyed" to the publisher, and neither the author nor the publisher has received any payment for this "stripped book."

Special thanks and acknowledgment are given to Caridad Piñeiro for her contribution to the CAPTURING THE CROWN miniseries.

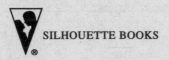 **SILHOUETTE BOOKS**

ISBN-13: 978-0-373-27498-7
ISBN-10:   0-373-27498-X

MORE THAN A MISSION

Copyright © 2006 by Harlequin Books S.A.

All rights reserved. Except for use in any review, the reproduction or utilization of this work in whole or in part in any form by any electronic, mechanical or other means, now known or hereafter invented, including xerography, photocopying and recording, or in any information storage or retrieval system, is forbidden without the written permission of the editorial office, Silhouette Books, 233 Broadway, New York, NY 10279 U.S.A.

All characters in this book have no existence outside the imagination of the author and have no relation whatsoever to anyone bearing the same name or names. They are not even distantly inspired by any individual known or unknown to the author, and all incidents are pure invention.

This edition published by arrangement with Harlequin Books S.A.

® and TM are trademarks of Harlequin Books S.A., used under license. Trademarks indicated with ® are registered in the United States Patent and Trademark Office, the Canadian Trade Marks Office and in other countries.

Visit Silhouette Books at www.eHarlequin.com

Printed in U.S.A.

Books by Caridad Piñeiro

Silhouette Intimate Moments

Darkness Calls #1283
Danger Calls #1371
Temptation Calls #1390
More Than a Mission #1428

*The Calling

CARIDAD PIÑEIRO

attended Villanova University on a Presidential Scholarship and earned her Juris Doctor from St. John's University. Caridad is the first female partner of an Intellectual Property firm in Manhattan. Caridad is a multipublished and award-winning author whose love of writing developed when her fifth grade teacher assigned a project—to write a book for a class lending library. She has been hooked ever since.

Look for *Death Calls* and two other books in THE CALLING Vampires series beginning in November 2006! Book #2 in the series, *Danger Calls*, was a *Catalina* Magazine Top 5 read for 2005 and *Darkness Calls* was an *Affaire de Coeur* 2004 Reader's Poll Finalist for Best Paranormal. Look for *Sex and the South Beach Chicas* in September 2006 from Downtown Press.

When not writing, Caridad is a wife, mom and attorney! You can contact Caridad by visiting www.caridad.com.

To my mother-in-law, Mary Scordato, who opened her heart to me and has always been there when I needed her! I couldn't ask for a more loving and wonderful mother-in-law.

Chapter 1

She's to be taken alive, Aidan Spaulding reminded himself as he walked the streets of Leonia, trying to become familiar with the lay of the land before heading to his latest assignment—identifying the killer of Prince Reginald, the man who would have been king of Silvershire.

Corbett Lazlo, Aidan's boss, had received information that a world-renowned female assassin was behind the killing. The Sparrow, as she was known, was believed to have poisoned the prince. Aidan was to confirm that and try to capture the elusive gun for hire.

Aidan had more personal reasons for wanting the Sparrow caught. Two years earlier, he and his best friend, Mitchell Lama, had been on the trail of a suspected terrorist as part of another Lazlo Group detail. They had been about to close in on their suspect, unaware that the man they were seeking was also being sought by the Sparrow.

Mitch and he had split up in the narrow and twisting alleyways of Rome's Trastevere section, communicating via walkie-talkie as they attempted to corner their man.

When the walkie-talkie in his hand had gone dead, Aidan had realized his friend was in trouble. After years in the military together, Mitch knew better than to go incommunicado without signaling his partner. The nature of the mission had changed suddenly as Aidan raced through the alleyways, now trying to locate Mitch. He had finally found the friend who was almost like a brother sprawled on the ancient cobblestones of a back alley.

Mitch had been nearly gutted and was barely alive. Somehow, though, his friend had managed one last word before he died in Aidan's arms—*Sparrow*.

He had been looking for her ever since, intent on avenging Mitch's death. Now here she was, being handed to him on a silver platter. The only problem was, he could do nothing about it until after the Lazlo Group had all the answers it needed regarding Prince Reginald's murder. But after that…

Nothing would keep him from giving the Sparrow just what she deserved.

The young woman they suspected of being the Sparrow— Elizabeth Moore, aka Elizabeth Cavanaugh—ran a restaurant in this modest seaside town. The restaurant—apparently a cover for her real occupation—had become quite well-known for its seafood and Silvershire-inspired cuisine.

He had seen the help wanted sign go up late yesterday morning in her restaurant's front window, so it was the perfect time to see about applying for the bartending position.

Pulling his PDA off his belt as he approached the Sparrow's restaurant, he used the walkie-talkie adapter he had built into the unit to cue Lucia, the Lazlo group's top computer specialist, to see if she was picking up the signal from the earpiece he was wearing.

"Mixmaster to Red Rover. Come in Red Rover. I'm about to go in."

Lucia's chuckle crackled across the airwaves a moment

before she said, "Mixmaster… Do we really have to do this stupid name thing?"

Aidan smiled. Lucia was never one for clandestine shenanigans. Shutting off his walkie-talkie, he replied, "No problema, Lucia. Can you hear me?"

"Loud and clear, Blender Boy," she responded.

He immediately asked, "Kir Royale?"

There was a barely noticeable pause before Lucia said, "One part creme de cassis to five parts champagne."

Satisfied that the wire was working, he started walking toward the restaurant and said, "Let's get this show on the road."

The sun was warm on her back as she tended the garden at the front of the restaurant. Wildly spreading nasturtiums lapped over onto the large granite slabs that made up the patio where guests shared drinks while they waited for a table inside the ivy-covered stone building that housed her restaurant.

Carefully she deadheaded older blossoms and picked others for inclusion in one of the seasonal salads she was offering on this week's menu. She was just about finished when she heard a footfall behind her. A man walked through the opening of the low stone wall that separated her property from the main road. A very attractive man.

Slipping the basket holding her gatherings onto her arm, she strolled toward him, easing off her gardening gloves as she did so.

"May I help you?" Elizabeth asked as she met him by the path leading to the restaurant. She realized she had to look up slightly to meet his gaze. He was about half a foot taller than her with a lean athletic build that accentuated the long lines of his body.

He motioned to her front window with one hand and replied, "I noticed the sign. I'm here to apply for the bartender's position."

She examined him more carefully, from the faded and

sinfully tight jeans to his logo T-shirt and black leather jacket. He looked more like a tourist on vacation than someone interested in permanent employment. "I'm sorry. I didn't quite catch your name."

He held out his hand with a brisk, almost military snap. "Aidan Rawlings. Are you the owner?"

With a quick glance at her hand to make sure it wasn't too dirty from her gardening, she shook his hand and said, "Elizabeth Moore. Chief cook and bottle washer. Literally."

He smiled with teeth too white and too perfect for normal humans. They seemed apropos with his shaggy and sunstreaked blond hair and eyes so blue she couldn't believe he wasn't wearing colored contacts. His smile broadened as he noticed her perusal of him and that she was still busily shaking his hand.

Yanking it away, she wiped her hand down on the gardening apron she wore, realizing her palm had gotten sweaty from the brief contact. "I'm sorry. You said you were here for the bartender's job?"

He nodded and tucked his hands into his jeans pockets. Or maybe it was better to say, tucked the tips of his fingers into those pockets, since the jeans were so tight they didn't really leave a lot of room for anything else besides his long lean legs and...

She stopped herself from proceeding with the perusal.

"Is the job still available?" He rocked back and forth on his heels as he asked, apparently growing uncomfortable, but then again, so was she. Not much of a surprise considering she generally avoided strangers, in particular, men like this one.

Handsome, danger-to-your-common-sense kind of men.

"Do you have experience?" After she asked, she began to walk toward the door of the restaurant and he followed beside her, keeping his paces small to accommodate her shorter legs.

"I've worked in a number of bars," he replied with a careless shrug.

She supposed that he had, but not as a bartender. There was something about him. Something in the way he moved and in the slight swagger that screamed Bad Boy. She could picture him as either a bouncer—he had an air that said he could take care of himself—or an exotic dancer, but not a bartender.

As she reached the door, she faced him. "I'm sorry, Mr....Rawlings was it?"

"How about you just call me Aidan?" he said with a practiced smile that had probably swept more than one woman off her feet. Aidan, however, was going to get a swift lesson in the art of Just Say No!

"I appreciate you coming by, but the position—"

"Is still available, right?"

She responded to his statement with a subtle drop of her head as if she didn't want to acknowledge it. "Quite frankly, my restaurant isn't the kind of place for a Tom Cruise *Cocktail* redux."

He actually jerked back as if slapped and a stain of color came to his sharply defined cheeks. "Excuse me?"

"I just don't think you're the right type." And he definitely was not used to being turned down by a woman.

Surprise appeared once more on his face, followed by what she would possibly call admiration until he carefully schooled his expression.

"And what type are you looking for exactly?" he asked and placed his hands on his hips.

"Someone more...professional. This is a four-star restaurant and my patrons expect—"

"Uptight and pompous? Fair enough." With that, he turned and walked away, but she couldn't help but notice just how nice a derriere he had. Not that it would change her mind.

She needed someone who wouldn't cause trouble and, although pleasant to look at, Aidan Rawlings was trouble with a capital *T*.

Chapter 2

"Crash and burn."

Lucia's words cut rudely across the airwaves and into the earpiece as he hurried from the Sparrow's restaurant. He was at the edge of the property when something compelled him to look back.

She was standing at the door, still watching him, and when their gazes collided from across the distance, a becoming blush stained her cheeks before she escaped into the building.

Aidan smiled. Good. The lady was not as unaffected as she let on.

"Shut up, Cordez," he whispered beneath his breath.

"All bad moody are we? What do you plan on doing now?" Lucia asked while he continued on to the hotel at which the team was staying, only a few blocks from the restaurant.

"If she wants someone a little more professional, that's what she'll get."

He was already at the door of the hotel when Lucia quipped, "That may take a lot of work."

He ignored her dig and headed up to their suite. Inside, Lucia was busily working on her laptop.

Not that they'd needed it today, Aidan thought as he walked over and stood behind her, watching as she entered a date onto a list she was compiling.

"What's that?" he said and motioned to the screen.

Lucia looked up over her shoulder. "Corbett's contacts—"

"So it's Corbett now is it?" he teased, well aware that Lucia had a crush on the mysterious head of their group.

"His contact at MI6 provided a list of kills that they attribute to the Sparrow. That's in this column." She pointed to one list and Aidan scrutinized the schedule, which comprised nearly a dozen incidents in the last six years. The Sparrow had been busy. There was just one glaring error.

"Mitch's name is not on the list."

Concern flashed across Lucia's face a moment before she said, "MI6 can't connect Mitch to the Sparrow."

"Well, they're wrong. I know what Mitch said to me." He sat on the edge of the desk and crossed his arms.

Lucia laid a hand on his forearm as if to comfort him. "Maybe Mitch was trying to tell you something else about her."

He thought about it, but what kinds of things did a dying man think important enough to say? In his book, first was the name of his killer. "The Sparrow did it. End of discussion."

Seeing that he had gotten his defenses up, Lucia said nothing else, but instead began entering another set of dates onto the list. A number of the dates and locations matched those for the Sparrow's kills. "What are you doing now?"

"More than you are, clearly," she teased, but then added, "Whoever spilled the beans to Corbett about Elizabeth being the Sparrow wasn't completely sure. So I did a search to see where she might have gone. Contests, expos, vacations and…"

Fingers tapping away on the computer keys, she finished her entries. Beside a number of the dates that had already been there courtesy of MI6, there were now four entries for Chef Elizabeth Moore that matched.

"Seems like we have a pretty good candidate for the Sparrow," he said.

"It appears that way. There's just too much coincidence, including this weekend here." Lucia motioned to one entry on her list. "She was at a cooking expo in the town next to the prince's estate. He was found dead that weekend."

"Poisoned, which seems to be a favorite method for our assassin." Which could be why MI6 hadn't listed Mitch, although some of the Sparrow's other kills had been the plain old get-up-close-and-kill-them type. Which made him wonder just what motivated her. Sticking a knife in someone... Seeing that look of surprise fade to a lifeless stare...

He knew it well, having had to kill more than once on his assignments as an army Ranger. It wasn't easy even if you told yourself that you had to do it. That it was either you and your men, or the man whose life you had just taken. But that look never left you. Not even when you slept.

Like the final expression on Mitch's face. One of surprise and possibly even regret. For months after Mitch's death, that image had chased him through his nightmares.

"Aidan?" Lucia asked, apparently sensing that she had lost him.

"I'm going to review the Elizabeth Moore file. Do you think you could give me a copy of that when you're done? And can you add Mitch to the list and see if she was in Rome then?"

"You got it."

He went to his room, slipped out the earpiece and placed it on a mahogany desk that held an assortment of other electronic gadgets he had designed. Grabbing the file on Elizabeth Moore once more, he plopped down onto the bed and began to review the facts.

Elizabeth was an only child whose parents had been local

merchants. When she was fourteen, her parents had been found murdered in their fish shop. The murder had never been solved. The file hinted at possible involvement by members of the Royal Family's ministers to quash parts of the investigation.

He paused, wondering if that was what had set the Sparrow on the path she had chosen? He was still lucky enough to have his parents and couldn't imagine what it might have been like to lose them at such a young age, especially to an act of violence, and then find justice denied.

The photo of the Sparrow stared at him from the left side of the file. No hint of the wide and engaging smile he had seen earlier today. The photo had apparently been taken in Prague when an MI6 operative on another mission had noticed her standing in a square. The serious-looking young woman had fit the description of the Sparrow that MI6 had gleaned over years of investigations. With the renowned assassin suspected of being in town, the operative had decided to take the picture just in case.

It might not even be her, he thought. There must be millions of women who matched the general description— five foot six, brown hair, brown eyes and a slim build.

Not that he would have called her hair just brown. As she had stood in the sun, he'd noticed the vibrant melange of reds, browns and even hints of blond. And her eyes—they had been more like the color of a rich sherry. As for the slim build, definitely slender but with curves in all the right places.

Losin' it, he chastised himself. The lady might be attractive, but that did nothing to change the fact that she was suspected of killing nearly a dozen people. Including Mitch.

It was up to him to get close to her, to confirm whether or not she was the Sparrow and whether she had murdered King Weston's heir, and then she could be punished for her crimes.

Which meant he had to attempt yet again to get her to hire him for the bartending position that was now vacant since Corbett Lazlo had arranged for a friend in London to hire away Elizabeth's bartender.

Lazlo's connections were part of what made the Lazlo Group tops in what they did—handling delicate and often-times dangerous investigations, like this one involving Prince Reginald's murder.

Pampered and spoiled royals like Prince Reginald held little appeal for Aidan. From what he had read in the dossier provided to him, Prince Reginald had been a selfish dilettante who probably would have made a hell of a bad leader for the centuries-old island kingdom.

Not that he involved himself in politics, since his nomadic life rarely gave him reason to grow attached to any particular place, and he had no interest in what happened in this tiny little town. At least, not in anything that wasn't related to this mission.

As for the Sparrow, he thought, she wanted professional? He would give it to her.

The bartending part was under control thanks to the earpiece and the program he had loaded on his and Lucia's PDAs. He'd resorted to that after his best attempts at memo-rizing an assortment of drink recipes had failed. He was a magna cum laude grad of MIT in a number of majors, none of which included Mixology 101.

But now he had to deal with his other dilemma—getting the Sparrow to hire him. He walked to the closet. Inside were an assortment of jeans, but also a few suits. He wasn't normally a suit-and-tie kind of guy. In some ways, he found them too much like the uniform he'd had to wear for so many years in the military. Now that he was in the private sector, he preferred his clothes to be casual. It suited his rebellious nature better.

In fact, the last time he had worn a suit had been to Mitch's funeral two years ago. It was one of the suits in the closet. Somehow apropos, he thought, as he reached for it and pulled it out. The suit was dark charcoal-gray and designer—Hel-mut Lang. Mitch, who had always insisted that his clothes and women be top-drawer, had forced him to buy it, claiming that his friend was never going to meet the right kind of woman if he looked like a Hell's Angels reject or a derelict surf dude.

Aidan had to admit the suit was gorgeous. Maybe it was just what the Sparrow had had in mind when she'd said that her type was someone more professional.

Watch out, Sparrow, 'cause here I come.

Elizabeth was running late. After doing all her shopping and advising her sous chef and assistants as to what to prep for inclusion in that night's dinner specials, she'd decided to tackle the slightly overgrown flowerbeds in the back of the restaurant during her afternoon break. In this backyard garden, which faced the shore, she had created an area for alfresco dining and dancing beneath the stars.

She was rounding the corner of the building on the way to the front door when she smacked into someone heading toward the back patio. Hard hands grabbed hold of her to keep her from falling. "I'm sorry," she said, noticing not just the strength in the hands clutching her, but the fine fabric of the suit jacket as she grabbed tight.

She finally looked up and the familiar blue of his eyes gazed down at her, nearly laughing. "No, *I'm* sorry. Your sous chef said you were out back."

He released her and took a step away, which allowed her to get a complete picture of his total transformation. A suit the color of deep slate—definitely expensive—accented his lean muscular build and broad shoulders. His shirt was a pale gray and he was wearing a silk tie that had a stylish Keith Haring kind of pattern in maroon on a dark blue-gray background. His shaggy hair was brushed off his face, the longish strands secured somehow, exposing the sharp lines of his cheeks and jaw.

He cleaned up well, she thought, although a part of her was remembering yesterday's bad-boy look and regretting the change.

"Mr. Rawlings," she said with a polite nod of her head. "I must confess that I wasn't expecting to see you again."

He offered his arm and she looped hers around his, slightly

surprised by the gallant gesture. She walked with him around the side of the building and to the front door.

"I'm not a man who's easily dissuaded, Ms. Moore," he said as they stopped at the entrance to the restaurant.

"And what if I told you the position had been filled?" she asked with an upward arch of her brow.

"A gentleman such as myself wouldn't dare call a lady a liar, but…" He pointed to the help wanted sign that was still posted in the front window.

Heat rose to her cheeks, much as it had yesterday when he had caught her appreciating his backside. Definitely not good. The last thing she needed around here was someone who would be distracting her from all that she had to do. "Mr. Rawlings—"

He stepped to stand in front of her, held out his arms and said, "You wanted professional. So here I am."

"I did say that, only—"

"I know my way around a bar," he jumped in.

"I suspected as much, but—"

"What have you got to lose?" he interrupted yet again.

Elizabeth gripped the handle of her gathering basket tightly and examined him once more. Dressed like this, she could definitely see him preparing drinks for her patrons. Heck, he was dressed nicely enough to be one of her patrons. But could he mix a mean cocktail?

"A martini," she said out loud.

"Excuse me?" he asked, clearly confused.

"How do you make a martini?" she clarified and nervously swung the basket back and forth a bit, hoping for failure on his part.

He raised one sunbleached eyebrow as if to say, Aw, come on. Try something harder. Then he rattled off, "One and a half ounces of gin. Dash of dry vermouth." He paused, smiled and said, "Shaken, not stirred."

She had to chuckle at his imitation of Sean Connery because it was dead-on. "Too easy. How about a…" She hesitated, trying to think of one of the more unusual drinks with which she was familiar. "A B-52," she finally said and watched him squirm, but not for long.

"The drink, right, and not the alternative band from Athens, Georgia?"

Smiling, she confirmed, "Right. The drink."

"One ounce each of Bailey's Irish Cream, Kahlua and Grand Marnier." He picked up his hands, mimicked the shaking, and she got the rest of the recipe. Not to mention getting the very appealing way the man could move his hips.

Fresh heat came to her face. She gave it one last try to attempt to convince herself it was insane to consider him for the job. "You'll never get this one—Mexican Sunset."

He grinned. It was an appealing little-boy kind of grin. A gotcha grin. "Too easy. Bottle of beer, preferably Corona, garnished with a slice of lime and less a sip so you can add the sloe gin. I'm assuming the sloe gin is homemade. I understand there's a great abundance after the fall harvest of the local blackthorn bushes."

He knew his stuff. She had to give him that. "You don't strike me as the type that will stay for long," she said, firing the last salvo she had held in reserve.

He hesitated since she had scored a direct hit and the grin ran away from his face as he grew serious. "You're right. Dad was an army man so I'm used to a wandering kind of life."

"I know the type," she interjected, thinking of her sister Dani and all her travels.

"So you understand, then. But the way I see it, you need a bartender and I'm here. Not going anywhere for a while and I promise that when I do decide to go, because it *will* happen, that I'll give you plenty of time to find someone else before I run."

Promises. She knew just how often they got broken. But he had a point—she needed a bartender. The past few nights had been horrendous as she tried to cook while at the same time helping out the wait staff with the drinks. "It doesn't pay much, but tips are generally good. If you get here by five, dinner's included. You can start tomorrow."

He smiled and held out his hand to seal the deal. She hesitated before she shook it, and he said, "To new adventures."

"I'm not the adventurous type, Mr. Rawlings," she replied, hoping to make it clear that she had no interest in anything he might propose.

His grin broadened. "Aidan, please. And, Ms. Moore—"

"Elizabeth. All my employees call me Elizabeth," she corrected and pulled her hand from his since it was starting to feel rather warm. Again.

"Elizabeth," he said and took a step toward her. "I think it's going to be quite an experience working together."

She suspected he was right. "See you at five, Aidan. And while the suit is…nice, a white shirt and dark slacks will do."

With that, she turned and walked into the building.

"Score one for the Mixmaster," Aidan heard in the earpiece as he headed for the street.

"Told you she couldn't resist my charm," he replied and hurried back to the hotel, eager now that it looked like the investigation might finally get under way.

"And here I thought it was those drink recipes I was feeding you, only… How did you know about the sloe gin?" Lucia asked.

"You never go into unknown territory without doing your research, Cordez. So I did a little fact-gathering on this town. Did you know that…" As he walked, he recited the details that he remembered, being careful not to be noticed whenever he walked by someone.

He was back at the hotel within ten minutes and found that besides Lucia, Walker Shaw, the Lazlo group's psychiatrist, waited for him in the suite, as well. "What brings you here?" he asked and patted the other man on the back in greeting.

"Snazzy," Walker said as he perused Aidan's clothing.

Aidan held out his hands. "The lady fell for it."

"Well, that's good. At least there's some progress going on here." The frustration was apparent in Walker's demeanor. "We haven't been able to do anything yet with the information Zara and I found. So for now, we're relying on whatever details the two of you manage to get."

"Not too much pressure," Lucia quipped and handed Walker a piece of paper.

It was a copy of the list she had provided to Aidan yesterday. Walker examined it and then looked up at him. "Seems like we're on the right track. It's just too much coincidence that Elizabeth Moore turns up in a lot of the same spots as the Sparrow."

"Including Rome," Lucia added nervously, shooting a half glance at Aidan after she said it.

"What?" He ripped the list from Walker's hands and quickly read until he came to the date and location of Mitch's death. Beside it was a new entry indicating that Elizabeth had been in Rome as part of a contingent for the Silvershire Tourist Board.

"When did you find this out?" He jabbed the air in Lucia's direction with the paper.

"Late last night."

"What?" he repeated, his voice a little louder than before. "Why didn't you say something *before* I went to see her?"

Lucia shook her head. "Duh. I didn't think it would accomplish anything besides getting you angry."

"Angry? You're right that I'm angry. You're part of *my* team and you withheld vital information," he nearly screamed at her.

"Because you're totally capable of compartmentalizing your emotions to maintain neutrality about this job?" Walker said facetiously. He, more than any of them, knew how hard Mitch's death had been on Aidan, who blamed himself for making the decision that the two of them should split up. He had been as responsible for Mitch's death as the Sparrow.

"Cut the psychobabble bullshit, Walker. I understand the nature of the assignment."

"Which is to find Prince Reginald's killer. Period." The other man's tone brooked no disagreement.

Aidan knew that on one level, Walker was right. They had been hired to identify Prince Reginald's murderer, not Mitch's. Taking a deep breath and relaxing his hands—he hadn't even realized he'd made them into tight fists—he let his anger flow out of him. Anger was a distraction. There was no room for distractions with a killer as savvy as the Sparrow.

"I understand and I'm sorry. It's just tough at times, but…I've only failed once at an assignment." He didn't need to mention that Mitch had died as a result of that failure. "I won't fail this time."

Walker stood and laid a hand on Aidan's shoulder. "We all understand, Aidan. And we're here for you."

"Together we will figure this out," Aidan reassured Walker and Lucia, but then excused himself.

Tomorrow he started working for the Sparrow. He had to be alert and ready to handle any kind of situation that presented itself. Which meant that he needed to do some additional research, and prepare a few gadgets that would allow him to keep a close watch on Elizabeth Moore.

He also needed to get a better sense of the town. With that in mind, he quickly reviewed a map of the area that had been included in his dossier and then headed out again.

Leaving the hotel, he walked briskly to the furthest edge of the town where the docks were located. He stepped from the main street onto the large and very old granite slabs that led to the docks. Although it was late in the day, fisherman were hauling boxes and bushels with their catches onto the docks to be transported to the nearby fish market.

The scene reminded him of one of the seaside towns he had lived in briefly before his father's army career had demanded they move somewhere else. Although he didn't consider himself a settling-down kind of guy, it occurred to him that if he ever did decide to let some moss grow under his feet, it might be in a town like this one.

Mitch and he had always loved to go surfing, sailing or fishing whenever their assignments gave them a break. His best friend who was dead. Murdered by the woman who had hired him earlier that morning.

With that thought in mind, Aidan hastened his pace, familiarizing himself with the area around the Sparrow's restaurant. He noticed the clean and tidy homes along the streets, a combination of older stone buildings and slightly more modern stucco-and-wood edifices.

Nearing the edge of the village, which was not all that far from the wharf, mom-and-pop-type stores appeared here and there, interspersed with the residences. Eventually, he was within sight of the restaurant once more.

He couldn't help but admire the carefully kept gardens and manicured lawns surrounding the central building. As he slowly strolled past, he noticed a cottage way in the back, close to the shore. It was similar in style to the restaurant building, made of stone with a slate roof, but with two stories. Colorful blossoms graced the front of the cottage while in back, tall sea grasses waved with the ocean breeze.

If he recalled correctly from his files, the cottage was the Sparrow's home. Her nest.

In time, he would get in there and locate the information he needed. He was sure about that. He would do whatever he had to in order to complete this mission since it was more than a mission to him. It was long-denied payback for his friend's death.

He only hoped that once the mission was completed, he would finally have the peace of mind that had eluded him for the past two years.

With that thought in mind, he hurried back to the hotel to prepare for his first day of work for the Sparrow.

Chapter 3

The early-morning hours at the markets were the ones Elizabeth liked the best. She enjoyed investigating the stalls to search out ingredients for something new and playfully haggling with the vendors over the prices. As she walked past one merchant or another, they shouted their greetings. Most of them had known her since she was a child.

Sometimes, if she finished with the shopping early enough, she would walk down to the water's edge and take the long way back home. If the tide was just right, she could skirt the edges of the tidal pools lingering along the shore and find what the ocean had left behind. Small crabs, seashells and even some lobsters every now and then.

From the shore just past her cottage, she could see the mile or more to where fisherman harvested mussels from the pilings of an ancient stone bridge. The Romans had built the bridge centuries earlier to join Leonia to the smaller seaside town of Tiberia across the narrowest part of the harbor. She served those fresh mussels every day in a garlic-and-white-wine-infused broth. Her parents used to sell them in the fish shop they had owned at the time of their deaths.

She could understand why her sister, Dani, found it so hard to be in Leonia. Everywhere she went there were reminders of their parents.

Elizabeth continued walking along the shore, the bag filled with her purchases dragging at her arm. Memories dragging at her heart as she recalled her mother, father and Dani strolling together along the beach. At times, she felt totally alone with all of them gone. Forcing such thoughts away on what had started out as a delightful day, she trudged onward, trying to enjoy the warmth of the sun and the caress of an ocean breeze sweeping along the coast.

At the beach behind her cottage, she detoured up a rocky path until she was at the edge of the back patio to the restaurant. She paused but a moment to appreciate all that she had built with her hard work. Then she was striding across the yard and to a side door by the vegetable garden. As she neared the entrance, the sounds of activity welcomed her. Walking into the kitchen, she greeted Natalie, her friend and sous chef, who inclined her head in the direction of the front of the restaurant. "Someone's up there for you. Says he's the new bartender."

Elizabeth placed her bag on a prep table and shook a cramp out of one arm. "If you could unpack, I'll see what he needs."

Elizabeth walked to the bar tucked into a far corner at the front of the restaurant. The driving rhythm of the B-52s' "Love Shack" greeted her—Aidan had a boombox on the polished surface of the mahogany bar and was rocking along, his arms and hips moving to the beat. She couldn't help admiring his grace and the sexy shift of his body to the music. It reminded her of her earlier observation that exotic dancer might well have been his previous employment.

When he realized he had been caught in mid–hip grind, he stopped dead. "In honor of the day you hired me," he explained, but quickly added, "It's not too loud, is it?" Hot color rode on his defined cheeks as he crammed his fingertips into those tight jeans' pockets and shot her an embarrassed grin.

"Not at all. It's just a little different from our usual musical fare," she said and motioned to the sound system tucked onto a low shelf behind the bar.

With a quick look at the stereo, Aidan shrugged. "Didn't want to mess with anything until I was familiar with things. It's okay that I came early to get acquainted, right?"

Getting acquainted, huh? Elizabeth told herself not to read too much into his choice of words. He was, after all, someone who would eventually leave, and getting acquainted with him could cause nothing but problems. "Feel free to familiarize yourself with the liquor stock and other supplies. The music selection is generally a bit more sedate. When you're ready, I'll show you the wine cellar."

Great, Aidan thought. A wine cellar meant another list with which he would have to deal. In his ear, Lucia advised, "I'm on it. Make sure to bring home copies of the wine list and menu."

"I'll let you know when I'm ready for the wines," he said to Elizabeth, and then continued. "In the meantime, I'll see if we're low on anything." After he finished, he examined Elizabeth's face, trying to gauge whether she had overheard Lucia. There was nothing there but interest of a different kind.

Or at least that's what his guy radar was telling him. He hoped it wasn't wrong because it might make the task of getting close to the Sparrow that much easier, although he was a little disconcerted about how someone supposedly as elusive as the Sparrow was apparently so easy to read.

Unless she's a very good actress and is stringing you along?

"Thanks," she replied and pointed with one finger to the back of the restaurant. He noticed then that she wore just clear polish on short, blunt-cut nails. No rings or jewelry of any kind. The hands of someone who used their hands to earn a living. Either chef or assassin.

She continued. "I'll be in the kitchen. If you need limes, cream or anything else, it's in the large fridges. Jeremy, the old bartender, would keep some supplies handy in the fridge beneath the bar."

"Got it," he replied with a quick salute and his most engaging smile as a way to see if his earlier read had been wrong.

Elizabeth delayed briefly, seemingly unsure of whether to go or stay. Then with a shy wavering smile, she bolted from the bar and to the kitchen.

Aidan waited until he was sure she was gone and not returning, and then went to work.

From a well-worn knapsack he had tucked beneath the bar, he pulled out what looked like four fat sewing needles and slipped them into the back pocket of his jeans. Stepping from behind the bar, he scoped out where he could hide one of them, but still get a clear shot from the fiberoptic cameras built into the ends of the thick needles.

He settled on easing one into the stopper on a commemorative liquor flask sitting on the top shelf behind the bar. The empty flask was obviously kept for decoration and would not be moved often. That camera should give Lucia a clear shot of anyone in the anterior part of the building.

"Are you reading this signal?" he said softly and when Lucia confirmed the view was good, he moved to the other side of the dining room. On an end table tucked into a corner, a candlestick, flower basket and brass lamp in keeping with the restaurant's traditional-style décor had been placed.

Dark woods and floral wallpaper graced the walls of the room. Landscapes of the Silvershire countryside were scattered here and there, and at one end of the room, a large stone fireplace held logs ready to be lit if the weather called for it. The curtains at the windows were sheer, offering gorgeous views of the gardens and the shore beyond.

The flowers on the end table were fresh and sure to be discarded shortly and while the candle was newer, it, too, would be subject to regular handling and replacement. He settled on working the camera into the top edge of the ivory-colored lampshade, focusing it on the dining area.

Lucia confirmed that the signal was clear, and, satisfied with what he'd done, Aidan paused for a moment to consider how to approach bugging the kitchen. That area was busier than most and usually occupied. Plus, he really had little cause to go in there, except for those supplies Elizabeth had mentioned earlier. Deciding to use that as an excuse to inspect the area, he hurried back to the bar and was thankful that the fridge Elizabeth had mentioned was empty of anything other than an old-fashioned glass bottle of cream.

Quickly striding to the kitchen, he pushed through the door to find Elizabeth and another young woman standing before a table, glumly looking down at something.

"It's okay, Natalie. It just takes practice," Elizabeth said, laid a hand on the other woman's shoulders and gave a comforting pat.

He moved behind them and with his greater height, peered over their shoulders to examine the dish sitting before them. Whatever it had once been, now it was a pile of stuff colored a muddy shade of brown. Blackened edges tenaciously gripped the sides of a white cooking dish. The center had sunk down, creating a network of cracks in the surface that revealed something gooey and unappealing beneath. "What is that?"

With a sniff and a quavery voice, Natalie replied, "My final exam."

"Oh."

"It's a chocolate soufflé," Elizabeth corrected with a glare over her shoulder and once again patted Natalie's back in a reassuring gesture. "We'll work through it together, Nat. By tomorrow, you'll be an expert and ready for the test."

Natalie sniffed one last time as she picked up the dish with oven-mitted hands. "Let me dispose of this mess."

When she walked away, Elizabeth faced him, clearly annoyed. "She's just learning," she explained, defending the younger woman.

Aidan held up his hands to ward off further comment. "I didn't mean anything by it. I just came for some supplies."

Elizabeth accepted his apology and gracefully motioned with her hands to the spacious and orderly kitchen. "Well while you're here, I may as well lay out the rules for this area. One—don't annoy the chefs and two—don't touch the chefs' knives. You've already broken rule one."

Great. He'd pissed her off. As for her knives… "Your knives being—"

She slipped past him to go to one of the work tables. On its surface was a cylindrical leather pouch tied with a ribbon of leather. He followed Elizabeth and watched as she nimbly undid the tie, grabbed one side of the pouch and with a quick toss, unfurled it to reveal a collection of about a dozen different blades. "*My* knives," she said and held her hand out to emphasize the point.

Before he could say anything else, she whipped one large knife from its holder and with a batonlike twirl of the handle through her fingers, she then slipped the blade into a holder on the belt riding low on her hips. A practiced move done with ease. Too much ease, he thought, replaying in his mind how quickly she had taken the knife—one that was easily about eight inches long—and gracefully maneuvered it onto her belt.

Had she gutted Mitch with as much skill?

He bit back his anger and said, "Neat trick. Where did you learn it?" Even as he said that, he was reaching for another knife, but she slapped his hand away.

"Remember— Don't touch the knives. As for where—in cooking school," she explained, one hand resting on the table near the pouch, the other just above the knife at her belt. Her hip was cocked to one side, like a gunslinger ready to draw. He wondered if she was getting ready to use the knife on him. If he had pushed too far.

When he met her gaze—that sherry-colored, drown-in-me gaze—he realized she was almost testing him. Seeing if he'd follow the rules she'd laid down, as if thinking he wouldn't or that maybe he was the kind of guy who liked to touch—and not just knives. Her jaw was set in a determined little jut, confirming his read wasn't all that wrong. "I get it, Elizabeth. Don't touch."

Elizabeth nodded and realized that Aidan had gotten the dual message in her words. It both pleased and disappointed, but she told herself not to be disappointed since Aidan was just passing through.

"Glad you get it. It will keep things simpler. Do you want to see where the wines are kept?" She motioned to an old wooden door, made from a few hand-hewn planks, at the far side of the kitchen.

He gave her the go-ahead curtly. "May as well get it over with. I can collect my supplies later."

Elizabeth walked to the door, which led down into the cellar, Aidan close behind her. She opened it, flipped a switch on the wall, and then went down the flight of stairs to a large space that ran beneath the entire restaurant. As she reached the bottom step, she pointed to the far wall where a series of racks held her collection of wines. "We keep the stock first by color and then by region. Whites closest to the floor where it's cooler. Reds along the top."

She continued walking, too conscious of Aidan behind her, but as they moved to the racks, it wasn't the wine that seemed to get his attention.

"What's that?" he asked and as she turned to look at him, she realized he was looking at the far side of the cellar, where there was a home gym, boxing bag, mat, lockers and a safe.

"A gym. You're welcome to use it during the hours the restaurant isn't serving meals. The equipment is too noisy otherwise."

A hard look came to his face, but he schooled it and gestured with his hand to the racks of wine. "Anything I can't touch down here?"

Elizabeth shook her head. "While all the wines are excellent vintages, they're generally moderately priced. No sense gouging the customers."

He walked to one of the racks, ran a finger along the bottles as he seemingly inspected the labels. He moved from one rack to the next in that fashion, perusing them intently.

She walked to stand by the end of one rack and clarified, "Italians and local wines are in the first two racks, Californian in the middle, some Australian, Chilean and French in the final section."

Pausing by the rack of Italian vintages and removing one bottle for a closer inspection, he said, "How do you choose which wines you'll carry?"

Elizabeth joined him, took the bottle from his hands and examined the label. With a nonchalant shrug, she said, "Tasting trips. Some are recommended to me by others. Like this one." She returned the bottle to him and continued. "I was in Rome a few years back and someone said I might like it."

This time his reaction to her statement was quite physical. His shoulders tensed and a muscle ticked ominously along his jaw. "Rome, huh?" he asked as, with almost exaggerated care, he placed the bottle back onto the wooden rack.

"Yes. A beautiful city. Have you ever been there?" she asked, wondering if there was something about that city that bothered him.

He faced her, the hard set of his jaw relaxing a little, and shrugged. "No. I tend to stay to the coasts since I like the water."

"Surf much?" Her question coaxed back that little-boy smile.

"Surf. Swim. Fish. I'm an ocean kind of guy."

"Leonia's a good place for all of that," she said and headed for the stairs once more, needing to get to work.

"I'll keep that in mind while I'm here, as well as the gym," Aidan said and followed the attractive sway of her hips all the way up to the kitchen level. The lady had a nice ass and being a guy, he wasn't about to ignore the view.

Once they were back in the kitchen, she made a beeline for the prep table, where Natalie and another young woman were busily laying out a variety of ingredients. Elizabeth joined them, suggesting one thing or another and giving instructions. Her tone with them was patient and friendly. Despite her easy demeanor, however, her mind now seemed totally on the work that needed to be done.

Which was perfect for him. He strolled to the large refrigerators in the kitchen, checking out the surroundings to see where he could place a camera. A speaker up at one side of the kitchen caught his eye after he had removed some limes and lemons from the fridge and was returning to the bar.

Perfect, he thought. He'd have to wait for a lull in activity in the kitchen first, but since they were all so busy there now, it gave him a perfect opportunity in the cellar. Grabbing a menu and a pad of paper as if to take notes, he went back down to the cellar unnoticed and once there, walked to the farthest part of the room, near the safe and lockers.

The lockers were like those you would find in a gym or a school. He opened the first few to find some empty and some holding assorted clothes and bags, possibly belonging to Elizabeth's staff. The last one had an ordinary combination lock that might not take much time to pick. He noted the make, model and serial number to see if there was a way to get a master key to simplify things.

Next, he turned his attention to the safe. Big, gray and old. A bit of rust along the edges, likely as a result of the sea air and dampness in the cellar. Despite that, the lock spun freely and the safe was in generally good condition. Again, he noted the information on the safe in the hopes of getting inside next time he could.

He suspected the safe would hold what most businesses would safeguard—important papers, cash and the like. But he wondered what else it and the locker might hold that wasn't related to the restaurant. The Sparrow's records and weapons?

A noise from above reminded him he had to get moving. Shifting back to the first locker, he found a spot for the camera.

"Lucia, come in Lucia," he said after he had finished positioning the surveillance equipment.

"Perfect shot. I can see the entire cellar."

"Did you see the label on the wine?" he asked and walked back over to the racks, where he once again pulled out the bottle he had been inspecting earlier.

"A little unclear," Lucia advised.

A harsh sigh escaped him before he said, "It's clear to me. This was one of Mitch's favorites."

Chapter 4

Elizabeth stretched a kink out of her back. Just a few hours to go until the start of the dinner service and everything was in order and ready. Which meant that she'd better take her afternoon break.

Natalie and Susanna, another of her assistants, had already left for some rest. Both young women lived nearby, as did most of the staff she employed. Which made her question where Aidan would drift?

She ambled toward the front of the building, but he had already departed. Not out of the ordinary, but she got a sense of something not right with him. It made her wonder if he was in trouble. If that was the reason he moved from place to place, never putting down roots. She made a mental note to ask him for some references if he survived his first night on the job.

Closing up, she went to her cottage, changed into jogging clothes and checked out the tide. Low enough still that she could run along the shore instead of the hard asphalt road toward the center of town.

Even though she stayed on the wetter hard-packed sand, her heels dug deep with the force of her strides and so she pushed a little harder. Her arms pumped as she ran, passing behind the main buildings in town and the public access ramps to the beach. As she skirted a protective stone jetty close to the old Roman bridge before turning around, a fine sweat glistened on her bare arms and legs from her exertions.

"Elvis has left the building," Lucia called out from the central area of the suite.

Aidan put down the microchip he had been laboring over and walked out to view the now-empty rooms of the restaurant from the monitors Lucia had set up in the common space of their quarters.

Grabbing a set of binoculars, he rushed to the corner of the hotel room, grateful that Corbett Lazlo had thought to rent a space with windows that faced the shore and the restaurant. Scoping out the area with the high-powered binoculars, he tried to locate the Sparrow, but couldn't.

"Damn. I'll have to get something in the cottage so we can monitor her better."

Lucia joined him at the windows, another pair of binoculars in hand. "Is that where you think she is?"

Aidan looked at his watch. "It's only three, so she's got a bit of time until she needs to get dinner going. She could be anywhere, but my money is on the cottage. She strikes me as a homebody."

"When she isn't busy being an assassin?" Lucia tossed out.

"So you're finally convinced it's her?" he asked and glanced over at his colleague.

Lucia shook her head before bringing up the binoculars once again. "Either that or there's a hell of a lot of coincidences."

"Hmm." He turned his attention to searching out the grounds of the restaurant and the cottage, but he could see nothing.

A moment later, however, Lucia chuckled loudly. "A homebody, huh?"

Aidan stepped to her side and tracked the line of sight of Lucia's binoculars. He caught the blur of movement along the shore. Training his binoculars on the area, he increased the magnification until he could finally identify Elizabeth.

She was running. He couldn't call it jogging since the pace was too fast. Almost punishing. Her arms pumped smoothly while the hair swept up in a pony tail bounced in rhythm to her long and graceful strides. A cropped dark-maroon T-shirt was plastered to her body by a combination of sweat and a breeze.

She was cold.

He grew increasingly interested as he noticed even more about her. The firm muscles at her midriff and legs shifting and bunching. The running shorts she wore weren't scant, but her legs were long for her height. Very long, which brought disturbing visions of what she could do with those legs.

He groaned.

"Aidan?" he heard from beside him and realized Lucia had been talking to him.

"What? I'm sorry. I was concentrating."

"You are such a guy," she teased with a wide smile.

He had to shake his head and laugh. There was just something refreshing about Lucia's forthrightness when you were used to dealing with people who were generally deceptive.

Like the woman running along the shore, he reminded himself, fighting her sexual pull.

"Okay, so she's…cute," he confessed.

Lucia laughed and let her binoculars drop down on the strap hanging around her neck. "I hope you're a more convincing liar when you're around her."

"You'll find out soon enough," he said and headed to his room, intent on testing the waters in more ways than one.

Elizabeth was nearly back to the cottage when she noticed first the lone swimmer moving toward her from the docks and then the pile of clothes and towel sitting on the beach just behind her home.

Finishing her jog, she paused by the towel and placed her hands on her hips, took a few deep breaths as she watched the swimmer head into shore. His strokes were sure and even. They propelled him through the water elegantly as his head turned from side to side in a rhythmic breathing pattern.

She recognized that head, she realized—Aidan. This was confirmed as he reached the shallows and got caught up in a surge of water. He body-surfed the wave in before he rose up out of the wash of the breakers.

Elizabeth gulped and this time, had to force herself to breathe. He was all lean muscle and athletic grace. As he headed toward shore, he picked up his arms to slick back the longer strands of his hair from his face and all that muscle rippled beneath smooth tanned skin. He wasn't wearing the loose shorts that so many American men wore, but a sinfully slinky Speedo that barely covered him. Barely being the operative word.

Breathe, girl. Breathe. She fanned her face and blamed the hot flash on her jog.

He smiled as he noticed her and hurried from the water, jumping over one wave and then battling the backward pull of the wash until he was standing before her. "You were right about how great the waters are. Although a little rough in spots."

"The swimming and surfing beaches are up more toward town. It's a little rocky here. You've cut yourself," she said and motioned to a raw scrape along his collarbone. "Let's get that cleaned."

Aidan looked down to where a bit of blood mingled with the salt water and ran down his chest. He hadn't planned it that way, but he wouldn't waste a prime opportunity. Especially since he had noticed how she was checking him out as he had come onto shore. "I'll be fine," he said and met her gaze directly.

She blushed and stammered, "W-we really should clean it. You wouldn't want it to get infected."

Again it occurred to him that she was too easy to read, but then again, he hadn't been all that obscure up in the hotel room with Lucia. Was it a cosmic joke that they should both obviously find themselves attracted to one another? Spy *v.* Spy Sexcapades before they had to do each other in?

"Thanks," he said, bending to pick up his clothes and looping the towel over his shoulders. She walked toward the cottage but didn't offer to let him in as he had expected. As he had hoped, since in the pocket of his pants, he had another set of cameras ready to install. Instead, she pointed to a rustic outdoor shower by the back door.

"Rinse off over there while I get some first aid stuff."

Elizabeth walked into the cottage and he waited for her to return before he stepped beneath the shower and turned on the water. He wanted an audience for his show. When he was certain she was observing him, he made a point of getting good and wet. Slick. Then, he ran his hands all along his body, as if wiping away some dirt, and as he did so, he could feel her gaze on him, tracking his every movement.

Knowing she was a voyeur to his little act brought an immediate and unwanted reaction. The upside of it was that in turn, his rather obvious excitement created a riot of color along Elizabeth's cheeks. She ripped her gaze from him then and nervously fingered the plastic box in her hands—the first aid kit.

He stopped and shut off the water, grabbed his towel and dried himself as he walked toward her. He toyed with the idea of wrapping the towel around his waist, but decided against it. In this game, you used every advantage available.

She had put the kit on a low stone wall by the shower and was fumbling with opening it as he approached.

"Here, let me," he said and took the kit from her hands, opened it and laid it back on top of the wall. He removed a tube of antiseptic cream, squeezed a little onto his finger. Working it into the scrape, he made sure to skip a section so that it might require her further attention.

"There." He was closing the tube when she reached out and took it from his hands.

"You missed a spot."

Bingo, he thought.

She placed a dot of the cream on her index finger and after, rubbed that finger along the top portion of the scrape. The action brought her close and he lowered his head, got into her personal space. Despite her run, she still smelled fresh. Feminine, although there was no hint of any perfume. An assassin couldn't afford to leave even something as simple as a scent behind, Aidan realized, but then turned his attention back to her, putting himself where she couldn't avoid him.

Elizabeth stroked the cream into the scrape. His skin was warm beneath her finger. As she skipped her gaze up to his face, she finally realized how close they were. And that she had to reach past him and brush even closer to remove a bandage from the kit. She didn't hesitate leaning toward him, even though her breast brushed his chest as she did so.

Her nipple, already peaked from the chill of the ocean breeze, tightened even more and she shivered.

"Cold?" he asked and rubbed his hands across her bare arms to warm her. It only brought another shiver. One that came from another place she didn't want to acknowledge, so she pulled away from him and shot him a glare. He was obviously used to playing this game quite well, but she didn't intend to be another notch acquired in his wanderings.

"Don't touch, remember?"

Aidan didn't push, although she could see that he was tempted to find out just how far he could.

Stepping away from her, he held his hands up as if in surrender. "I get it. Thanks for the help." With that, he grabbed his clothes, walked back to the beachfront and turned toward town.

Elizabeth watched him go and wondered whether hiring him had been a mistake. She'd hoped getting a bartender would solve her problem, but this guy...

As she watched his Speedo-clad backside saunter away, it

confirmed her original impression that he would be nothing but trouble. When he turned, caught her observing him… again…and winked, she knew she was right.

Aidan was going to give her nothing but grief. She had to keep a close eye on him. She couldn't afford to let him get close or to work his way into her heart. The price to be paid for that was just too great.

Chapter 5

*F*rustration.

That was the only word Aidan could use to describe his feelings on so many levels.

A few days had gone by and he had yet to be able to charm his way into her cottage.

Forget charming his way into her pants. The lady might as well have on a cast-iron chastity belt given how effectively she countered his every attempt to get close. She was a master, he'd give her that.

Not to mention that in the days that he'd been in the restaurant, he'd seen a woman who was patient and kind and all-so-nice that it was hard to imagine a side of her that could kill a man in cold blood.

Frustration. Again.

On a positive note, he had actually managed to fake being a halfway decent bartender the first few days with Lucia's help via the earpiece. Luckily, tastes in Leonia were rather pedestrian. By the end of the week, he had memorized the most commonly requested libations and discovered the many attributes of the restaurant's favorite wine. It was from a local vineyard along the coast and not all that far from Prince Reginald's country estate. He wondered if the Sparrow had bought the wine before or after killing the prince.

He and Lucia were partaking a glass of that vintage as they monitored Elizabeth's activities thanks to the strategically placed cameras. Although the restaurant had closed nearly an hour earlier and all of the staff had gone home, Elizabeth continued to work.

She finally gave a little nod of her head and seemingly satisfied, went back through the kitchen and out the rear door. Once in the backyard, another camera that he had set up in a hanging flower pot on the patio picked up her movement toward the cottage. She entered, closed the door and lights snapped on inside.

"The Sparrow's in her nest for the night," he muttered and took another sip of the wine. He sat there, watching the silent screens, still pondering how he would get into the cottage to plant the other surveillance equipment.

There was generally too much activity during working hours. Every night for the past few days, Elizabeth had gone straight home after work, making it impossible for him to sneak in.

About half an hour later, he was still considering whether he could break in tomorrow between when he left the restaurant for the night and Elizabeth finally closing up, when he noticed the lights in the cottage snap off. The Sparrow was ready for bed.

Surprisingly, however, Elizabeth walked out of the cottage a second later, clearly not dressed for sleep. She had on a black form-fitting cocktail dress. Strapless, it exposed the paler skin of her shoulders and arms, and dropped down to only mid-thigh, gracing him with a view of those sinfully long and lusciously toned legs.

Aidan bolted upright in his chair. "It's eleven-thirty. Where could she be going?"

"Homebody, huh?" Lucia quipped again, but Aidan glared at her.

"We need to track her."

"Time for *you* to track her. Time for me to plant some cameras," Lucia said and rose from the table.

Aidan grabbed the binoculars, turned on the infrared sighting and rushed to the windows. He immediately picked up her body heat moving down the walk leading from the restaurant to the street. Increasing the magnification, he could make out Elizabeth's body shape turning onto the road before the building. "She's coming into town."

"It *is* Friday night, Aidan," Lucia said.

When he faced her, he realized she had changed into all-black clothes.

"You'll bug the cottage?"

She confirmed that she would with a nod of her head. "You'll follow our little bird?"

Glancing at his watch, he realized he only had a few minutes before Elizabeth walked past the hotel. No time to change from the jeans and T-shirt he had donned upon returning to the suite. So he just slipped his earpiece back in and grabbed his leather jacket.

"Keep me advised of what's going on," he instructed and Lucia picked up one of the walkie-talkies set to the same frequency as the earpiece.

"I'll need about half an hour," she advised and he raised an eyebrow at her comment.

"Don't think I can keep her occupied for that long?"

Lucia laughed and shook her head. "Come on, Aidan. So far you're batting zero in that department."

He was annoyed that she was right, but he had his reasons for not pushing too hard. If Elizabeth was the Sparrow, and there was little so far to contradict that possibility except his malfunctioning intuition, he couldn't let himself rush things and maybe make a mistake. He had done that once before and Mitch had paid the price.

"I'm a patient man, Lucia. Some women can't be rushed," he responded.

"Whatever," she replied with a flip of her hand. "Just give me half an hour."

With that, she left the suite and he hurried after her, but took the elevator while she went to the stairs so as to remain inconspicuous.

He stood there, impatient, tapping his foot while he waited, hoping he wouldn't miss Elizabeth as she passed by the building. Not that she would be all that hard to find. There weren't that many places she could go on a Friday night at nearly midnight.

As the elevator arrived and he stepped in, he made a mental list of the dozen or so establishments he had noticed on one of his earlier walks, imagining which of those someone like Elizabeth might favor.

A nice quiet pub somewhere? Then he recalled what she was wearing. Not what you wore to hoist a pint with the locals. As he reached the ground floor, he hurried through the lobby and paused by the entrance to the hotel. Peering out, he caught sight of her about a block up, just turning onto one of the side streets, and smiled.

The Sparrow was about to find out just how persuasive he could be.

The Women's Artists' Cooperative was one of those places that became whatever you needed it to be. During the week the site hosted various literary events, displays of local art and the Wednesday Wing Woman social for women over sixty-five. On Friday and Saturday nights, it transformed into a club featuring local female bands of differing persuasions.

For the women of Leonia, there was no better place to be on a Friday night than the WAC as it was affectionately known by the female population. For the men, the term WAC had a whole different meaning. Not necessarily a positive one.

Most men in town knew to stay away on the weekends since the women at the WAC went there to be free of the pressures of man/woman mating rituals. It was a way that women could bond and enjoy themselves without any inhibitions.

Elizabeth loved that about the WAC. Within its walls, she could spend time with the few women she counted as friends.

Tonight they were meeting at the WAC to celebrate Natalie successfully passing her final exam. With her help, Natalie had learned the secrets to a scrumptious chocolate souffle. She smiled, thinking of the young woman's excitement as she had told her.

As she stepped through the door, she spotted her friends seated at a table near the dance floor and rushed over. On stage, a band of women barely past their teens energetically played a No Doubt tune. The singer was doing a passable imitation of Gwen Stefani and had even styled her dress and hairstyle to mimic the celebrity.

At the table, she hugged all her friends and once she sat, they ordered another round of drinks and toasted Natalie's success. Talk came quickly and easily with the other women as did the desire to dance as the band launched into their own version of "Cruel to be Kind."

Inclining her head in the direction of the dance floor, she said, "Anyone care to join me?"

Natalie and Samantha, a designer with her own clothing shop in town, jumped at her suggestion. The last woman at the table—Kate, the owner of an upscale bath and body store—shook her head. "I'll hold our spot."

Together, the three women eased onto a free spot at the edge of the dance floor and Elizabeth gave herself over to the beat, moving in time to the bass line of the song. Smiling and feeling relaxed for the first time in days, she danced through the song and then stayed on the floor when the band began another tune with a similar beat.

She was enjoying the music and her friends until Natalie leaned over and said, "Check out what just walked in."

Elizabeth followed the direction of Natalie's gaze. Aidan. He was sauntering past a score of women near the long runway from the club's entrance to the main section of the WAC. As he passed and made his way to the bar, heads turned to watch him go by.

She felt only a tiny bit of vindication that she wasn't alone in her attraction to his physical attributes. That feeling was chased by an emotion she normally didn't experience—jealousy.

And then that unsettling feeling that had been plaguing her for the last few days resurfaced. She finally realized the cause of it—Aidan.

Looking away from him, she moved until her back was to the bar and tried to rededicate herself to the music and the fun she had been having just moments earlier. A difficult thing to do with Aidan sitting at the bar. She told herself just to relax, but it was impossible.

Returning to the table, she grabbed her glass to quench the thirst she had worked up while dancing, only to find it empty. Looking around, she realized there wasn't a waitress in sight. She had only one choice—head to the bar or suffer being parched.

As she glanced toward where Aidan was sitting barely twenty feet away, she noted his broad shoulders filling out the black leather of his jacket. Remembering the strength of them when he had been swimming the other day, she cursed beneath her breath.

She would be damned if she let him wreck her night.

Chapter 6

He was drowning in a sea of estrogen, Aidan thought as he sipped on the beer he had ordered. Picking up the long-neck bottle, he took another slug as he tried not to look stupid surrounded by the dozens of women packed into the club. He'd obviously made a major gaffe.

Either Elizabeth was gay—and he couldn't believe that his radar was that off—or he'd stumbled into what was clearly intended to be a ladies'-only club.

No wonder the bouncer, a rather burly woman he recalled seeing on the docks, had given him an odd and unfriendly glance as he had paid the admission fee.

He shook his head at his own stupidity and his failure to reconnoiter the location. He also wondered how he would ever approach Elizabeth without seeming all stalkery. Best that he not—

"Following me?" she said and leaned one elbow on the surface of the bar as she signaled with a wave of her hand for the bartender.

Busted. He looked up at her and faked disinterest. With a shrug, he said, "Heard the band from out on the street. They sounded pretty good. Decided to see what was up."

A furrow appeared between her brows as she considered him. "Judging from your choice of music the other day, female bands of the indie persuasion are possibly your type. Although the black biker jacket screams hard-rock guy to me."

He gave another indifferent shrug and tossed back a slug of the beer again. "I'm a man of eclectic tastes. And you?"

She crossed her arms after finally sliding onto the bar stool beside him. Signals definitely mixed, he thought. "The same. Men generally stay away on Friday and Saturday nights. It's an unwritten rule."

Chuckling, he swiveled his head back and forth as if to check her statement and teased, "Well, color me stupid. I hadn't noticed."

She surprised him by laughing. When the waiter brought her drink—a glass of red wine—she laid some money on the bar and said, "Gotta go."

With a cool nod and another sip of his beer, he replied, "See ya."

Elizabeth strolled back to her table, making sure to add what she hoped was an enticing little sway to her walk, certain that he was watching no matter his attempts to seem disinterested.

Or maybe it was totally egotistical of her to think Aidan was here because of her. Maybe he really had just been looking for some good music, although there were a few other clubs in Leonia that offered entertainment on the weekends. Some of them were probably more suitable for someone like Aidan.

As she sat at the table with her friends, Natalie inclined her head in the direction of the bar. "Brave man."

Elizabeth settled into her seat and picked up her glass of merlot. Peering over the edge of it at her friend, she replied, "Either brave or stupid."

Natalie narrowed her eyes as she considered Aidan once again. "Doesn't strike me as the stupid type."

"He's yummy," added Samantha, shooting a glance over her shoulder.

Wanting to downplay his presence, Elizabeth tried to act cool. "If you like that kind of man."

"Girl, what woman doesn't go for that whole bad-boy routine?" Kate hooted with a nudge to Elizabeth's shoulder.

She held up her hand as if to be counted. "Me, for one. Bad boys don't linger and I've had enough of people leaving in my life."

Her comment cast a pall over what had been a fun gathering. She immediately regretted it, heartfelt as the comment had been. Attempting to regain that earlier lightheartedness, she said, "Although I have seen him in a bathing suit. A rather brief Speedo to be exact. There's not an inch of him that needs manscaping."

Natalie nearly spat out her drink. As it was, she gave a noisy snort. "You're not kidding, are you?"

Elizabeth looked over to where Aidan was sitting, arms spread across the bar, long-neck bottle dangling lazily from one hand. As their gazes met, he smiled and picked up his bottle as if in a toast.

She mimicked his actions, earning a round of snickers from all her friends.

"Right, not interested. Tell us another one, Lizzy Bee," Natalie joked, using Dani's nickname for her.

"So what are you doing here, when Tall, Blond and Dangerous is over there?" Kate chimed in and pointed to Aidan.

"Why, I'm dancing, of course. Anyone care to join me?" She rose from the table.

All three of her friends looked from her to Aidan before Samantha finally stood. "I'm game."

With a glare at Kate and Natalie, Elizabeth quipped, "Cowards," before working her way through the crowd and back to the dance floor.

The band had switched to a classic Bangles tune. Definitely danceable, she thought and once again gave herself over to the energetic beats, trying not to think about the man sitting at the bar, possibly watching her. Every now and then, as her dancing and the crowd shifted her into a different position on the floor, she would catch a peek of him. Still lounging there, sipping his beer.

She wondered if it was his second bottle or if he was still nursing the first. Then she wondered why she cared. She wasn't one for meaningless involvements of any kind, especially with someone like Aidan who wasn't the kind to linger for long.

Faltering to the beat, she forced her mind away from thoughts of Aidan and back to the playfulness of the music. She was just loosening up a bit when the song ended and the band announced that they had a request.

Suddenly, Aidan was at her side, holding out his hand. Samantha was moving back to the table where Kate and Natalie sat, watching with extreme fascination.

The lead singer crooned the opening bars of Gloria Estefan's "Words Get in the Way."

"I'm not interested," she said, glancing down at his hand before shooting her gaze up to his face.

"It's just a dance," he replied, the tone of his voice low. A bedroom voice, perfect for whispering endearments. Lush with sensual promise. A well-rehearsed voice that had likely worked for him on many an occasion.

"I'm your boss," she hissed back and peered around to realize they were starting to attract attention, which was the last thing she needed. She liked her privacy and didn't need the village gossips wagging their tongues over her.

"I promise I won't claim harassment." He grinned and wiggled his fingers, again urging her to dance and rather than risk a scene, she snared his hand and joined him in the slow dance.

Bad boy that he was, he took advantage of the opportunity

to come close. Inclining his head, he whispered in her ear, "Relax."

Hard to do when she was so aware of him physically. Close, but not as close as he maybe wanted. She would give him credit for that. He wasn't a total cad.

His chivalry didn't stop him from keeping his hands at her waist for the longest time while she slipped both of her hands to his shoulders—those broad, leanly muscled shoulders she remembered from the other day.

Finally, he exerted just the tiniest bit of pressure to urge her closer until she barely brushed his chest as they moved to the music.

An annoying tingle of awareness awoke again. A little shiver danced through her when he bent his head and asked, "It's not so bad, is it?"

No, it wasn't. If anything, it was a bit too good. She found herself pressing her cheek to his and moving an inch closer. Which brought a shudder and made her fight her way back from him to avoid her attraction.

She hated how she responded to him and took to mentally counting the seconds that passed in an effort to distract herself.

"Relax," he urged again, smoothing his hands up and down her back. Pressed her to shift nearer.

Reluctantly she went, still counting. Finding that ineffective, she opted for another tack. "Gloria doesn't strike me as your type, either."

He chuckled. "Eclectic, remember? Besides, her music soothes me."

She jerked away and eyed him dubiously. "Soothes you?"

Aidan smiled and cradled the side of her face. "Yes, soothes. As in, to relax. To let yourself go." As he said that, he stroked the side of her face and then eased that hand to the nape of her neck and pressed her close once more.

Once there, he continued, gently whispering in her ear. "Listen to the words. What she's trying to say."

Despite her best efforts, she found herself doing as he

asked. She let the words slip into her, let herself finally relax against him, moving her body to those sensuous beats, and he did the same.

When the song ended and the band abruptly resumed with a loud and fast number, it yanked her from the mood.

"That was—"

"Nice?" he filled in for her, a hopeful look on his face as she realized he was still holding her hand.

Too nice. "I've got to go."

He released her and with a nod, she returned to her table of friends.

Instead of going to the bar, however, he followed her, his hand at the small of her back, as if to remind her of his presence. Not that she could drive away her awareness of him no matter how she tried.

At the table, she glared at him, hoping to make it clear that she wanted him gone, but he obviously either didn't get her hint, or more than likely, the rebel chose to ignore it. "Mind if I join you ladies?"

Her three friends, or maybe it was better to say three ex-friends, shifted to make room for a chair he secured from another table with an irresistible smile.

Elizabeth stood there, reluctant to stay, but unwilling to let Aidan spoil her night. For that matter, she was unwilling to acknowledge that she was attracted to him. He was probably used to women falling all over him constantly. And she suspected he was All-Access Aidan to anyone who was willing.

Which she wasn't.

Hesitantly, she took a seat next to Aidan and allowed her friends to engage him in conversation while she sat back, trying to gauge whether he was as he appeared—a happy-go-lucky guy, intent on just having fun as he drifted from place to place.

But when he leaned away from the table and their gazes locked, there was something else there. Something painful. She noted it as his glance fell on her, as if he, too, was trying to decide just what she was.

She realized then that he wasn't what he appeared to be. Which was fine. She wasn't as she appeared to be, either.

The WAC closed its doors at two, Aidan discovered.

What amazed him was that after a long day of work, none of the women at the table seemed inclined to leave until that hour.

And so he stayed until the announcement was made for last call, and, after, he walked out of the club surrounded by Natalie, Samantha and Kate. Elizabeth was directly behind them as they ambled up the block.

Samantha and Kate lived along the town's central road. He bid each woman goodnight at their doors. That just left Natalie, her arm looped through his, and Elizabeth, who had finally moved up to walk beside them. At a street directly in front of the hotel, Natalie paused.

"This is my stop," she teased and gave him a playful kiss on the cheek. "See you later."

Aidan waved as Natalie crossed the street, and then faced Elizabeth. "Guess it's just the two of us."

Elizabeth immediately protested. "There's no need for you—"

"A gentleman always walks a lady home," he said and offered his arm.

Ignoring him, she walked in the direction of the restaurant, but Aidan followed, matching his paces so that they were side by side. He was silent, since he knew that to say anything would just drive her further away, something he didn't want to do given that he had made some inroads this evening.

Although he had watched her tonight much as he had watched her all week, he was still uncertain. Maybe even troubled by what he had seen. The Elizabeth he was getting to know didn't jibe with what he knew her to be—a ruthless killer.

The Elizabeth he had discovered had been kind. Patient with the staff and the sometimes demanding patrons. Determined, but at times—and he didn't want to admit that those times had been around him—decidedly insecure.

But of course, in his line of work, deception was a way of life.

Elizabeth had to be very very good at it, he thought, as they continued walking onward silently, moving closer and closer to the restaurant. When they reached the low stone wall marking the boundary between her property and the main road, Elizabeth stopped and faced him.

"Although I didn't ask you to, thanks for walking me home."

He shrugged, the buckles on his black leather biker jacket jangling with the action. "It's the least I could do."

She arched one eyebrow, half in question, half in challenge. "Really? And you expected nothing in return?"

Aidan chuckled and smiled at the audacious tone behind her words. "Well, maybe one thing."

That perfectly shaped brow curved ever upward. "And what would that be?"

Chapter 7

She had tossed down the gauntlet and should have known better than to think he wouldn't pick it up.

One side of his mouth quirked as he slowly leaned toward her until he was barely an inch away. He surprised her then by saying, "Last chance."

His breath was warm against her lips. She imagined just how much warmer his mouth would be on hers. The voice of her daring side screamed, "Stop running, girl! Go get him!"

And so she did, closing that last little distance and covering his mouth with hers. Experiencing the warmth over and over again as he answered her kiss. Tasting him when she opened her mouth and he did the same, slipped his tongue in to dance with hers.

Their lips were the only points connecting them and she found herself reaching up, laying her hand on his leather-clad shoulder to ground her since her head was beginning to spin. And then suddenly, he yanked away.

"I'm sorry," he stammered, although he wasn't quite sure why he was apologizing. After all, this was what he'd been after all week long—a way to get closer.

Even in the dark, the rush of color to her cheeks was painfully obvious. "Sorry? You're sorry?"

Again she was throwing him for a loop. "Yes, I mean, no. I mean, I know you didn't want it to go that far," he offered as an excuse.

She crossed her arms and cocked her hip. That eyebrow crept upward again as her sherry-colored eyes burned with annoyance. "Already running, Aidan?"

"I think we'll probably both be thankful in the morning that we stopped when we did."

With a nod, and without waiting for her reply, he hurried away.

He rushed into the suite eager to see what Elizabeth would do once she was within range of the cameras Lucia had set up in her cottage.

A purely professional interest, he reminded himself, but as he caught sight of Elizabeth in her bedroom, he knew it for the lie it was.

Sitting beside Lucia, he watched as Elizabeth reached behind her and undid the zipper on the back of the basic little black dress that hugged her slim curves. The fabric loosened, and then with a dip of her shoulders, the dress slipped off and pooled at her feet on the floor, leaving her standing in nothing but lacy black underwear. Very feminine, highly revealing underwear.

He swallowed hard.

"A woman doesn't wear black unless she wants someone to see it. Especially black like that." Lucia nudged him with an elbow.

"She didn't know I'd be there." He continued watching, waiting for the undergarments to drop, as well, but then Elizabeth grabbed something from the edge of the bed.

She headed to a door at the far end of the room and Aidan

reached for the monitor controls to switch the view, only Lucia batted away his hand.

"I didn't bug the bathroom. There's no way out of that room besides the window."

Chagrined, he replied, "You're right."

Lucia punched a few buttons at that point and a view of the back of the cottage popped into place on one monitor. The light from the bathroom window was visible, a bright beacon against the dark stone of the cottage, but not much else.

"She can't go out that way without us knowing," Lucia explained, and then yawned.

"Maybe we should take turns the rest of the night?" Aidan suggested. "I'll take the first watch."

With a knowing grin, Lucia bid him goodnight.

Aidan settled in, anxious to see Elizabeth again while he replayed over and over that enticing kiss and the confusion surrounding it. He was embarrassed that he had lost his objectivity, forgetting why it was that he was kissing her and actually enjoying it.

Maybe he just wasn't as cut out for this part of the spy business as he thought. He could handle the surveillance and fighting after his many years as an army Ranger, but the rest...

That had been Mitch's specialty. He had been the kind who could charm even a snake-oil salesman. Not that his friend's charisma had been enough to save his life. The Sparrow was apparently immune to it, although tonight...

Had it been his imagination that Elizabeth had responded?

Had she fooled Mitch in much the same way before plunging the knife into his gut?

His mood different, he looked at his watch, wondering what she could be doing in the bathroom for so long. And then he caught a glimpse of motion in another of the monitors at the furthest end of the table. He squinted at the picture; it was so dark, he was barely able to discern much beside the general height and body shape of the individual.

Cursing, he grabbed the monitor controls and flipped a switch that turned on the night vision for that camera. The picture improved, not that he would be able to get much information about the suspect. At first glance, the black-clad figure was built much like Elizabeth, but the identity would be impossible to confirm thanks to the ski mask covering the suspect's face.

The Sparrow? he wondered and glanced back to the monitor in the bedroom where there was still no sign of Elizabeth.

How had she gotten from the cottage to the cellar of the restaurant? A tunnel between the two buildings?

His gaze fixed on the black-clad figure, he watched her move to the safe. With a few quick spins of the dial, she opened it and removed a moderate-sized foot locker from the bottom shelf. Placing the foot locker on the floor, she undid yet another lock and flipped open the top of the locker. The angle on the camera made it possible to see what was inside— an assortment of knives and bottles.

Don't touch the knives, he repeated Elizabeth's warning.

Elizabeth—the Sparrow—reached into the bottom of the foot locker and extracted a holster and gun. She took the time to check the clip and firing mechanism on the gun—a Heckler & Koch Mark 23. He recognized the weapon immediately.

The HK Mark 23 had been specially commissioned by the Pentagon for its Special Operations Command. A friend within SOCOM had raved about the gun and insisted both he and Mitch should check it out. Their friend been right. Both he and Mitch had loved the double-action .45-caliber gun that could be fitted with a silencer. His friend's pistol had disappeared on the night he'd been killed.

More and more evidence was piling up against the Sparrow in Mitch's murder. He had to remind himself that his friend's death was not the reason for this assignment. His goal was to find Prince Reginald's murderer. But maybe one of those bottles in the foot locker held a poison similar to the one that had killed the prince.

Aidan observed the Sparrow holster the gun and slip on the holster, quickly get the foot locker back in the safe and close it once again.

She turned, glanced over her shoulder as if sensing that she was being watched. Pausing, she examined the room, then moved to the one locker closest to the safe. Again with a few quick turns she opened the combination lock.

He wondered what she was up to and was surprised when she pushed aside some clothes hanging in the locker, stepped inside, and then closed the door behind her, disappearing from sight.

Shit. Standing, he rushed to Lucia's room and pounded on the door. "Lucia! The Sparrow's flown the nest!"

As Lucia opened her door, she grumbled, "This better be good, Aidan."

He motioned to the monitors. "The Sparrow is armed and dressed to kill. She headed out of the cellar through some kind of hidden passage in one of the lockers."

"Then you better arm yourself, as well," she said, but he bent and picked up the hem of his jeans leg to reveal the mini six-shot Glock 36 tucked into an ankle holster.

Lucia let out a disbelieving chuckle. "If it's the Sparrow, you'll need more than that pea shooter." She reached into the pocket of her robe, extracted her larger Glock 34 and held it out to him.

Aidan snagged the weapon from her grasp and, as he headed for the door, called out, "Keep an eye on the cellar. Call me if there's any activity."

"Where do you think you're headed?"

"To the beach. It's the most likely place for the tunnel to end. I should be able to see where she's going from there."

He'd raced off the main street and down to the shore, running along what little was left of the beach thanks to the high tide. By the time he got behind the cottage, his shoes and the bottoms of his pants were soaked all the way up to the knee.

The light in her bathroom still spilled into the night.

He pulled out Lucia's Glock, crept up the rocky path from the beach and scoped out the dunes and gardens adjacent to the cottage. No activity besides the movement of the marsh grasses in the dunes from a slight ocean breeze. Crouching down, he kept to the edge of the garden that Elizabeth had crafted behind the restaurant.

Still no sign of anyone.

Moving to the side yard, he examined that area, and then paused, glancing down at the luminous face of his watch. Nearly fifteen minutes had passed since the Sparrow had slipped into the locker. He recollected her pace as she'd run the other day. If she had escaped into an open area and decided to run, she could be a good distance away already.

Cursing beneath his breath that he might have lost her, he pressed toward the opposite side of the yard, but could see nothing in the backyards of the neighboring shops and homes. A dog's bark caught his attention.

He squinted through the night in the direction of the noise.

That was when he thought he saw something moving down at the water's edge, close to the old stone building that was Leonia's fish market. Concentrating, he focused on where he had seen the motion.

Was that something moving in the shadows behind the fish market?

"Come in, Blender Boy. The Sparrow's in her nest," Lucia advised over his earpiece.

He ignored Lucia and peered down to the market.

Definitely something, he thought. Maybe even two people behind the building. "Red Rover, confirm, Red Rover. I think I've got something here."

"Sparrow just came out of the bathroom. What do you have?"

Aidan squinted and cursed that he had forgotten to bring his binoculars. But Lucia had a pair up in the suite. "Red Rover. Focus on the back of the fish market. At about two o'clock."

Some noise came over the wire and in his mind, Aidan

counted the seconds of delay as Lucia grabbed the binoculars, headed to the window and monitored the area he had pointed out. Moving nearer, he tried to confirm what he'd seen earlier, but the closer he got, it seemed to him that he might have imagined it. Or maybe it was two fisherman making an early delivery.

"Nothing in sight. Are you sure you saw her there?"

He wasn't certain and he should have been. He had been one of the army's best and here he was, being led around in circles by a slip of a woman. "Not sure, Red Rover. Returning to base," he advised, then slipped the gun back into his pocket and walked through Elizabeth's gardens to the road.

Once there, he raced back to the hotel and to the suite where Lucia was seated in front of the monitors. In one picture, Elizabeth slept soundly in her bed.

He walked up behind his colleague. "I don't get it. I saw someone preparing for a job. I saw her leave the cellar."

Lucia looked over her shoulder at him. "I'm not saying you didn't. But if she did all that, she wasn't gone for long. Or maybe it was someone else."

"Maybe," was all he could admit. Plopping down into the chair beside her, he returned her weapon and moved his feet, which squished noisily.

Lucia finally examined him and shook her head. "Maybe it's time for you to get clean and get some rest. You need to be back on the job—"

"At ten. The restaurant opens for brunch at eleven."

"I'll take over your watch. Plus, I'll fill Walker in later this morning." She tucked her gun back into the pocket of her robe.

Right, fill in Walker, he thought. But there was one thing he needed to tell her before he went to sleep. "The weapon she had—"

"A Sigma SW9F? That's what ballistics said about her two pistol kills," Lucia interrupted.

Aidan met her gaze squarely and shook his head. "She had an HK Mark 23."

"Mitch's gun." She reached out, laid a hand on his arm. "I'm sorry, Aidan."

"I'm not. Whoever was in that cellar did it. Chances are that it was the Sparrow. I plan on proving that she killed the prince, as well. When you call Walker, make sure and find out if he has any new info."

"Will do," she acknowledged and turned her attention back to the monitor, not that there was much going on. Just Elizabeth still in her bed. Peacefully at rest.

Aidan wondered how she could sleep so soundly. Didn't all her kills haunt her the way Mitch's murder haunted him?

But then again, sociopaths didn't have the same kinds of reactions that normal people did, he thought. Walker would be the first to tell him that. Yet her behavior earlier that night and her kiss…

She had been just a normal woman, enjoying a night out with friends. Friends who might be able to give him more information on the real Elizabeth. Although he had to be at the restaurant by ten, that still left him an hour or so in the morning to visit both Kate and Samantha's stores and talk to the women.

Maybe they would give him some insight on what made the Sparrow tick, because, so far, she had him totally confused.

Chapter 8

Elizabeth was awake long before the alarm went off, chirping stridently to remind her she couldn't linger in bed.

Saturdays and Sundays were always the busiest days of the week thanks to the brunch the restaurant served, but they were also the most profitable. Well worth the extra effort.

She was in the kitchen with time to spare before Natalie and her other assistants appeared. She fixed herself a large mug of coffee, and took a moment for a stroll through the back garden, pausing to pick a dead flower here and there.

In about four hours, her patrons would begin to arrive, but for now, she grabbed a seat on the low edge of the stone wall between her cottage and the beach. As she sipped her coffee, she gazed out at the ocean and observed the fisherman put out to sea.

She had often sat in the early-morning hours in her parents' fish shop near the docks and seen a similar sight. Her mother would sometimes make her a special breakfast of eggs and kippers, while her twin sister Dani—ever the more adventurous one—would tag along with their Da to greet those fisherman who were already inbound with their catch.

She hadn't been able to reach Dani in days and wondered what exotic part of the world her sister was visiting. She only hoped that Dani's busy schedule would soon allow time for a call home for news of when they might be able to get together again.

With her coffee becoming lukewarm and the growing heat from the rising sun reminding her that time was short this morning, Elizabeth headed to the kitchen. She was still the only one there. She used the time to experiment with a new dessert recipe she wanted to enter in the annual Silvershire Cooking Contest at the end of the month—a trifle doused with a sour cherry liqueur that a local distillery was making.

Concentrating, she selected a recipe for the cake portion of the trifle that would be firm enough, but not too heavy. She hoped that when the competition came in a few weeks, she would be able to place in the contest once more.

Not that she needed the glory. But the awards had brought her work to the attention of editors at magazines like *Gourmet* and *Bon Appetit,* resulting in invitations to other cooking expos and contests. They had given her a chance to see more of the world.

She smiled and thought that maybe she wasn't all that different from her wandering sister. Easing two pans with the cake batter into the oven, Elizabeth was turning her attention to the filling and sauce for the trifle when Natalie popped into the kitchen.

"G'mornin', Nat," she called out and wiped her hands free of some cake batter with the towel tucked into her apron strings.

Natalie walked over and slipped an arm over her shoulders. "Is it a good morning, Lizzy Bee?" she teased with a too-obvious wiggle of her eyebrows.

Elizabeth rolled her eyes upward. "Nat, even if it were a good morning that way, do I strike you as the type to kiss and tell?"

Natalie pointed her index finger in Elizabeth's face. "So

you did kiss. You don't need to tell me since it's obvious from the look on your face."

Elizabeth raised her hands to her cheeks as if to hide what Natalie had seen, but then dropped them back down as the guilt behind that action registered. "You absolutely cannot know that from just one look at my face."

Chuckling, Natalie headed to the door to the cellar, but paused before going down. "You're right. I can't. But you haven't denied it, so I guess I'm not so far off base."

With that, the younger woman flounced down the stairs, leaving Elizabeth to wonder what she would do when Aidan showed up for work. *If* he showed up for work. He had seemed conflicted last night.

Join the club, she thought, admitting that she had been just as puzzled by their rather pleasant, but equally awkward interlude.

But she was here this morning and ready to face him. She had to be here. Plus, she couldn't let him get the wrong idea about what was happening and how much he affected her.

She wondered again what he would do this morning if he came to work. She got the sense that whenever things got too complicated or didn't go his way, Aidan was the kind who left.

She only hoped that if he did decide to go, he would honor his promise and not leave her in a lurch. Especially not over the weekend when things would be crazier than ever.

With that thought in mind, she returned her attention to the dessert, the day's menu and a last-minute trip to the markets for ingredients to complete the chef's specials for the day.

A footfall close by made him bolt from bed, gun in hand. Whenever he was on assignment, he slept with his weapon within easy reach, tucked beneath the mattress with the handle sticking out for a quick draw.

Lucia held up her hands in surrender. "I'm sorry I woke you, but Walker's here. He's got some news."

Aidan lowered the gun. "Give me a few minutes, please."

Once dressed, Aidan stepped out into the main area of the suite where Walker Shaw sat on one of the couches, a shuttered look on his face.

"I gather there's problems," he said and took a seat opposite Walker.

"You look like hell," his colleague said. "Rough night?"

"Late night with the Sparrow. First at a local club and then after, when she went for an early-morning stroll," Lucia advised and brought over a tray with a pot of coffee and some cups. "I had room service bring this up. Figured you could use the jolt, Aidan."

"Thanks, Lucia," Aidan said.

Walker added his own thanks and then asked, "Were you able to see where she went? MI6 says there's been a lot of chatter on the wires lately about the Sparrow. She may be on another assignment here."

Aidan shook his head while filling up a cup with the heavenly smelling brew. He loaded it up with a few sugars, but kept it black since as Lucia had guessed, he needed a jump start this morning. "Someone slipped out through a secret passage in the cellar of the restaurant. Definitely dressed for a covert op and she was armed...with Mitch's gun."

Walker paused with his coffee cup halfway to his mouth. "How do you know that?"

"Although earlier ballistics had the Sparrow carrying a Sigma SW9F, she tucked an HK Mark 23 into her holster. Mitch's gun was the same make and has been missing since his murder. Plus, it's not that common a weapon," Aidan advised.

"Connect the dots, huh? But what about connecting the dots to Prince Reginald's murder?" Walker challenged and shifted his gaze to Lucia.

"Nothing yet."

Walker cursed beneath his breath. "Not good, guys. Corbett called this morning. A friend has warned him that the local tabloid—"

"The *Quiz?*" Lucia asked.

Walker nodded. "The *Silvershire Inquisitor,* or, as you noted, the *Quiz.* Seems one of the reporters has a lead on Prince Reginald's last night alive."

"If this *Quiz* is a gossip rag, why the worry?" Aidan wondered out loud as he sipped on the hot sugar-laced coffee.

"Because unfortunately, the story seems to have some truth behind it," Walker advised.

As Lucia fixed herself a cup of coffee, she asked, "So what is the story?"

"It seems the prince met an attractive young lady earlier in the day—slim athletic build, dark-haired."

"The Sparrow?" both Aidan and Lucia said in unison.

Walker shrugged. "Fits the description, doesn't it? Anyway, rumor has it that the prince locked himself in the room with this lady for a night of pleasure."

Aidan laughed harshly. "From what I saw in the file about the prince, that seems to be pretty routine behavior. So why the worry about this magazine's article?"

"Cocaine and murder," Walker answered quickly. "There had been some hint of drug use before with the Prince. A few months ago, immediately after the prince's death, the *Quiz* ran an article claiming that the prince had overdosed. No respectable news service would touch the piece."

"And now?" Lucia pressed.

"The paper claims to have proof positive that the prince was not only using drugs on his last night, but that he was murdered."

"Do the results of the toxicology reports confirm the drug use?" Lucia questioned and at that, Walker leaned down and extracted some papers from his briefcase. Laying them out on the coffee table between them, he motioned to the results.

"I've reviewed them myself and it seems clear. The prince had cocaine in his system along with a poison. The drugs are embarrassing to the royal family and the murder—that may add more fuel to the political fire the Union for Democracy keeps stoking."

Aidan leaned over, grabbed one of the papers and turned

it so he could get a better view. Examining the results, he said, "So the prince got his coke and in addition, a little something extra—digitalis."

"Not a hell of a lot, but enough to stop his heart," Walker explained, and then continued. "The thing is, it wasn't pharmaceutical-grade digitalis."

Lucia peered at the documents, obviously unsure, and inclined her head toward the papers. "How do you know?"

Walker flipped through a few pages of the report until he got to one page. He offered that to Lucia who took it and read while he explained further. "When digitalis is sold commercially, whether for injection or as a pill, it's generally mixed with other ingredients. The analysis of the chemical breakdown solely showed the basic components of digitalis and cocaine."

"And one gets close to unadulterated digitalis how?" Aidan jumped in.

This time it was Lucia who offered up the explanation. "According to this report, digitalis can be extracted from the leaves of a relatively common plant—*digitalis purpurea*— otherwise known as foxglove."

"Foxglove?"

At his question, Lucia handed him the report, which included a picture of a plant.

Aidan read aloud some of the description of the plant. "'The common foxglove can be found widely throughout Europe and the British Isles. Foxgloves have hairy leaves and spiky purple flowers in July. The leaves and seeds can be used for medicinal purposes as they contain cardiac stimulants.'"

"Elizabeth's gardens are full of all kinds of plants, but I don't recollect seeing anything tall and purple."

There was silence for a moment as both Lucia and Walker considered his statement. Then Lucia said, "It's August. That description mentioned that the plant flowers in July."

"So it's possible the plant looks very little like this picture right now. Do you think you can get some more information on the Net while I talk to Elizabeth's friends this morning?"

"Don't you think that might make Ms. Moore suspicious?" Walker asked and began collecting the assorted papers he had laid out for inspection.

Aidan took a last gulp of his coffee and rose from the table. "It might, but it doesn't seem like we have much choice. If the *Quiz* knew about the cocaine and the murder, what's to say they won't find out about the Lazlo Group and blow our cover?"

"Aidan's right. We need to act quickly to get more information," Lucia added.

Walker hesitated, clearly uncertain about their plans, but he finally relented. With a nod, he said, "I'll have to trust your judgment. Especially since it seems from past info that someone is feeding the *Quiz* news in order to discredit the royal family. In the meantime, do you have anything to definitively identify Elizabeth Moore as the Sparrow?"

"Like someone with her body type sneaking through the cellar of her restaurant with Mitch's gun?" Aidan said facetiously, growing irritated with the other man's reticence regarding that part of the investigation.

Walker held up his hands as if in surrender. "Okay, I get it. Too many coincidences that can only point to our chef being the Sparrow and Mitch's killer. What we need to do is connect the Sparrow to the prince's murder," Walker reminded. "First, we have Elizabeth being near the estate at the time of the murder."

Lucia counted down another reason. "And a woman matching her description was seen with the prince."

"If the prince died with a smile on his face, Walker, do we have any DNA at the scene?" Aidan questioned.

The other man shook his head. "Not yet. I've brought in our own team to go over the area and reprocess the prince's body. If the prince and the Sparrow engaged in sexual activity, there will be fluids. We should also try to find any DNA evidence that may tie the killer to the digitalis. If it is from a plant, maybe the DNA can provide a signature to its origins."

"Maybe I can find something similar in Elizabeth's assorted gardens," he tacked on.

Walker glanced at his watch and then at Aidan. "You're on at ten this morning and finished at eleven tonight?"

Aidan smiled suggestively. "Unless I can entertain the lady the way I did last night. If I can…" He pointed to Lucia. "There's a special fiberoptic camera I've been working on. I think you can use it to help pick the locks on the safe and locker since we haven't been able to track down a master key due to their age."

"Not without backup," Walker advised. "I'll be back by ten this morning so that you can prep, Lucia. We'll play it by ear after that."

"Sounds like a plan," she confirmed.

With a nod, Aidan grabbed his jacket and walked out the door. He had a little over an hour left before Elizabeth expected him for work and a lot to do.

He was optimistic, however, that the information from her friends might help seal the deal on Elizabeth being the Sparrow. It might also help him drive away his attraction to the enigmatic woman he'd come to know in the past few days.

Chapter 9

Nothing could have prepared him for what was going on in Samantha's shop. A multitude of women, some of them familiar from last night at the WAC, jockeyed for position around the merchandise, cramming every inch of the store looking for bargains. The young fashion designer was apparently running an immense clearance sale.

Samantha and one of her associates were very busy behind the counter, ringing up and packaging purchases. Clearly the likelihood of talking with Samantha was nil, and when one particularly aggressive woman shoved past him with a shoulder an NHL hockey player would envy, he decided to turn his attention to the other young woman he had met last night.

Kate's shop, which was just a block away from Samantha's, was very much like the woman he had met at the WAC. Quiet. Subdued. Elegant. Everything in her shop sat neatly in order on the shelves and display tables scattered throughout the intimate store.

He browsed around the store while Kate helped a customer. There were an assortment of lotions, salts, perfumes and soaps. Aidan paused at one table and eased the stopper off a bottle. A heavy and rather cloying floral fragrance immediately filled the air before he could replace the top. He wrinkled his nose and quickly put the bottle down.

Moving to the next table, he took note of the assorted flowers being used in the preparations. Plumeria. Peony. Lavender. Lily of the Valley. No foxglove.

He wondered who prepared the floral essences for Kate or whether she did them herself. If it was the latter, it occurred to him that maybe she had been an unwitting accomplice to the Sparrow's kills. Maybe Elizabeth had asked her friend for something of a medicinal nature.

Or maybe Kate had managed to pull off a grand charade, he thought, as he examined her while she worked behind the counter. She was gift wrapping the customer's purchase. Her hands were nimble as she worked. Quick and sure with the scissors, he noted.

Kate was about the right height, although not slim. Definitely more voluptuous and of a slightly larger, but arguably medium build. Her hair leaned toward black more than brown, but of course, a woman's hair color could easily be changed.

As Kate finished and walked over, he gave her his best smile, but like Elizabeth, the lady seemed unaffected.

"You don't strike me as the gardenia type," Kate said and motioned to the bottle he held.

He shot the label a quick glance. "I was looking for something for Elizabeth. Do you know what she might like?"

Kate narrowed her eyes and took a long moment to scrutinize him. "Lizzy Bee doesn't strike me as your type, Aidan."

"Lizzy Bee?" he repeated and recollected her friends calling her by that nickname last night. "Cute," he added.

Kate adopted what some might consider a wary stance, arms across her midsection, head cocked to one side. "What do you want from Lizzy?"

Smiling, he put down the bottle of gardenia oil and moved to another table, Kate trailing behind him. "How about this? Do you think Lizzy Bee would like this?" he asked as he picked up another bottle.

Kate gently removed the fragrance from his hands and put it back in place. "Only her friends call her Lizzy Bee."

He wasn't winning any points by being nice, so maybe some shock factor would help this conversation move along in a more helpful direction. "Well, I'd definitely say that what happened last night could be called friendly."

She surprised him then by getting right in his face, her early wariness brewing into anger. As she poked a finger in his chest, he took a moment to examine her roots—all the same color as the rest of her black hair. Either recently colored or her natural shade.

Kate jabbed him once with her finger as she said, "Look, Mr. Travellin' Man. Lizzy has had enough grief in her life. She doesn't need the likes of you causing any more. Get it?"

Recalling the information in the file about her parents and hoping to elicit further explanation from the now prickly Kate, he urged, "What about Lizzy's family?"

Kate's look turned even harder and her poke this time actually registered on his pain meter. "You'll probably hear it anyway if you linger—Lizzy's mom and dad were killed a long time ago. Best you don't bring that up around her."

"I'm sorry to hear that. Accident?" he asked, his tone conciliatory and finally, a break appeared in Kate's armor.

"Murdered," she replied in soft tones and a telltale sheen erupted in her eyes.

With a slight incline of his head both in recognition of her statement and in deference to the deaths, he said, "I hope they got the bastard who did it."

"Unfortunately not, although if there is such a thing as karma, the prince got what he deserved." She spun away from him, heading back to the counter.

Aidan grabbed a bottle from a table along the way as he

followed her. Once she was there, he placed the bottle on the glass top of the counter holding an antique brass cash register. "Care to explain?"

Kate considered him carefully, as if deciding whether or not his interest was sincere. Apparently he passed muster, because she sighed and picked up the bottle, toying with it nervously as she explained herself. "Rumor had it that Lizzy's parents were accidentally delivered a load of fish stuffed with drugs. Whoever was bringing in the load must have found out and gone to retrieve the drugs."

"And Lizzy's parents were in the way?"

"Or maybe they had already found the hidden drugs and needed to be eliminated. Who knows? A suit from some ministry decided to use his pull to quash the investigation."

"Because the prince was involved in the murders?" Aidan pressed, needing to know because on some level, it justified to him what the Sparrow had done to the prince.

Kate shrugged. "Probably not directly. He was too young. But rumor has it he was a party animal. People like him are as responsible as the dealers who killed Lizzy's parents."

She finally looked down at the bottle in her hands. "Lizzy doesn't wear any perfume. You're better off buying her something she'll use."

She took the bottle with her as she walked away from the counter, placed the oil back on the shelf, paused by another table to pick up a small round jar and returned to where he stood. "Here. This is her favorite hand lotion. Slight hint of plumeria. Her hands get chapped."

That she used something on her hands was good, he thought. It might have left a residue on something at the prince's retreat that would help connect Lizzy—the Sparrow he forced himself to remember—to the murder.

"Thanks. Could you gift wrap it, please?" He dug into his jeans pocket for cash. While he was counting out the money for the lotion, he asked, "So who helps you create the formulas for everything?"

Kate punched up the sale on the antique register. With a loud clang and kachunk, the drawer opened and she finally responded to his question. "Most of them I do myself. Every now and then I ask Lizzy. She's a whiz with plants."

Elizabeth had been prepared to keep her cool around him, wanting to create some distance after what had happened on Friday night. Despite her desire to do so, she found herself surprisingly annoyed when it was Aidan who kept his distance.

He had shown up for work the next day, surprising her. She had been prepared for him to run.

He'd been courteous and respectful. No subtle mentions of Friday night's make-out session. No hint that it had left any kind of impression on him or even that he was inclined for a repeat performance.

Color her annoyed. Saturday and Sunday night had come and gone without any kind of move on his part and as for her—she'd be damned if she'd throw herself at him. Lord knew he'd probably had his share of women doing that, what with those blond good looks and that amazing body. Not to mention that whole swagger thing.

Elizabeth paused in the midst of her workout on the boxing bag as she considered that she was just losing focus about Aidan Rawlings.

A light sweat covered her body from her workout. She grabbed hold of the bag, which was rocking a bit from her last blow, and steadied it, considering as she did so that she'd done just fine in her life without a man. She definitely didn't need one to mess up her life right now.

Punch, punch. Jab followed by a drop kick.

The bag swung away again from the force of the blow and she timed its return arc, swung out with a roundhouse kick, imagining as she did so that it was Aidan's head.

From behind her came the sound of someone approaching. In her peripheral vision, a man's arm came into sight, reaching for her.

She grabbed the arm, high up close to the elbow, and with a shift of her hip, sent him flying over her shoulder and onto the mat face down. Once he was there, she twisted the arm she still held and placed her knee smack in the center of his back, pinning him forcefully to the mat.

Aidan, she thought from the familiar sight of his shoulders and that shaggy mane of sun-bleached hair. She was tempted to release him, but there was a bit of anger there, so she maintained her hold and warned, "Don't sneak up on me."

He turned his face to the side, the only movement he was capable of without dislocating a key body part. "Good mornin', love. I thought I'd drop by and see if you wanted to have breakfast. I guess not."

She released her hold a little. A mistake she quickly realized as he reversed their positions and nailed her to the ground. He had her wrists pinned to the mat in a tight grip. She was breathing a little roughly from her workout, and the motion seemed to drag his attention to her breasts.

Typical man, she thought as he loosened his hold much as she had earlier, giving her enough slack to roll and assume the upper position with Aidan now trapped below her. "We're closed Mondays. I wasn't expecting anyone."

He flexed his hips beneath her, right where she was busy straddling him in a very intimate position, she suddenly realized. "And a very good morning it is. Now," he teased.

"You're no gentleman," she said, freed him and rose, grabbing a towel from inside an open locker.

He was reaching out for her again, but she batted his arm away, disliking his assumption that one kiss gave him the right to touch. "Don't," she warned.

"Like to play rough?" he questioned playfully and as if to test how far he could push, extended his hand toward her once more.

As she had done before, she batted it away, but he teasingly repeated the gesture. Tossing down the towel with which she had been drying off, she once again flung away his arm and took a step toward him. "Mister, if you want to learn about rough, I'm game."

"Oooh. Big tough chef—"

He didn't get a chance to finish the statement as she dropped and swept his legs out from under him. He went down onto the mat in an ignominious sprawl.

He leaned up on his elbows and grinned at her. Damn him, she thought, but stayed out of his reach since she suspected he would be more than capable of taking her down. "Pretty nice moves. Where did you learn them?"

He was just full of questions, it seemed. Kate had told her that he had been by her shop on Saturday, prying into her private life. She wasn't about to satisfy his curiosity. She didn't trust him enough yet to tell him anything. "Let's just say a girl needs to know how to defend herself."

A moment of hesitation played across his face, which afterward, grew serious. "On account of what happened to your parents?"

She knew Kate had spilled the beans about her family history. Despite that, she had not been prepared for him to raise the subject. There wasn't anything really personal going on between them. Yet, the daring little voice in her head tacked on.

Walking back to the locker, she picked up the towel from the floor and began collecting her things, intent on going ahead with her normal Monday routine.

Out of the corner of her eye, she watched as Aidan stood and dusted himself off. He took a step toward her, then seemed to reconsider the wisdom of that. Grasping his hands in front of him tightly, he said, "Could we start over?"

Juggling her bag and towel in her hand, she half turned and said, "Meaning?"

"Good morning, Elizabeth. Would you care to have breakfast?" he asked in that husky bedroom voice of his.

She picked up her chin a defiant notch, determined not to let his charm affect her. "Sorry, but breakfast was two hours ago."

He glanced at his watch and with a carefree tone said, "How about lunch then?"

Determined, she would give him that. Smiling, she replied, "That's not for another three hours. Maybe four since I had a nice big breakfast."

In response, his stomach growled. He rubbed his hand over his midsection to silence it. "So what do you plan to do in the meantime? It is your day off after all."

"There's never a day off," she replied and walked to the stairs.

Aidan was immediately there, following her. Was it her imagination that he shot an inquisitive look at the safe and lockers? she wondered, but then realized that his gaze was securely fixed to her Lycra-clad backside.

With a roll of her eyes, and a little extra swing to her hips, she went up the stairs, advising him as she did so, "I plan on shopping."

"Shopping?" he croaked and shot a glance up at her face to see if she was serious. When he realized that she was, he said, "Shopping, huh. Well, I guess I'm game if it includes taking you to lunch."

She paused on the top step and examined his face. He was clearly sincere with his response. She told herself not to be too flattered that he'd risk shopping in exchange for lunch with her. Some men would do anything to impress a girl and Aidan definitely seemed to be that kind of man. Despite her awareness of that, she didn't feel like turning him down. He intrigued her too much, as dangerous as she knew that might be.

"It's a deal. Come back in half an hour. I need to shower."

"I'll just hang in the garden," he replied and once they were on the ground floor, she walked to her cottage while Aidan sat on the stone wall by the cottage path, perusing the various plants.

It occurred to her that there was something odd about his behavior since the other night. Maybe their little excursion would be just the thing to find out what he was really up to.

Her intuition told her Mr. Rawlings was interested in something she might not like.

Chapter 10

Aidan turned his attention to the assorted flowers in the restaurant's backyard and alongside the cottage. He didn't have a clue what most of the plants were and didn't care. His mind was focused on looking for the tall, spiky, purple-flowered plant that would put the final nails in the Sparrow's coffin.

As he searched and snapped photos with his PDA for good measure, cautiously walking along the edge of the garden, it occurred to him that today's little display of martial arts had almost iced it for him. What he couldn't understand is why that bothered him? For two years he'd been searching for the Sparrow and now that she was almost in his grasp, he was actually almost regretting it.

It wasn't because of the fact that she was attractive. He'd had his share of beautiful women to enjoy.

Was it because she was basically a really nice person from what he had seen of her behavior? Possibly. It definitely wasn't because of their kisses, or how good it had been with her riding him during their little physical interlude that morning.

He cursed when excitement awoke at the recollection of her above him, pressed tight, rousing him.

Shooting a glance at the cottage, he realized she was already inside. He switched the functions on his PDA just to confirm it. He had rigged his equipment last night to accept the signal from the assorted cameras and with a few swipes of his stylus, he got to the video feed from her bedroom.

She was undressing for the shower, her back to the camera. Totally unaware that anyone was keeping an eye on her.

He swallowed hard as she tossed aside her workout pants and eased off her panties. Her ass was perfection—and those legs…

He swiped at the sweat that popped out on his forehead and blamed the sun and leather jacket he was wearing, but he couldn't pull his gaze from the PDA.

"Mixmaster. Come in, Mixmaster," Lucia called out over the earpiece.

"What is it, Red Rover?" he snapped as Elizabeth slipped her fingers under the band of her sports bra and eased it up and over her head, displaying the long sweet line of her back, the flare of her breast as she bent to toss the bra and T-shirt on her bed.

"Bad, bad boy, Aidan. You're supposed to be looking at the flowers."

Cursing beneath his breath again as he realized Lucia was observing him, he shut off the video feed on the PDA and returned to camera mode so he could snap off a few photos for additional review. He would send them in via the satellite uplink in his PDA. "Copy, Red Rover. Prep yourself. In half an hour you can try and pick the locks if you've got the backup."

"Walker should be here shortly," she advised and Aidan extended his search for the foxglove to the front yard. Like the gardens in the back, this was a riot of colorful flowers mixed with green leaves and accented with foliage of burgundy, white and gold.

Nothing resembled the foxglove, and Elizabeth would be down shortly.

He strode across the front yard and was stalking around

the corner of the building when he noticed a patch of plants with little spikelets of flowers that weren't quite purple in his book. More a deep rose color, but the blooms were bell-shaped. As he bent and examined the leaves, he realized they were fuzzy. Fuzzy probably passed for hairy in the plant world and foxglove was supposed to be hairy.

Upon closer examination, he realized that the plants had at one time had another larger, central stalk. It prompted a recollection from the materials Lucia had downloaded for him—it was common to cut down the main flower spike after it was past its prime to produce a secondary flowering.

Bending, he took a plastic evidence bag from his pocket and, careful to use the bag to safeguard the integrity of the sample, snipped off leaves from a few different plants. He also took a moment to snap a picture.

"Find something?" Lucia questioned.

Aidan nodded, aware that she would see him via the garden camera. "You might say the mother lode. Let Walker know. I'm e-mailing you all the pictures now for someone to examine."

He placed the bag back into his pocket, quickly dispatched an e-mail with the digital photos, and returned to the backyard, settling himself on the low stone wall to wait for Elizabeth.

When she emerged, she nearly took his breath away. White capri pants emphasized those amazing legs and slim lines. A white crop top with pink polka dots left most of her sculpted midriff exposed. Her thick mass of hair was tied back with a pale-pink scarf, pulling his attention to her amazing eyes and the full lips he had liked kissing so much the other night.

Damn. She was dressed to kill and as her gaze met his, he realized it was not by accident.

She didn't know why she had chosen this particular outfit, but the flare of heat in Aidan's eyes proved she had made a good choice. That is, if she wanted whatever was happening between them to progress to the next level. Which her daring side was thinking she might, immediately before her more repressed side argued that it was totally insane. Daring side being ahead two to nothing at this point.

Reaching into the denim drawstring bag she was using as a purse, she pulled out her keys and dangled them before him. "We need to get the car. It's garaged a few blocks down."

He fell into step beside her as they walked to the main street and then toward the docks. They had gone only a short distance when she stopped by the garage next to the fish shop her parents had used to own.

Aidan seemed quick to pick up on that, for he asked, "Your parents' old store?"

With a nod, she slipped the key into the lock on the garage door. "After they died, a cousin took over running the shop in exchange for buying it out. It helped pay some of the bills."

"But not all?" he questioned.

"Not all," she answered truthfully. If Aidan was after something other than time with her, best he know now that money wasn't necessarily something of which she had a lot. The restaurant turned a profit, but only enough for her to be comfortable.

When she reached for the handle to lift the door, he said, "Let me."

She stepped aside and he grabbed hold of the garage door handle and lifted the door to reveal her father's prized roadster.

Aidan let out a low whistle. "That's a beauty. What is it?"

She walked into the garage and ran her hand lovingly over the hood. "A 1962 Gaston convertible. It was my Da's."

Sleek and sporty, the car screamed speed, she thought, and lovingly ran a hand over the smooth line of the driver's-side fender.

Aidan walked around the car, smiling. "This is a classic. Eight-cylinder engine. Chrome fenders, exhaust and spoke-wire wheels. Even the racing stripe," he said with the unadulterated glee of a boy on Christmas morning.

"Da's pride and joy. Silvershire's finest, he said. I even bought one of the Gaston new hybrids a few years back, but gave it up to keep this one."

"I can see why," he replied and ran his hand along the buttery-smooth leather of the passenger seat.

"Help me put the top down," she replied after Aidan had finished his inspection of the roadster.

He did as she asked and once the top was down and secured, eased into the passenger seat. She started the car and even with its age, the engine was as smooth as ever. She made it a point to have the car regularly serviced as her father might have if he was still alive.

Wheeling the low-slung roadster out of the garage, she turned onto the road leading away from town and Aidan looked at her quizzically. "Where are we headed?"

"Everywhere and anywhere. Just trust me," she said, smiling as the sun shone down on them and the wind blew into the cab of the car as she picked up speed.

Aidan's gaze met hers, and for a moment it seemed as if he was wondering if he could trust her. As quickly as that emotion came it fled, and he was grinning at her, his blue eyes even more startling in color in the bright sun and clear, cloudless day. He settled back into the leather seat of the Gaston, and she turned inland, deciding to save the coast road for the afternoon trip home.

Besides, they were going to have to do their shopping if she was to have fresh things for the restaurant and something they could eat for lunch. Maybe even dinner together if the day turned out right. She wouldn't consider that breakfast was a possibility. She had not met a man special enough to stay overnight in quite some time.

She drove along the woodland country roads for a quarter of an hour or so until they neared the prince's retreat. As they passed the tall wrought-iron gates that marked off part of the grounds, Aidan asked, "Is that private property?"

Peering toward the gates, she said, "It belonged to the prince, God rest his soul."

"Funny thing for you to say," Aidan quickly replied.

"Why do you think that?" she wondered, but kept her attention to the road. Deer were quite common in these woods as no hunting was permitted on the royal estate.

"According to Kate, you believe he's responsible for what happened to your mother and father," Aidan said, his tone almost…condemning.

She finally shot him a glance out of the corner of her eye, trying to understand where he was coming from. Wanting him to know just where she stood on the topic of the late prince. "People like him…don't care that their fun might hurt others. So that makes him responsible in a way."

With a shake of his head, he stressed, "But the royals don't get treated like you and me. If he did drugs, he and his friends were never going to pay for what harm they caused with that."

He was almost baiting her, wanting her to admit she had wanted the prince dead. When her parents had first died and the investigation had apparently been shut down by the royal family's minions, she had wanted to understand why and she wanted retribution. Had been prepared to seek it out herself. But then reason had replaced her anger and she had realized that eventually whoever was responsible would get what he deserved. If Reginald's drug habit had started that early, his life had probably been hell anyway.

"Whether on this plane or another, Reginald was eventually going to face the consequences of his actions," she finally answered, but her response did little to appease Aidan, she realized as she shot another quick glance at him. If anything, his face grew harder and a muscle clenched along his jaw.

When he spoke, his words were curt and filled with pain. "If it was someone I cared about, I'd want him punished. Now, and not in some afterlife."

The emotion was so intense, it compelled her to stop the car. After she did so, she faced him and laid her hand over his clenched fist where it rested on his thigh. "You lost someone like I lost my parents?"

Aidan knew he was close to blowing it, but her calm acceptance that the prince would get his punishment flew in the face of what he suspected she had done. And not just to the prince. But as she placed her smooth palm over his hand and her gaze met his, it was hard to believe she could commit those acts.

Her touch was gentle. The empathy in her gaze nearly undid him. *Nearly* being the operative word. He reined in his desire to test her reaction to Mitch's name and instead, decided to use her own ploy against her.

"My best friend."

"I'm sorry," she said and rubbed her hand over his in a gesture meant to soothe.

Aidan pressed. "If I knew who did it, I would kill them."

Her hand stilled. Her eyebrows knitted together as she contemplated his words. Finally, in a tone so soft he barely heard her, she said, "Then that would end two lives instead of one, wouldn't it? Your's and the killer's."

She met his gaze then, dead on, her chin in a slightly defiant tilt. Her sherry-colored eyes had deepened to the color of a fine aged cognac. He was hard pressed to know whether she was challenging him or troubled by the prospect of what he had claimed he would do.

Given the Sparrow's track record, he couldn't imagine that she would be worried about his coming after her. She'd proven herself too worthy an opponent already. As for the possibility that she was challenging him, that would mean that he had maybe blown his cover, and she knew he was referring to her and Mitch.

If he had done the latter, there was possibly one way to know for sure. "His name was Mitch," he said and waited for her reaction.

"Mitch? Was he the friend who was killed?" she asked, no hint of any recognition on her face.

He went for broke. "Someone knifed him in an alleyway in Rome."

No hint again of anything on her face or in her tone indicated she had a clue what he was talking about. "Was it a robbery? Or a fight over something?"

"Does it matter?" he replied and finally her face reflected some emotion—pain.

"No, it doesn't. Dead is dead. Out of your life. Never to hold you again. Or laugh with you."

She whirled in her seat, then started up the car and pulled onto the road again. As she drove, she occasionally swiped at her eyes, but said nothing else.

Great. He had made her cry. He hated to see women cry. Call him a sucker, but the waterworks always did him in.

And somehow, he couldn't imagine the Sparrow allowing herself the luxury of tears. Which just confused him even more. Elizabeth's words and actions contradicted what he had expected.

Again he told himself to remember that the Sparrow was likely a sociopath and perfectly capable of such a deception. Walker would remind him of that. He suspected the earpiece he still wore had exceeded the range for transmission back to the hotel. A shame. If Walker had been listening in, he might have been able to get a better read on Elizabeth.

Elizabeth, he thought and examined her again. The pale-pink scarf securing her hair matched the polka dots in her shirt. The color brought out the hints of red in her lush hair. The wind was tossing about the few strands that had escaped the scarf. She must have sensed him watching her for she glanced his way for a moment before returning her attention to the road.

"What's so interesting?" she asked, seemingly uncomfortable with his perusal.

"You. You're beautiful," he said, wanting to change the

mood that had taken over since their earlier discussion. Hoping that change would lead to other things. He told himself that was what was necessary for him to break down her barriers and really determine what was going on with her.

But it wasn't a lie that he found her...*attractive* wasn't quite the right word. She was...stunning. Interesting. A woman with multiple layers he wanted to peel back. He suspected that so far he had only managed to scrape the first few layers.

She smiled and a touch of pink in a shade darker than her scarf stained her cheeks. Sparing him yet another glance, she said, "I bet you say that to all the girls."

Grinning, he replied, "Only the pretty ones."

Chapter 11

Elizabeth drove around a bend in the road that led out of the woods and to the first of her regular stops. Up ahead, another car was already parked at one side of the road while along the other, a fence kept an assortment of goats and cows in an emerald-colored pasture thick with summer grass.

She slowed as she pulled up behind the other car, and Aidan asked, "Is this where we're shopping?"

"We call it 'hedge veg,'" she explained and parked the Gaston along the side of the road.

"'Hedge veg?'" Aidan repeated and cocked his head to the side in question. "Is that like the Silvershire version of green markets?"

She shook her head and tucked a few loose strands of hair back. "It's not just greens and typically, we don't stop at markets. Come with me and you'll see."

Not waiting for his reply, since at this point he was basically her captive audience, she slipped from the car and walked to meet him where he waited by the chromed front bumper of the Gaston. As she approached, he offered his arm and touched by the chivalrous gesture, she eased her arm through his. They strolled past the other parked auto and toward a modest covered stand by the side of the road and in front of a well-kept farmhouse. A man who had apparently just made a purchase strolled past them, bag in hand.

"Hi, Addy," she called out once they were closer to the stand.

The older gray-haired woman behind the counter smiled broadly and walked around to give her an enthusiastic hug and Aidan an inquisitive look.

"And this would be?" Addy asked as she shook Aidan's hand.

"Aidan. I'm Elizabeth's new bartender."

Once again, Addy's look was speculative as it passed from Aidan and back to her, but she ignored it. "What do you have for me today?"

Addy grabbed her hand and nearly dragged her over to the counter. "The goat cheese is out of this world today and the husband just finished up a batch of mozzarella," she said and motioned to the samples spread out on the table.

Elizabeth first tasted the goat cheese. Creamy, with a full-bodied flavor. She scooped up another bit on a cracker and offered it up to Aidan, who had come to stand beside her.

He opened his mouth and she popped it in. After chewing, he nodded emphatically. "That's good."

Next, they sampled the mozzarella. Still warm from the vats where it was prepared, the cheese had a rich creamy flavor, milder than the goat cheese and with a firmer consistency. She smiled at Addy to show her approval and said, "I'll take a dozen each of both these cheeses if you have that many. Only, I'm not headed straight back to town. I could pick them up tomorrow…."

Addy waved off her suggestion. "Not to worry, luv. My George has to pop into town during the morning, so he can drop them off."

"Thanks so much. In the meantime, we'll need something

for a picnic lunch. How about the…" She glanced over at Aidan and waited for him to make the selection.

He shrugged, seemingly unsure at first, but then he pointed to the goat cheese.

"Great choice," she confirmed, and Addy quickly wrapped up a round of the cheese in some grape leaves, dropped it into a bag, and passed it to Aidan to carry.

"You two have a nice day now," the older woman called out as they returned to the car.

Aidan tucked the bag into the space behind the front seats that arguably passed for a back seat. It brought a memory to Elizabeth of her and Dani crammed onto that narrow leather bench as young girls while her family did the hedge veg together.

She was smiling as she eased behind the wheel and Aidan must have noticed it, for he said, "Penny for your thoughts."

"Only a penny?" she teased, starting up the car and steering it back onto the main road.

Aidan examined her face carefully, wondering what had put that enigmatic smile there. It was a smile filled with pleasure, but also with a hint of…nostalgia. Surprisingly, he knew the thought wasn't one about him, although how he could read her that well, he didn't know.

Or maybe she was just acting once again. She *was* the Sparrow after all. Or at least, that's what he forced himself to remember.

The next stop was barely a few miles away: a farmhouse where the yeasty aromas of fresh-baked bread wafted all the way to the roadside. As before, there was a stand and this time, a few other patrons were already lined up for the homemade wares.

Just as at the other location, the older woman behind the counter was clearly pleased to see Elizabeth, but then again he told himself, why wouldn't she be glad to see someone who was probably a good customer? Although, as with Addy, there appeared to be something more personal there, which was confirmed when at one point, the two women stepped to the side and Elizabeth eased her arm over the older women's shoulders.

A more serious discussion obviously ensued. Definitely one that wasn't about the assortment of breads and rolls the woman had for sale. At the end of the conversation, the two exchanged an emotion-packed hug before returning to the stand where the woman placed a number of different rolls in a brown paper bag.

Elizabeth paid her, grabbed the bag and handed it to him. "So I'm the bag man, is that it?"

She grinned at him playfully and nudged his shoulder with a closed fist. "You've got to earn your lunch somehow."

He bit back a rather risque comment on how he could earn that lunch.

With a nod, he followed her back to the car, tucked away their purchase and they were off to another stop and then another and another. It took hours to run from one roadside stand to another, sampling the assorted items available for sale. At one small farm that barely looked inhabited, a rough-hewn ramshackle table held a meager sampling of thumb-sized pear-shaped tomatoes. Beside what was left of the tomatoes, a basket contained some money, obviously payment for prior purchases.

Elizabeth perused the tomatoes, selected a few dozen, and deposited some bills into the basket.

"How do you know that's not too much money?" he asked, and then quickly added, "And how does the farmer know people will pay?"

"Dan, the farmer, he's a bit shy. But he knows people will pay for what they take. It's the honor system."

"The honor system," he repeated, but unfortunately couldn't keep the tone of disbelief from his voice.

Elizabeth smiled and shook her head. "Mr. Rawlings, you've clearly seen your share of places where things are…different. In Silvershire, we are simpler. Some things, like honor, still exist."

With that, she walked back to the car, her bag of tomatoes in hand.

He watched her go, intrigued. Perplexed. From their earlier conversation to this one, from the way everyone they met interacted with her, Elizabeth was clearly well-liked and respected, trusted and, last but not least, honorable.

Aidan forced himself to remember that even amongst thieves honor existed.

Back in the car, Elizabeth advised they would make one more stop before heading to a special place for a quick bite. That last location was a vineyard within sight of the water. "Hector makes a wicked collection of pinots. It has to do with the way the coastal fog covers the grapes in the morning and the way the blackthorn and other wild berry bushes surround the vineyard," Elizabeth explained as she drove.

"Is this the ever-requested Lionshead wine?" he asked and Elizabeth nodded as she steered down a short winding road lined by brambly bushes—probably the berries Elizabeth had mentioned.

At the end of the road was a stone building, similar in size and construction to Elizabeth's restaurant—a one-story building made of stone and covered by vines in spots. After they parked the car in the crushed-seashell-covered lot, they walked to the open door of the building.

Inside there were two long counters with some smaller tables and chairs before them—a tasting room from the looks of it, he thought, recalling one Mitch had dragged them to many years earlier during a layover in California's Napa Valley.

"Hector? Are you open?" Elizabeth called out and walked toward the counters.

A man immediately popped out of the back room. Once he realized it was Elizabeth, a broad smile came to his face. *"Mi amiga,"* he said, arms opened wide as he strode toward her.

"Como estas, Hector?" She embraced the handsome man. He was maybe in his mid thirties and attractive if you liked the dark swarthy types, he thought and bit back the little pang of jealousy.

Hector shot a glance at him. An unfriendly one confirming to Aidan that maybe the feeling was mutual. "And this is?" Hector asked after releasing Elizabeth and walking to one of the long counters, where he picked up a bottle and opened it, removing first the foil seal at the top and after, the cork.

Elizabeth held her hand out to Aidan. He slipped his hand into hers and sat next to her at the counter as she said, "This is Aidan. My new bartender."

"Oh," Hector said, but made no effort to take the introduction beyond that. Instead, he placed a glass before each of thcm and said, "Try my new vintage."

Pouring a bit of wine into each glass, he waited for Elizabeth to offer her comments.

Aidan just picked up the wineglass and took a large sip, earning a murderous glare from Hector. Elizabeth on the other hand, held the glass up to the light, then tilted it on its side. "Good color and tone."

Placing the glass on the counter, she grabbed the stem and rotated it to swirl the wine. Once the wine had settled down, she picked up the glass and sniffed the wine. "Wonderful robust bouquet."

With more of a slurp than a sip, she finally sampled it. "Exceptional, Hector. You can really taste the berries. Mostly…blackberry?" she questioned.

Hector enthusiastically confirmed her guess. "So, you like?"

Nodding, she said, "I like, a lot. Can I get a case delivered to the restaurant and one bottle for now?"

Glancing in Aidan's direction as he realized he would likely be the imbiber of the single bottle of wine, Hector glared at him again, but Aidan merely smiled at the man.

With a grumble beneath his breath about wine heathens, Hector stalked into the back room and a few seconds later, emerged with the single bottle, which he lovingly entrusted to Elizabeth. "Enjoy it, *amiga*," he said, but all the time he scowled at Aidan.

Elizabeth leaned over the counter and gave Hector a friendly kiss, seemingly unaware of what was going on between him and Aidan. As they exited the tasting room, she met his gaze and smiled. "Ready for that late lunch?"

Aidan shot a quick peek at his watch and realized it was nearly four. "A very late lunch. Possibly early dinner."

She stopped and checked her own watch. "I'm sorry. Time just seemed to fly. Would you rather return to town?"

He stood before her. She looked so troubled that he needed to ease her discomfort. Cupping her cheek, he ran his finger along the smooth skin there, which had a touch of color—the kiss of the sun from their drive. "I've had a great time so far. It's been…enlightening."

An odd choice of words, Elizabeth thought as she examined him. He seemed sincere enough about having enjoyed the day so far, and so she said, "All right, then. We're off to lunch."

Back behind the wheel of the car, she continued onward to the coast road and turned in the direction of Leonia. As she drove, she alternated glances between the coastline to her right, the road before her and Aidan in the passenger seat. He was looking toward her and then past her to the rugged shoreline.

It took another fifteen minutes or so to reach the spot. Her spot. One free of ghosts.

She had discovered it one day many years back during one of her hedge-veg runs. Pulling the car over to a switchback along the coast side of the road, she parked the Gaston and faced Aidan. "Ready?"

He confirmed, "Ready."

She leaned into the back of the car and grabbed just a few of the packages stored there and handed them to Aidan. "I just need to get something from the back," she said.

They both stepped out of the car, but he waited by the front fender while she went to the back. Opening the trunk, she removed the blanket and picnic basket her mother had always kept there for an impromptu stop. She slipped the blanket under one arm and grabbed the basket with that hand. Walking toward Aidan, she offered him her other hand and he took hold of it.

Hand in hand they walked down the grass-covered slope until they were at its rocky edge. Once there, they paused for a moment to appreciate the view. To the left were the imposing palisades and rugged shoreline of Silvershire's North Coast. To the right, Leonia Bay with the sister towns of Leonia and Tiberia nestled at its foot. In the bay, sailboats and fishermen's boats travelled to and fro, or put out to sea.

"Beautiful," he said, but as their gazes met, it was clear he wasn't referring to the view.

The intensity of his interest created a funny little feeling inside her. Bolstered by that feeling, she smiled at him, took a step closer and cradled his cheek. Beneath her palm there was the rasp of his evening beard and the warmth of his skin. She ran her finger along that beard and then to the edge of his lips, fascinated by them. By him.

She dragged her gaze from his lips and up to his eyes. Against the backdrop of sky and sea, they seemed even more blue than before. "Are you hungry?" she asked, but the question suddenly had little to do with food.

Aidan placed his hand on her waist, on the bare piece of skin exposed by the crop top. His hand was hot. His palm rough against the soft skin of her midsection. "Famished," he replied and closed the last little bit of distance between them.

She had to look up at him with his greater height. She watched as he bent his head until his lips were almost on hers. "Is this crazy?" he asked and again, she was puzzled by his choice of words.

Brushing her lips against his in the barest of kisses, she said, "Is it because I'm your boss?"

He pulled away then and his face mirrored his bewilderment and withdrawal. "Let's eat," he said and held the basket so she could lay out the blanket.

She hesitated for a moment, equally confused and…hurt.

She wasn't normally one to just throw herself at a man and now that she almost had…

Denied, her repressed side almost gloated. It stung a bit, but she wasn't going to let that ruin what had been a wonderful day.

Spreading out the blanket on the prickly grass by the rocky bluff, she then took the picnic basket from him and placed it to one side. Then she accepted the remaining items from him, including the bottle of wine, and worked on creating a spur-of-the-moment meal.

The goat cheese went on one plate and she surrounded it with the pear tomatoes, drizzling them with the fresh-pressed virgin olive oil she had bought. She took a bit of sea salt and, with her fingers, sprinkled it all over the cheese and tomatoes.

She placed that plate in the space between her and Aidan, who had taken a spot on the opposite side of the blanket.

On another plate, she placed the rolls and slices of a dry-aged ham similar to a prosciutto purchased at one of their stops. That plate joined the other, and then she handed Aidan the bottle of wine, a corkscrew and some glasses.

"Are you always this prepared?" he asked and took the items from her.

"We always picnicked," she explained. "Sometimes it was after a shopping expedition or a hike. Sometimes a day at the beach."

"It sounds like your family had fun," he said and she nodded, but battled the mix of sadness and happiness the memory brought.

"Yes, we did. I miss them a lot."

Her voice had a tight feel to it. As he looked at her again, he could see the glint of unshed tears. He picked up his hand and moved it toward her, wanting to comfort her once again, but then quickly let it drop back down. This was crazy, he thought, much as he had told himself earlier. Crazy because there were too many secrets between them. Too many doubts.

So instead, he concentrated on opening the wine and

pouring glasses for each of them while she put out the final plate—a dish piled high with an assortment of summer berries.

He handed her a glass filled with Hector's wine, and offered up a silent toast. He waited for her to take a roll, break off a piece and then scoop up a bit of the oil-drizzled cheese. She popped the snack into her mouth and smiled. "Delicious." After, she reached for one of the tomatoes and did the same.

Aidan joined her, ate some of the bread and cheese. The flavors were…amazing. The tang of the cheese and fruitiness of the oil. The creaminess of it all against the crustiness and yeasty taste of the bread. He reached for a tomato and like the bread and cheese, the flavor was intense. Earthy and sweet. "Really, really good."

"Try this," she said and offered a bit of the ham that she had wrapped around a chunk of the bread. He let her feed him the morsel. Again, the tastes and textures were alive in his mouth.

"Hmm," he replied and washed down the bite with a sip of the wine. It was, as she'd noted in the tasting room, quite good. And he could taste the hint of berries.

Or maybe it was his imagination, since from beyond the rim of the glass he was busy watching Elizabeth toss back a bit of the wine and eat a strawberry. As he brought the glass down, their gazes collided and he realized that no matter what he thought she might be, he found her incredibly interesting. Complex. Desirable.

And the feeling, it occurred to him as her gaze travelled over his face and settled on his lips, was apparently decidedly mutual.

Take it slow, he told himself. He needed to explore all the nuances of the woman sitting across from him, just as he could with the wine in the glass. Maybe he could uncover other things about her, as well, during this little…interlude.

He reached for a strawberry—a big, red ripe one. Picking it up, he brought it to her lips.

She covered his hand with hers, as if to steady it. A sweet touch. Gentle.

She took a bite of the berry and the juice from it escaped onto her lips, reddening them. She licked the juice away with her tongue.

He nearly groaned as he imagined that tongue licking other things. As it was, he had to shift his position on the blanket to ease the pressure of his erection against his jeans.

Men were sometimes too easy, Elizabeth thought. But as she took note of other things, her mouth suddenly went dry and she realized, maybe men and women weren't all that different, as parts of her suddenly became…ready.

Physical response notwithstanding, she knew nothing about Aidan other than he would leave, and he in turn knew little about her. Not who or what she was. Not what she wanted from life.

But then again, maybe this didn't have anything to do with any of that. Maybe this was one of those carpe diem times. Time to seize and be seized in return without any thought as to where that would lead. When the voice of common sense rose up to tell her it would lead to nothing good, she batted it way, tired of being sensible.

Grabbing another bit of bread and cheese, she once again offered it up to him. A little smidge of cheese remained on his lips and he must have sensed it for he was reaching up to wipe it away when she said, "Let me."

He stopped, his gaze on her face as she shifted on the blanket to move closer and then, flicked her tongue over his lips to remove that one errant piece of cheese.

He moaned then. Or at least she thought he did, but he made no move to take it any further.

So maybe he wasn't as easy as she had thought. It wasn't going to stop her from doing the seizing. She was a modern woman after all.

Aidan took a deep breath to control himself since he wanted nothing more than to kiss her and lay her down on that blanket and take off every last piece of…

He gritted his jaw and told himself to maintain perspective. He was investigating her. She was likely a renowned assassin who would gut him quite easily with that little knife she was using to remove the skin from a pear she had pulled out of another bag.

With the pear peeled, she made slices which she placed on the plate beside the strawberries. Once she was done, she sipped her wine, grabbed a little more of the bread, cheese and ham. Another tomato.

He watched her enjoy the food with such gusto. He wanted to join her in that sensation and so he did the same, eating more of their purchases. He reached for a slice of pear but was waylaid as she offered her slice to him; he, in turn, offered her his slice.

The pear was sweet and so ripe that the juices dripped onto his fingers and downward. His gaze was locked with hers as they brought the slices of fruit to each other's mouths. Their eyes never wavered from each other as they both bit down and ate the pear slices.

But when nothing was left and he would have reached for another piece, she did the unexpected.

She grabbed hold of his hand and brought it close to her mouth. Slowly, she licked the pear juice from each of his fingers and then finally, slipped his index finger into her mouth to lick it some more.

It was his undoing; he nearly burst the seams on his jeans.

He grasped her head in his hands, but some last little crumb of chivalry reared its head as he asked, "Are you sure about this?"

"No," she said, and he had to smile at her honesty.

Thieves, he reminded himself as he closed the distance between them and said, "Me, neither," just a moment before he finally kissed her as he had wanted to all day long.

Chapter 12

The other night hadn't been an aberration, she thought. He really was an amazing kisser. His mouth was hard and soft. Gentle and rough. Warm.

Unbelievably delicious, she thought, as she licked his lips and tasted the pear and berries and cheese, and, beneath it all, the elusive but heady taste of Aidan.

She whimpered. Or, at least, she thought she did, which made him back away for a second until he realized it was a good kind of sound and he smiled.

She could feel that smile against her lips which in turn, made her chuckle.

He seized the opportunity then and dipped his tongue into her mouth, increased the pressure of his hand on the back of her head. She met his tongue with hers, tasting him. Exploring the different sensations of his mouth, tongue and lips. Of his warm breath coming roughly against her mouth as he expelled a ragged groan.

"Lizzy Bee," he said, but she pulled away from him then, afraid of the intimacy in his tone.

"Don't call me that." She added hastily, "Please."

The warmth in his eyes grew cold. "I guess only your friends call you that," he said and withdrew from her.

Talk about ruining the moment, she thought and plucked at the fabric of her pants. "I'm sorry. I didn't—"

He cut her off with the curt motion of his hand. "It's okay, Elizabeth. Really. I remember the rules—don't touch."

She struggled for the right words. "It's not that. It's just… You're right that only my friends call me that. And my family. And you're—"

"Neither," he quickly shot out and peered at her, his gaze condemning.

"Neither," she repeated lamely. "But I'm…attracted to you and…"

Her hands searched in the air as if she might pluck her explanation from there, but could find nothing better than, "I like you. I want to get to know you. I thought I could do this right now, only—"

She didn't get to finish as he suddenly resumed where they'd left off—kissing her with his lips and tongue until she moaned, and he finally eased away. "We need to take this a little slower, right?"

"Definitely," she confirmed and smiled. "Sometimes you can't rush things."

"Right," he said and picked up his glass. "Like a good wine—"

"It takes patience and…nurturing," she finished for him.

"Caring," he surprised her by saying, and, for a moment, it seemed as if he'd surprised himself by admitting it, so much so that there was almost a physical reaction on his part as his body tensed and he sat up straighter.

"Aidan?" she asked and he forced a smile.

"This is…new for me," Aidan replied. It wasn't a lie. It was new for him on so many levels. He had never lost control with another woman before as he had with Elizabeth. He had never lost his perspective while on an assignment, but here he was, clearly in jeopardy of doing so. Or maybe he had already, since he found himself reviewing over and over again all the things he'd learned about her in the past few days, trying to weigh them against the evidence that he knew pointed to her being the Sparrow.

When she gave him a shy smile and the blush of the sun's kiss deepened on her face, it became even harder thinking of her as an assassin.

"It's new for me, too," she said.

He nodded in resignation, uncomfortable with where this was leading. "Let's finish up and head back."

"Let's," she said as if sensing that to push more right now would only cause problems. "The coast road is beautiful during the day, but at night it can be a little difficult."

He had been so distracted by her, he hadn't realized how much time had gone by and how quickly dusk was coming upon them. Perusing the shoreline, he caught glimpses of the road they would take back to town. It wound wickedly along the coast. In spots, the road hugged the edges of the rocky palisades before it led downward toward the two towns nestled at the base of the harbor.

He helped her put away the food that remained and fold up the blanket. Once everything was carefully stowed in the trunk, Elizabeth got back behind the wheel of the car and he slipped in beside her. As she started up the car, he said, "I had a nice time today."

Grinning broadly, she replied, "I did, too, but the day's not over yet. You're going to love the views on the road home."

He was kind of loving the view right now, he thought, but didn't say so. It would just embarrass her. Instead, he contented himself with watching her out of the corner of his eye as she steered onto the road and they began the downward trek along the coast.

It was as beautiful as she had said: the harsh imposing cliffs and rocks against the cerulean blue of the ocean and baby blue of the sky, Elizabeth in her pink a vibrant contrast in the foreground.

She handled the car well, maintaining a controlled pace along the downhill road with its constant curves, some of which came precariously close to the rocky edges of the cliffs. They were about halfway down the road, along a stretch that was a little straighter, when an SUV suddenly appeared behind them.

Aidan was a bit surprised he hadn't noticed the car before, or maybe it had just turned onto the road behind them. Something bothered him about the car. Okay, maybe more than one thing. The windows were tinted so darkly it was impossible to see inside. The black of its oversized hulk loomed behind them as it picked up speed, getting closer and closer.

Elizabeth had noticed the car, as well, and muttered, "Wonder where he's going at that speed. It gets kind of hairy up—"

She didn't get to finish as the SUV suddenly lurched forward and bumped them from behind. The Gaston swerved wildly as Elizabeth battled for control, but she quickly regained it and centered the car in her lane.

Aidan gripped the wooden dash with one hand, Elizabeth's seat with the other as he braced himself for another possible impact. He looked back and noticed that the SUV had fallen behind by at least a car length. Elizabeth had sped up to avoid the other vehicle.

But a second later, the black SUV hurtled forward like a battering ram, smashing into their back bumper once more. The sickening crunch of metal and tinkling of glass sounded. The impact whipped them back and forth within the car, which fishtailed once more with the blow.

Elizabeth, however, didn't panic. If anything, a determined glint came into her eyes. Her jaw set into a tight line. She expertly steered out of the fishtail and into the middle of the road. This time, she kept dead center, ignoring the white lines for the lanes as if to give herself room to maneuver.

Aidan looked back and out of the corner of his eye, noted Elizabeth using the rearview mirror to keep the SUV in sight while staying aware of the road ahead. A road that was veering sharply to the right. To the left—nothing but sky and sea. Not even a guard rail.

Shit, he thought, until Elizabeth—looking more like an Indy race-car driver than a chef—downshifted and hit the gas. Wheels squealed as they shot around the curve and created a few car lengths of good distance on the bulkier SUV, which barely managed to stay on the road.

Dirt kicked up as the driver of the other vehicle skirted the warning edge along the coast side of the road, but then they were into another short straightaway and the SUV picked up speed.

So did Elizabeth.

"Elizabeth," he called out to her, for the wind was rushing past them, noisy and wild.

"Hold on, Aidan," she screamed at him before she steered confidently through another curve, increasing the distance between them and the SUV, which fishtailed before coming through the curve more slowly.

But as before, on the straightaway the SUV made up some distance until it was nearly on their tail.

And then Elizabeth did the unexpected.

With another cliff-edged curve before them, Elizabeth pulled over hard to the right, did a one-eighty into a switch-back and stopped, tires skidding on the soft shoulder.

Surprised and unprepared, the SUV shot by them and then Elizabeth became the chase vehicle, pulling out and staying close to the SUV as it now tried to outrun them.

"Get the plate numbers," she called out to him, but the car in front had no plate.

As soon as she realized that, she dropped back, slowing down as their attacker increased the distance between and then finally, after one last barely controlled turn on a curve, the SUV sped out of view.

Elizabeth pulled over then. Her hands were fisted against the steering wheel, her knuckles white from the pressure. She was breathing roughly, as was he, he realized. "You okay?"

She nodded, obviously unable to speak.

"Would you like me to finish the drive?" he asked and she nodded, popping out of the driver's seat.

He got out of the car and met her halfway, at the back of the Gaston where she had stopped to look at the damage. Tears filled her eyes and she wrapped her arms around herself tightly.

Embracing her, he winced at the dented chrome bumper, scratched and bent trunk, and the jagged glass shards that remained of her taillights. Her father's pride and joy, he recalled, and trying to comfort her, said, "We can fix it."

She nodded brokenly and tears finally slipped down her face as she replied, "But it will never be the same."

Chapter 13

Aidan hated leaving her, but she insisted she was fine.

When he mentioned calling the local police to report the incident, she had grown agitated and insisted that it made no sense. They had no ID of the driver and no plate number.

All good reasons, except that any normal person would think that the police just might be interested in an attempted murder. But Elizabeth was clearly not a normal person, he thought as he walked back to the hotel and recalled the professional way she had handled herself at the wheel.

Back at the hotel, both Lucia and Walker were waiting for him.

Lucia jumped out of her seat and stalked over to him. She gesticulated wildly with her hands as she demanded, "Is there some reason you've been incommunicado all day?"

Aidan cursed and stopped her hands in midair. He reached into his jacket pocket for the earpiece that he had taken off when he'd realized they were beyond its range. Hoping he would get up close and personal with Elizabeth, he had not wanted to risk her seeing it. "Sorry. We were out of range."

"All day?" Walker asked and examined him carefully, anger darkening his normally blue eyes to a slate gray. "You look…confused."

Aidan plopped himself down on the couch. Lucia and Walker joined him, sitting on the chairs opposite him. "It was an odd day." He recounted what they had done, leaving out some key personal parts. Finally, he provided a detailed account of the SUV attack.

"Tinted windows. No plates. Sounds like someone was intentionally after you," Lucia said, and then added, "Any idea on the make?"

"Big. Relatively fast. Might have been a Hummer. It was dark and too much was happening too fast."

Lucia added her two cents. "I'll check through the island's DMV records and see what I can dig up."

"But there's more that's bothering you, isn't there?" Walker asked, leaning forward and resting his forearms on his thighs as he clasped his hands together. "Want to tell us what it is?"

Aidan slumped down into the cushions of the sofa and looked up at the ceiling, unable to meet Walker's discriminating gaze. Afraid the psychiatrist might see too much. "Everywhere we went, people were so happy to see her. She seemed to really take an interest in them." He then recounted the talk about the prince and after, the one about honor and still believing in it.

"But she refused to call in the police. She had something to hide," Lucia reminded him before Walker piped in with his opinion.

"The Sparrow is a stone-cold, remorseless killer. A pathological liar who is unable to form commitments of any type, but can fool people exceptionally well. Classic antisocial behavior."

"Elizabeth seems to have lots of commitments: her friends, all those people we met today." He didn't add that for a moment there, she seemed to have been getting committed to him.

"These kinds of killers are by nature glib and superficially charming. If it came down to it, the Sparrow would do as she pleased with little regard for that supposed friendship or affection," Walker reminded him.

"Like Mitch," he said out loud and finally met Walker's gaze.

"Or like you, Aidan. Don't let this woman trip you up with her charm and beauty," Walker warned.

"What made her like this?" he wondered aloud, still trying to reconcile what the Sparrow had done with the woman who was getting a little too close to his heart. Who threatened his mission.

"If she's a psychopath—nothing. She was born that way. But I think Elizabeth is likely a sociopath, slipping into this behavior due to the deaths of her parents."

Aidan recalled Elizabeth putting up the walls whenever talk turned to her parents. Her tears about the car came to mind. The tears hadn't been about crunched metal and broken glass. Certainly their deaths still plagued her. "You may be right about the why," he admitted. "She's still deeply affected by her parents' murders."

"You need to be careful around her," Lucia reminded, clearly concerned that he had lost perspective.

And maybe neither she nor Walker were all that wrong. Elizabeth was making him doubt who she was. Making him want to find a reason why she did what she did if she was indeed the Sparrow. A reason he could understand—like wanting revenge. He could comprehend that one well. It was what should have still been motivating him—avenging his friend's death.

He sat up and rubbed his hands along his thighs. "Lucia, were you able to get into the safe and the locker?"

She smiled emphatically. "Your little gadget worked like a charm. Broke right into both, only… There was no foot locker in the safe."

"She got it out of there without us seeing it? How?" he questioned sharply.

Shaking her head, Lucia answered, "There was nothing on

the cameras. I can't explain how she did it. And as for that secret pathway, it led into a series of tunnels which might take weeks to explore."

He turned his attention to Walker and suddenly recalled the evidence bag in his pocket. He tossed it to the other man. "Here's your foxglove. Maybe the DNA will match. Did the photos help at all?"

Walker admitted that they had, but motioned to the phone on the coffee table. "I think it's better that we get Xander on the line for this one."

Alexander Forrest, Xander to his friends and colleagues, was the Lazlo Group's DNA specialist and resident botanist. Lucia used her laptop to connect with Xander and his image filled the computer screen. After the preliminaries, he toggled the window on the monitor to display the photos Aidan had taken with his PDA.

"I assume you want a rundown on the Sparrow's flora," Xander said.

"Yes, please, Xander," Aidan confirmed and then the three of them settled back to listen and watch Xander's report. With swift strokes of his mouse, he instructed them on the assorted plants in Elizabeth's garden.

"The lady has a veritable pharmacy of poisons and medicines in her little gardens," he began. "These low-lying flowers are nasturtiums and completely edible."

He circled the bright orange and yellow flowers.

"But right next door and not so good—Lily of the Valley. Poisonous to cats, dogs, goats and, of course, humans. Next and a little further back, delphiniums. Likewise poisonous. But again, mixed in with this, there's some chamomile— good for stomach upsets. And some…"

Aidan listened and watched as the screen was slowly filled by Xander's strokes as he identified one plant or another. When that screen was filled, he went to the next shot and likewise detailed a number of other edible, poisonous or medicinal plants: calendula, valerian, echinaecea and peppermint.

Aidan had already been familiar with the latter since Elizabeth had shown him where he could get peppermint to use for drinks at the bar.

Last but not least, Xander flipped to the snapshot of what Aidan had suspected was the foxglove.

"*Digitalis purpurea* subspecies *mariana.* More commonly found in Portugal. Great choice for rocky areas prone to drought. Flowers are closer to rose than purple. But no matter how you use it—leaves or seeds—still deadly," Xander confirmed.

"So this garden—"

"Chock full of all kinds of plants that one could use for either good or bad," Xander interrupted.

Something went cold inside Aidan at Xander's words. Up until now, Elizabeth's actions had almost had him convinced that she wasn't what he suspected. That she might not be the Sparrow. But now...this was just one other thing to add to the ever-growing list of evidence against her.

First, her obvious presence in so many of the areas where the Sparrow had had a kill attributed to her.

Her physical condition and martial arts skills, not to mention her driving abilities.

Now the deadly garden plants. As he remembered his first day in the kitchen, he recalled her nimble handling of the knife. A killer's way with a knife.

If Elizabeth wasn't the Sparrow...

"Walker's got some leaves I snipped off the plants. Will you be able to do anything with that?"

Suddenly Xander's face filled the screen again. He held up a test tube. "I've already done the PCR testing on the sample our crew lifted off the prince's marble coffee table. Seems that's where he decided to do the lines of coke."

"So we were able to get more evidence at the crime scene?" Lucia asked her colleague.

Walker was the one who answered. "Our unit collected some remnants of coke, but no fingerprints, hair or fiber other than the prince's."

"What about fluids?" he asked, interested in a perverse and decidedly personal kind of way in whether the prince had shared himself with the Sparrow before biting the dust.

Walker looked at him and saw past the professional reason for the question. "No fluids at the scene," he replied, concern lacing his words.

"What about on the body?" he pressed.

"No indication of sexual activity," Xander advised over the speaker and Aidan glanced at Walker.

"What about good ol' saliva? I can't imagine that the prince would have had someone as attractive as the Sparrow in his room and not have traded spit."

Walker glared at him coldly. "Is that opinion based on personal knowledge?"

He stood, tired of Walker's and now Lucia's scrutiny. "You expect me to crack the Sparrow. That isn't going to happen unless I use everything at my disposal. Everything."

With that comment he started to walk from the room, but as he neared his door, he paused and faced Walker. "And may I remind everyone that I'm the lead agent on this assignment. While I appreciate your concerns, I need to do what I think is right to crack the Sparrow."

With that, he grabbed hold of the knob, but as he opened the door, Walker said to Xander, "Make sure we've got swabs of the prince's mouth. And if we don't, get them pronto."

Chapter 14

Aﬗs usual, Elizabeth was up bright and early, flitting around the garden like a beautiful butterfly or a vicious little bee. Snipping here and there. Filling her basket with murder and mayhem, Aidan thought.

It was a trifle early for him to go to work, but there was little reason for him to hang out in the hotel room. Grabbing the special surveillance equipment Lucia had used to crack the safe and locker, Aidan stepped out into the suite where, as ever, Lucia vigilantly perused the monitors while typing away on her laptop.

"Anything?"

"Just the Sparrow's typical morning routine." Noticing that he was dressed and holding the equipment, she asked, "Where are you going?"

"Figured I'd take a look in those tunnels. See what I can make of them."

Lucia gave him a heads up. "FYI— You'll find my footprints—size nine—for the first few feet in the main tunnel and then in the path to the right. Once I saw that way branched out into multiple tunnels, I stopped."

"Good job. Just keep an eye on Elizabeth and let me know if I've been compromised." When she returned to her busy pecking on the keys, he asked, "What else are you up to?"

"Hacking the Silvershire DMV."

"Why hack? We're on the government payroll," he began, but then he remembered Walker's earlier concern about the *Quiz* and their source for information. "I get it. You don't trust whomever we have to ask."

"Too much leakage of vital details. If there's a mole, I don't want them knowing what we're up to," she confirmed.

He patted her on the back, but as he walked away, Lucia called out to him. He stopped, turned.

She seemed hesitant to speak. Unusual for the normally feisty operative. "You and the Sparrow. It's just business, right? Because if it isn't—"

A sharp slice of his hand silenced her. "The Sparrow or Elizabeth. So far, we've got lots of things linking them, but nothing definitive."

"You're right. But it's hard to ignore everything we do have, isn't it?"

Aidan agreed despite his unease. "I still want definitive, Lucia. I want to solve this case. I want it for Mitch."

He didn't add that he wanted it for himself, because he was too conflicted. But Lucia knew. She might specialize in talking to machines, but she had great people sense, as well.

"Just watch your back," she noted.

"You help watch it for me." He motioned to the monitors and with a wave, headed for Elizabeth's cellar.

He had dressed in sweats. The gym bag he held contained assorted workout gear and the special surveillance equipment he had developed.

Elizabeth was in the front garden when he arrived, picking

things from the garden, presumably herbs for what she would cook that day. He waved and called out, "Good morning."

She walked over, examining him as she did so. "Working out?"

He pointed to the restaurant. "You did say we could use the equipment in the gym before the patrons arrived."

"I did." She nervously grasped and ungrasped the handles of her garden basket. "You were right yesterday," she blurted out.

"Right? About what?"

"The police. I called them this morning and filed a report. Called the insurance company, as well. An adjuster is coming in a few days to check out the damage."

Another decision that didn't make sense if she was the Sparrow.

Then he remembered her words to him about how things could never be the same and tried to reassure her, to work his way into her confidence. "Once it's fixed, it'll be like new."

"Right. Like new," she repeated, although she was clearly not on board.

"Right. So, I'm heading to the cellar. Unless you need help with something." *Or unless you want to pick up where we left off on the bluff,* he thought, wondering if that was possibly the way to the truth.

"No, no. I'm fine. I've got to decide on the day's menu. Prep a few things," she advised and turned toward the door.

He walked beside her and they entered the kitchen. It was empty, but she had clearly already been at work there. A number of bowls and items were laid out in anticipation of the day's meals. Tomatoes, basil and other herbs, fresh picked from her garden. He could smell their aroma as soon as they entered the room.

When she headed to her prep table, he peeled off and rushed down the cellar stairs. Just to be convincing, he decided to start on the boxing bag first. Grabbing the wrist wraps from his gym bag, he wound them snugly around his hands and wrists, and then began his routine on the bag.

Punch after punch. An assortment of kicks that would send noise up to the kitchen above. He wanted to make sure Elizabeth was aware of what he was doing. Afterward, he unwound the wraps and tossed them beside the bag. Hitting the center of the mat, he did crunch after crunch. As he'd expected, the sudden drop in noise drew her attention.

From his prone position on the mat, he was able to see the door to the cellar open. Her feet—petite feet he made a point to note, thanks to Lucia's earlier comment—were visible as were her toned calves, but not much else.

She was checking on him, and, seeming satisfied that he was up to just what he'd said, she closed the door.

Perfect. He quickly laid out some of the free weights on the mat, just in case she checked on him again. He needed to be able to grab one of the weights immediately as a cover. "Red Rover, I'm going in," he advised.

"All's clear. She's working in the kitchen."

He headed to the locker and with the combination Lucia had secured earlier, opened the lock and removed it.

Inside the locker it was much as he had expected. A sweatshirt and sneakers. He picked up the sneakers and noted the size—a six. A T-shirt lay tossed onto the floor above the sneakers. He held it up to his nose, but there was no scent. No fragrance.

Elizabeth didn't wear any perfume, just the hand lotion. A hint of plumeria, Kate had said when he had bought the jar. A jar he'd passed on for chemical review with the evidence from the crime scene.

There was no hint of plumeria. Actually, there was just a fresh-laundered smell that said the shirt hadn't been worn. He placed it back where he had got it, trying his best to rearrange it in the exact same position.

Leaning toward the back, he realized it would be a tight fit for him to go through the locker, unlike the Sparrow and Lucia, who were more petite. Tight, but doable.

The back of the locker appeared to be plain metal like any

other gym locker. He ran his hands along the edges of the metal and down at the bottom right-hand corner, behind the sneakers and beneath the T-shirt, he discovered a tiny button, right where Lucia had told him it would be. Barely the size of a pencil eraser.

He pushed.

The back of the locker swung smoothly inward into the tunnel.

Here goes, he thought, and wedged himself through the space into the opening.

His shoulder scraped against the metal and once he was in the passageway, he had to crouch to walk. It had definitely not been intended for a man his size. But a woman a few inches shorter, like Elizabeth, would have no problem moving about the tunnels freely.

The passage had been carved out of the dirt some time ago. Well before Elizabeth's time. Long-term water seepage had stained the walls a darker brown in spots or had calcified on them from mineral deposits. That might make the whole network of tunnels unstable. The tunnel was dimly lit by a series of light bulbs strung from wire at odd intervals along the earthen walls. There was enough light for him to see the footprints. Larger ones, likely Lucia's, moving straight ahead. Interspersed with them, both coming and going, a much more diminutive set. Elizabeth's? he wondered.

He bent and guesstimated the second set of footprints to be a size six, like the sneakers in the locker. For confirmation, he located two sets of prints adjacent to one another, laid down a coin for reference and snapped off a picture with his PDA.

Shoving the PDA into his pocket, he moved further into the tunnel. He heard a crackle in his ear and worried that he was losing the signal. "Red Rover. Copy, can you hear me?"

"Copy, Mixmaster. Not as strong as before though."

Conscious of that, he crept forward until he was at the spot where the tunnel branched. As Lucia had mentioned, her prints were clear in the sand of the passage to the right. Since she had already gone that route only to find it led to multiple tunnels, he chose the path to the left.

Careful not to compromise any evidence, he stepped cautiously, preserving the earlier footprints, hoping the Sparrow wouldn't be looking for his. As he moved deeper into the earthen corridor, he once again hailed Lucia. "Red Rover. Copy, Red Rover."

A snap, crackle and even a pop as she answered. "Barely...hear...you." Her words were punctuated by static.

"Copy, Red Rover." Up ahead, the path dipped downward, sloping lower below ground level. For sure the signal would be lost up ahead. He wondered how long he'd have to explore before Elizabeth would check on what he was up to in the cellar again. Without the connection to Lucia, he risked discovery...

"You may lose me in a moment," he advised and plowed forward, needing to determine what was up ahead. Where the tunnel led.

Nothing but earthen walls and bare bulbs. It was cooler though and for a moment he thought he heard something. He closed his eyes to eliminate any extraneous sensation from interrupting.

The ocean—it sounded like he was stuck in the middle of a giant shell. Another noise. The scuffle of a shoe?

He held his breath and there it was again. Louder. Definitely a footfall in the tunnel ahead of him. Elizabeth?

No word from Lucia, but then again, maybe he had finally lost her signal. And if he could hear the Sparrow's footsteps, he had to remain silent.

He held his breath and slowly inched back a yard or so toward a spot in the tunnel where a jagged outcropping of rock sprang from the earthen wall. Not very large, but enough for him to partially hide behind it. As he tucked himself tight to the outcropping, a faint and incontinuous signal came across his wire.

"...move...lost...beach," was all he could make out, and he tried to fill in the blanks.

The Sparrow was on the move and I lost her on the beach.

The beach being possibly straight down the passageway judging from the sound of the sea. He waited and listened for yet another footstep.

Nothing. Had the Sparrow realized he was there and run?

He cursed again beneath his breath. If he forged ahead, he might smack straight into her and if he did…

Proof positive that Elizabeth was the elusive assassin?

He didn't want to guess at why that thought now bothered him.

Another crackle of static and some scattered words pierced his ear. "Back…cellar…hurry…"

With a frustrated sigh, Aidan made the call and turned.

A sudden blur of movement caught his eye, but before he could register who or what it was, blinding pain smacked him in the middle of his solar plexus, doubling him up. It was immediately followed by a hard, swift kick to his head.

The force of that sent him flying against the wall, where his head connected roughly. As he dropped to the ground and his gaze darkened, all he could see before him were a pair of feet. Petite women's feet encased in running shoes.

Then everything went black.

"Aidan? Aidan?" Elizabeth repeated and wiped the damp towel over his forehead and the side of his face.

His eyelids flickered for a moment, and then he was instantly alert and in action.

He grabbed hold of her hands and shoved her down hard onto the mat, pinning her there with his greater force and strength. "What did you do to me?"

"What the hell's the matter with you?" she said and pushed at him, trying to loosen his grip.

He seemed disoriented for a second, looking around the cellar as if thinking he was elsewhere. When he realized where he was, he released her and sat back onto the mat, a puzzled look on his face.

Natalie came running down the cellar stairs at that moment, a bag filled with ice in her hand. "Here it is, Lizzy," she said and stopped short as she realized something was up.

Elizabeth rose from the mat, walked over to Natalie and took the bag of ice. She approached Aidan, who was looking a little dazed, probably from the blow that had put the bruise on the side of his face.

Not wanting to risk that in his current state he would take her down again, she paused well before reaching him and held out the ice bag. "Here. This might help."

Confusion reigned on his face again, finally forcing her to kneel before him and place the ice bag gently above the injury. He winced as she did so and roughly asked, "What the hell happened?"

She shrugged and Natalie piped in from behind her. "When you didn't come up for a while, Lizzy came down to see what you were doing."

"You were lying on the mat with one of the free weights beside you," she said and motioned to the equipment off to the side of the mat. "You were out cold, so I ran up to get some damp towels and asked Natalie to make an ice bag."

"Oh," he said and grasped the ice bag from her hand. As he held it to the injury, he winced again.

"Do you need to see a doctor?" she asked and Natalie broke into the conversation once more.

"You're not going to sue, right? After all, it was your fault the weights hit you," she said nervously, clearly concerned on her employer's behalf.

Elizabeth gritted her teeth. She knew Natalie meant well, but she wasn't helping the situation at all. While still kneeling before Aidan, she said, "Nat. Aidan is not going to sue—"

"You know how litigious these Americans are," her friend worried out loud, wringing her hands like an anxious old maid.

If it wasn't so serious, it would be laughable, Elizabeth thought. Trying to calm her assistant, she gave Natalie instructions that would remove her from the cellar. "Please finish up the prep work while I see to Aidan. I'll be up shortly."

Natalie seemed about to argue with her, but Aidan clinched it with, "I'm not going to sue. It was an accident. I think the weight slipped from my hand."

With that, Natalie scurried up the stairs, leaving the two of them alone.

She examined him again, reached out and eased the ice bag from the side of his face to take another peek. "There's a bruise already."

Aidan wanted to say, "Well, hello, duh. You kicked the shit out of me," but her look of concern was so real, it was hard to imagine she could fake it. "I'll be fine," he reassured, although a whopper of a headache was rapidly growing behind his eyes.

She dropped her hands to her thighs and rubbed them there nervously. "You scared me. I thought you were really hurt."

Again, apprehension, seemingly real and unpracticed, flashed across her face on his behalf. "I'm fine. And I know you have to get to work. I'm going to head back to my place to rest."

"That's not a good idea. You were out for a while. You could have a concussion."

She was probably right, because he was sure that at any moment, his head might split open. When he moved it too quickly, nausea set in along with a wave of dizziness. "So what do you propose, Lizzy?"

"Let's get you to the cottage. You can sack out there so I can check on you." As she said that, she slipped an arm beneath his shoulder, helped him to rise and then to navigate the stairs.

He appreciated her assistance, especially since his knees were wobbly. If it hadn't been for her support, he might not have made it to the ground floor. By the time they reached the door to the cottage, a fine cold sweat had erupted on his skin.

She must either have seen or sensed his discomfort since she asked, "Are you okay?"

"I need to sit down." No lie on his part. He worried he might keel over at any second.

She helped him to the sofa where she urged him to lie down and adjusted the pillows beneath his head until he was comfortable. When she examined him again, she said, "You look pale."

He wanted to upchuck, but manly man that he was, he forced it down. "Fine," was all he could manage, and he closed his eyes, hoping to make it clear that the one thing he wanted was to be left alone.

He sensed her continued presence by his side for a moment before she finally left.

Normally, he would have taken advantage of the opportunity to investigate the cottage at his leisure. Only now, he wasn't up to it.

And come to think of it, he hadn't heard a peep of any kind from Lucia. Reaching up to his ear, which was the side of his head that had taken the initial brunt of the kick, he dislodged the earpiece. It had tightly jammed into his ear canal from the force of the blow. It had also been accidentally shut off. Powering it back up, he slipped it into his ear and said, "Copy, Red Rover."

Chapter 15

Aidan maintained his prone position on the couch, his head pounding too badly to consider moving right at that moment. Even the slight crackle from the earpiece seemed overly loud as he waited for a response from Lucia. While he lay there, he recalled Elizabeth's concern for him. It troubled him. Had it been his imagination, or had he seen caring on her expressive face before he had closed his eyes against the pain? Could she be that good an actress?

He cursed under his breath as Lucia's voice finally came across the earpiece, too loudly. Pain stabbed through his temples from the sound of it. "What happened, Blender Boy?"

He wished he knew. He had no explanation for how Elizabeth had managed to elude him in the tunnel, nor how it was possible that Natalie thought Elizabeth had been with her in the kitchen the whole time.

Maybe because it was someone else who nearly took your head off?

"I don't know what happened. I heard someone and then they knocked me out."

"You should return to base," Lucia suggested, dragging a harsh chuckle from him.

"If I could, I would. Did *you* see anything?" He tried to keep his tone neutral, but even he could hear the pain and annoyance behind his words.

"Nothing. Someone jammed the signal," Lucia replied.

Damn. That was not so good, he thought and again it occurred to him that it would have been difficult for Elizabeth to do the jamming. It would take some sophisticated equipment and software to break into the encrypted signal and decode it. Not to mention jam it—or worse—listen in. Hopefully they weren't jacked into their current transmissions. For the moment, he had no way of knowing, however.

"Where was Elizabeth when I was decked? Did the jamming begin at the same time?"

"As far I know she was up in the kitchen until I lost the signal. I don't know how that fits into when you were attacked," Lucia answered. In the background he could hear her fingers flying across the keys. She was likely loading up images from all the various cameras just to make sure.

"Great. So someone knows how to jam us," he said with a tired sigh.

"Have we been compromised?"

Aidan shook his head, but then winced from the movement. His voice was tight as he held the ice bag to his face and replied. "Don't know. Easy to jam. Harder to break in."

"Don't know if this is proof that Ms. Moore is the Sparrow or that it's someone else."

Proof? Someone had attacked him and jammed the signal, but as far as they knew, Lizzy had been in the kitchen at the same time. But then again, maybe Lizzy had slipped away without Natalie noticing, Aidan thought. Again conflicting emotions rose up and he told himself it was possible that someone else had attacked him and done the jamming. As it was, he was already torn about how the kind, gentle and seemingly honest woman he had come to know could be an assassin.

"We need concrete proof, Lucia. Not just circumstantial evidence."

"That knock on your head do some damage, Aidan?" Lucia responded with some puzzlement in her voice.

"No damage, only… It just doesn't feel right. My gut tells me we're missing something here."

"Copy. When are you returning to base?"

"Give me half an hour or so. First I need to check on Lizzy in the kitchen," he answered, closing his eyes and shifting the ice bag on the side of his face.

He intended to take a good part of that half an hour to consider everything that had just happened and try to regain perspective. That, and let the pain behind his eyes recede.

Then he intended to track Lizzy down and try to find out just what was going on.

Chapter 16

Elizabeth didn't head straight back to the kitchen. She sat on the stone wall between the cottage and restaurant to take a moment to calm the shaking of her hands. To settle the knot in her stomach as she thought about what had happened to Aidan.

He could have been badly hurt. As it was, he seemed to be in pretty rough shape.

Maybe she should call a doctor. Make sure the nasty-looking injury wasn't serious. And, as Natalie's words came back to her, maybe she should make sure she did everything she needed to in case he did sue.

Americans *were* a litigious lot after all.

But Aidan wouldn't sue because she trusted him to honor his promise, she told herself. No matter that he was a nomadic man, she had the sense that he was true to his word.

She shot a glance at her watch. Only a few minutes had gone by since he had lain down. She'd give him half an hour or so and then go back and see how he was doing.

Rising, she walked to the kitchen where Natalie was assigning jobs to their two kitchen assistants. Satisfied everything was under control, she grabbed the list she had been working on earlier and reviewed the menu she'd devised for the daily specials.

It was going to be a hot day today according to the weatherman, so she wanted to keep the day's specials light.

Broiled hake served with a side of homemade tagliatelle covered with fresh pesto. She and Natalie would have to get to work on making the pasta soon. Next, fresh *haricots vert* tossed with a citrus vinaigrette and toasted almonds as well as a spicy gazpacho as first courses. For dessert she had a collection of wonderful fresh-picked berries. They would be great either alone, with some zabaglione, or around a scoop of fresh sorbet. Maybe mango, she thought and realized the sorbet would need to be prepped shortly for it to be set in time for dinner.

Satisfied with the specials, she returned to the prep table where Natalie was busy slicing what looked like morels. A basic, although pricier ingredient, for one of their staple dishes—a pan-seared duck breast in a red wine and morel reduction. But as she approached, she realized something didn't look quite right.

"Hold up, Nat," she called out and her sous chef's knife paused in mid stroke.

"Something wrong?" Natalie asked.

Elizabeth stood next to her and gazed down at the morels Natalie had been cutting. "These came in our regular delivery?" Even as she was asking, she plucked two slightly different-looking morels from the basket and laid them out side by side on the cutting board.

She grabbed a paring knife from a knife holder and carefully split each morel in half. "Damn," she muttered under her breath.

"Something up?" she heard and turned.

Aidan was at the end of the table, watching them intently, ice bag pressed to the injured side of his face.

"You are obviously. Are you sure that's wise?" she asked, concerned since he appeared a little too pale for her tastes.

"I'm feeling better. I just wanted to drop in and let you know I'd be back later," he said and walked directly over to where she was standing. "So, what's up?" he asked again and motioned with his head to the morels. He immediately grimaced, the action obviously painful.

He should have rested some more, she thought, annoyed that he was possibly making his injury worse. But first, she had to deal with the problem sitting before her on the cutting board.

She motioned down to the morel pieces. "The delivery we received this morning was tainted."

Was it her imagination or did Aidan's face harden at her words? She carefully explained to Nat, so that she would know for the next time. "See the differences between the two mushrooms here? The cap on this one is only connected at the top and the inside of the stem isn't hollow. That's a false morel."

"And that would be a problem because?" Aidan asked.

"It's poisonous. Not as poisonous as the aminita mushrooms, but definitely deadly," she replied.

His eyes turned cold, the lighter flecks of blue becoming like shards of ice. "You seem to know a lot about things like that," he challenged.

She twirled the sharp paring knife around once in her fingers before spiking it into the cutting board so that it stood upright, tip embedded in the wood. Expertly and efficiently. "It's my job to know things like that," she responded, angry with him on a variety of levels, including that he seemed to be questioning her expertise on culinary matters.

"I bet it is," he replied gruffly, tossed the ice bag to her, and walked out the door without a backward glance at the two of them.

"What's with him?" Natalie asked as she followed his stiff retreating back.

Elizabeth shrugged. "For the life of me, I don't know."

* * *

Her job. Yeah, right. World-renowned assassin. Aidan's head was pounding with all the facts running around in his mind and the conflicting emotions they raised.

He'd had his doubts about Lizzy, but with each passing minute, there was yet more and more evidence piling up against her. The tunnels. Shoe size. The attack. Those damn poisonous mushrooms and of course, the too-vivid reminder of her adroitness with a knife.

Back at the hotel, a concerned Lucia hovered over him like a hummingbird, inspecting the blow to his head.

He brushed her off with a weak swipe of his arm. "I'm okay. Really."

"Really?" she asked and examined his face, sensing that his anger was about a multitude of things beyond his injury. "Well, then I guess we can call Xander and hear what else he has to report."

In a way, it was almost the last thing he wanted to hear since he suspected that the DNA test would clinch the determination that Lizzy was indeed the Sparrow. But maybe it was better that way. Maybe that would allow him to regain full objectivity about her and complete a mission that was turning out to be more than he had expected. With a nod that brought fresh waves of pain and nausea, he sat down by Lucia's laptop and the speakerphone.

Lucia dialed Xander and he answered a moment later. "Alexander Forrest here."

"Xander. It's Lucia and Aidan," she advised.

"I was waiting for your call," he replied, an eager tone in his voice that told him that the younger man had good news.

Or bad depending on which camp you were in.

"Get on with it then," Aidan said grumpily.

"Whew. Wrong side of bed this morning," Xander said and after a short pause, his image filled Lucia's screen. The young man winced and with a chuckle said, "Or maybe the wrong side of someone's fist?"

Lucia was quick to explain. "I think it was a roundhouse kick judging from—"

"Enough," Aidan barked and regretted it as the word echoed painfully in his skull. "Get to the important stuff, Xander," he added more softly.

Xander shuffled some papers prior to beginning his report. "You were right about the prince not being able to resist the Sparrow. And may I say that I, too, find her babealicious."

"Xander," Lucia warned, heading him off before Aidan could admonish the young specialist.

"Okay, okay. On to the good stuff. Swabs from the prince's mouth yielded two sets of DNA. I did the PCR test and ran the unknown sample against some blood that Ms. Moore had donated during Silvershire's annual blood drive."

"When was that?' Lucia questioned and Aidan was thankful for her intercession, since his head throbbed so painfully, even speaking hurt.

"About two months ago."

"And? Do we have a match?" he finally asked.

"That's the strange thing," Xander said and immediately began flipping through his papers again. "We had a clean sample from Elizabeth. The one taken from the prince—well, it should have been fairly good."

"You're doubting the integrity of the evidence you were given?" Lucia pressed and shot a worried look at Aidan, obviously not liking where this was going. Too much information had already leaked from an inside source. To think that the same source could manipulate the evidence…

"There's nothing to say it was tampered with, only… It's not a complete match, but it's not far enough apart for it not to have come from the same person."

"What?" Aidan snarled in low tones. "What do you mean?" After he spoke, he leaned closer to the laptop to get a better view of Xander's face as he explained.

"About seventy-five percent of the DNA matched in the specimen from the prince and Ms. Moore's blood. But not all, which is weird. Unless the sample was compromised somehow or…" Xander chortled before continuing, "…unless Ms. Moore has an evil twin out there somewhere."

"You think the DNA can belong to someone other than Elizabeth Moore?" he pressed.

"Yes. Identical twins have identical DNA. Fraternal twins share fifty percent of the same DNA," Xander answered.

Aidan cursed under his breath. "But you said we had a seventy-five-percent match. So where does that leave us?"

"There's a theory about a third type of twin—polar body twins. Basically, the polar body is a remnant near the egg. Normally it dies, but if it should grow as large as the egg, it can be fertilized," Xander explained.

"Which means that both the egg and the polar body have the identical DNA from the ovum, but fertilization by different sperm causes the difference in the DNA," Aidan continued for him.

"And that results in what?" Lucia jumped in.

"In theory, twins that are nearly identical, but not quite. Of course, this is just a theory and some say that even if it is possible, it is quite unusual. Very, very rare."

Aidan glanced at Lucia, and, as he met her gaze, it was obvious what she was thinking. "This is getting to be a nightmare, isn't it?"

At her nod, he snapped at Xander. "Run the tests again."

"I can do that, only—"

"Xander. Just run the tests again," he repeated gruffly.

The young man nodded and signed off.

"Odds are the tests are going to come out the same way," Lucia advised.

Aidan shook his head, but regretted the action since it brought pain. In fact, his headache had been steadily growing during the entire conference. "She really nailed me."

"She did. *Elizabeth* did. Not some rare or nonexistent evil twin."

He hated to admit it, but the twin thing was a farfetched

idea. Nothing in the personal history suggested Lizzy had a sibling. But personal histories could be altered. The Lazlo Group did it all the time to protect its operatives and their families. It kept the cases away from their private lives. Or at least, that's what they tried to do.

The Sparrow, if she wasn't Elizabeth, could have done the same in an attempt to protect her twin.

"Aidan?" Lucia questioned, since he hadn't answered her earlier question.

"Your Lazlo bio says you're an only child. Are you?"

When she didn't reply, Aidan had his answer. "I'll try tonight to get more info from Elizabeth about her family."

"You plan on going to work? Do you feel well enough?"

"It's what I have to do," he replied and walked away, intending to get some rest. He planned on going to the restaurant, but laying low. He needed Lizzy to worry. He needed her to make the first move. If he did the approaching, it might seem too pushy, create a blip on her radar if she truly was the Sparrow.

Which, once again, he was unsure about.

Why? he asked himself. Maybe because Xander's report had only created doubt. He couldn't see her knocking him out in the tunnel and then faking the whole concern thing so well. Until he remembered the expert way she had handled that little paring knife and her knowledge regarding the poisonous mushrooms.

He was dumbfounded. Again.

But that's what she does. She creates the persona you think you know and then…the reasonable voice in his head reminded. It's what he was doing, except that he was finding it hard to reconcile all her many facets. In fact, he was fascinated by all her layers.

Somehow tonight, he'd find a way to reach her. To get more answers about her, because if they were on the track of the wrong woman…the real Sparrow was still out there. As deadly and dangerous as ever.

Chapter 17

Restlessness kept her awake. A restlessness created by all that had happened in the past few days.

First, that crazy-ass driver on the coast road the other night. Second, Aidan nearly killing himself in the gym this morning.

And last, but probably highest on the list, her feelings for Aidan, a man about whom she knew so little. A man whom she couldn't figure out. During their picnic the other day, she'd thought they had connected, but this afternoon he'd seemed…angry. Ready to attack. Maybe it had been the blow to the head, because later that night, he was a changed man. Alone and distant.

She had wanted to approach him, see if everything was okay, but it had been impossible thanks to an unusually busy Tuesday night and a party that lingered later than normal. She had hoped he would wait around after his shift, but he hadn't.

Maybe she had misread his interest the other day. Her radar was obviously off, which was to be expected. It had been so long since she'd played this man-woman game. Too long maybe. A reason to stay out of the game, the annoying voice in her head urged, even while she thought: nothing ventured, nothing gained.

Those dueling emotions were the reason for the unsettling feeling that her life had taken an unexpected turn thanks to this man. An unwelcome turn that wouldn't necessarily take her where she wanted to go. Especially since Aidan was just passing through. He had bluntly told her that the day he'd come back, trying to convince her to hire him.

She hadn't made a mistake with the decision to hire him. He had turned out to be a competent bartender. And a most competent kisser.

However, losing control with him had possibly been not such a wise decision.

She suddenly needed to take back the control she considered so necessary. It was what she had done her entire life. First, when her parents had been killed. Next, when Dani had left.

It was what she planned on doing now.

Changing out of her pajamas, she slipped on a pair of black jeans and grabbed the first shirt she laid her hands on—a black tank top sitting atop the clean laundry pile. She didn't bother with a bra. No one would be out on the beach at this hour and besides, she wasn't all that big anyway.

She tied up her hair with the pink scarf once more and slipped down the stairs barefoot, pausing at the door a moment to glance around her living room. She held her breath as she listened for the sounds of someone else, since the hairs on the back of her neck tingled as if she was being watched.

Only the susurrus of the ocean. It called to her and she listened.

She was on the move again, Aidan realized from the video feed on his PDA. He had been watching her for at least an hour or more. For the better part of that time, she had been standing by her bedroom window, looking out to sea. One arm wrapped around her midsection while the other hung down at her side. Occasionally she would reach up, rake back her shoulder-length hair or rest her hand at her mouth pensively.

Lizzy was clearly troubled. He wondered if he had even made the list of what she was worried about. He had tried to be distant tonight and it had worked. He had noticed her watching him, possibly interested in approaching, but it had not been possible. Too many restaurant patrons far too late into the night. And he couldn't just hang out and wait for her. It would be too obvious. So he had left. Tuned into the broadcast on his PDA of Elizabeth in her room.

Despite the late hour she'd returned home, Lizzy had obviously not been tired. She puttered around the cottage and then her room. After, she went to the window to stand until she abruptly sprang into action, changing into the black clothes and moving downstairs.

She waited at the door and cautiously looked around.

Aidan stood, yanked on his jacket as he watched her. Did she sense the surveillance? Was her assassin's radar that acute?

When she walked out the door, he rushed out of his room and nearly collided with Lucia.

"I was on my way to get you," she explained and he held up his PDA.

"I've been monitoring her."

She shot him a condemning look, apparently convinced that his interest had been anything but work-related.

"It's not what you think," he defended, even as he grabbed the binoculars and hurried to the windows.

Lucia said nothing, but instead joined him at the windows with her own set of binoculars. "She's headed for the beach again."

Aidan tracked Elizabeth's flight down the cottage path and along the rocky trail to the shoreline. "I'm going after her," he said and turned, but as he did so, some other activity on one of the monitors caught his eye.

He raced back to the table, certain he'd seen someone in black in the cellar of Lizzy's restaurant, but when he reached the monitor, nothing. It must have been his imagination.

"I thought you were leaving?" Lucia asked and craned her head over his shoulder while he kept his eyes trained on the feed from the cellar.

"Thought I saw something here." He pointed to the screen.

Lucia shook her head. "Not possible. We both know the Sparrow's on the beach."

"Right," he answered and yet his instinct told him something was off. Straightening, he motioned to the monitor as he hurried toward the door. "Keep an eye on that one," he said.

Lucia looked from him to the monitor, but, realizing he was serious, she confirmed, "Whatever you say, Blender Boy."

With a nod, he rushed out the door to chase the elusive Sparrow.

The sea at night could be so many things.

On some nights she sat and watched its movement and thought about how big it was. It made her feel insignificant and yet connected to it and the multitude of life deep within. It brought peace when she was troubled, as she was tonight.

On other nights, when a storm would kick up the waves, she would revel in its wildness and energy, imagining that buried within her there was more still to be explored. That she had the strength to do whatever was necessary.

As she walked along the moonlit water's edge tonight, the ocean was relatively calm, although there was the hint of a storm on the breeze blowing into shore. It matched the maelstrom of her emotions, seemingly calm on the outside, but within, restless.

She strolled for a bit further and was almost at the edge of town when she noticed the lone figure coming down one of the public-access ramps to the beach. It was too dark to see the person's face and yet she knew who it was.

Aidan.

Funny how in a few short days he had become familiar enough that she could pick him out even from a distance.

He strolled onto the sand, but then just stood there, staring out to sea, hands tucked into his jeans pockets. Eventually, he plopped down before one small dune to watch the ocean.

She had a choice to make: turn around or keep on walking. It took her but a moment to make the decision.

Chapter 18

"The Sparrow's at nine o'clock and approaching slowly," Lucia advised, but Aidan dared not move. Better not to let her know he was aware of her presence.

Instead, he whispered, "I'm going incommunicado, Red Rover."

Lucia's response came immediately, but he curtly advised, "I can't think personal knowing you're in my head, over."

With that, he removed the earpiece, turned it off and stuck it into the back pocket of his jeans. The front one would be too obvious if they got down to doing what he wanted to be doing.

Solely on a business level, he reminded himself.

The sand masked the sound of her approach. When her bright-pink-painted toenails were directly to the left of him, he finally looked up.

She stared at him intently, as if trying to solve a puzzle,

before she said, "If I didn't know better, I'd say you were following me."

Not quite what a normal woman would say, and a rein-
forcement of his colleagues' suspicions about her true
identity. Playing coy, he glanced over his shoulder behind her
and then up to the public-access ramp he'd descended to
reach the beach. Finally meeting her gaze directly, but with
an easy smile on his face, he replied, "Seems to me I'm the
one who's sitting near his tiny pay-by-the-night room at the
somewhat dubious Leonia Inn, while you, on the other hand,
are quite a distance away from your cottage. So, who's following who?"

She chuckled while shaking her head. "Touché." Without
waiting or asking she plopped down next to him and
mimicked his stance, knees drawn up to her chest, arms
wrapped around them. "What are you doing here?"

Playing it cool, he thought, but instead responded, "Watching the moon and stars and the ocean. And now, sitting beside
a beautiful woman."

Snorting inelegantly, she bumped his shoulder with hers.
"You are such a liar."

Pot calling the kettle black. "And you? What are you
doing here?"

A long pause followed his question. He was unprepared
when she said, "Wondering what it would be like to kiss you
again."

Barely containing his groan, he sneaked a peek at her.
Despite her audacious words, she was staring straight ahead,
a blush so bright on her cheeks that not even the indistinct
light of the moon could hide it.

"Okay, so you're right that I'm a liar," he said and shifted
slightly so that he might face her. As he did so, his butt sank
a little deeper into the sand and his knee brushed her side.

She turned so that she might also be able to see him better
and studied him intently. "So I'm *not* beautiful?"

Balls. The lady had them in spades and he liked it. Possibly too much. Cradling the side of her face, he ran his thumb along the blush of color. Was it his imagination or was her skin hotter? "That's not what I lied about."

She arched her perfectly waxed brow upward. It only emphasized her sexy girl-next-door look. "Really? So what—"

He slipped his thumb over her lips, silencing her. "I wasn't just watching the ocean and the stars. I was thinking of how nice it would be to kiss you, too."

"Liar," she repeated again, taking him aback.

"Huh?

"You were thinking about doing more than kissing and duh, so was I," she confessed, took his thumb between her teeth and gave a little love bite.

This time he did groan. When she licked the bite, it was impossible to ignore her offer.

He reached out and scooped her up into his lap, her knees splayed around his waist. He was totally hard and she couldn't fail to notice. He didn't rush it though, letting her get settled in a comfortable position. Bringing his hands to the middle of her back to slowly urge her forward until the tips of her breasts grazed his T-shirt front.

"You know that we might both regret this in the morning?" he tossed out for reflection.

"Possibly." Behind her words was a big hanging question. So he asked it, "But?"

"We might regret not doing it more."

The time for action was there. Right before him. Literally in his lap. It's what he had wanted—to break past the Sparrow's barriers.

And if she's not the Sparrow? the voice of his conscience warned.

"Lizzy—and I can call you Lizzy considering where this is likely to lead, can't I?"

Was he testing her or giving her one last out? Impossible to tell or at least that's what she told herself. That made it easier to push away her common sense and give into the desire she had been feeling since the other day. The desire that had given her the strength to brave taking a chance.

"Lizzy. I like the way it sounds coming from you," she confessed.

"Lizzy," he repeated and leaned forward, nuzzling her nose with his since in this position, they were face to face. "I want to take this slow, Lizzy."

His voice was soft and low. Slightly rough with want. His bedroom voice, only she didn't think she could wait to get to a bedroom. Returning the caress and shifting forward, she whispered in his ear, "How slow, Aidan?"

His breath hitched for a moment and she tugged on his earlobe with her teeth. "Aidan?"

He urged her the last little distance, licked the edge of her earlobe. "I want to touch you," he said, but made no motion to do so.

Her nipple was already hard and she wanted·what he wanted. Wanted the promise in his voice. Nuzzling the side of his face with her nose, she brushed a kiss against his cheek. Against her lips, his beard was rough with evening growth.

She cupped the hard muscle of his chest and grasped his nipple between her thumb and forefinger. "I want you to do this," she admitted as she caressed him through the insubstantial fabric of his T-shirt.

His harsh exhalation was warm against the side of her face. He said nothing, only complied with her request, bringing up both his hands and rolling the taut nubs of her nipples between his thumbs and forefingers.

A sharp mew of pleasure escaped her. She kissed the side of his face again and shifted her hand downward to his side where she eased it beneath his jacket and ran it up and down along his lean muscled flank. Needing more, she pulled his T-shirt out of his pants and slipped her hand beneath the edge of his shirt.

His skin was warm. Smooth. She imagined what it would feel like against her. Wanted it. Soon.

She worked her mouth to the edge of his lips, traced their outline before kissing him again.

He opened his mouth against hers, apparently as hungry as she for a greater intimacy. She granted it to him, opening her mouth and meeting his tongue with her own. Sucking and biting until there was a tight ball of need inside her from his hands caressing her, a little more roughly now, and the feel of his tongue making love to her mouth.

When she broke away from him, they were both breathing heavily. Their bodies trembled as they strained toward one another.

"Aidan?" she half asked as she cradled his head in her hands and lovingly kissed the side of his face. The side he had injured that morning.

He must have misread her actions since he said, "Do you want to stop?"

She chuckled sexily and dropped a quick kiss on his lips. "No. I want to go somewhere more…private."

He looked back at the public beach ramp, chagrin on his face. "My place—"

"Let's go back to the cottage," she offered and he nodded, smiled.

Somehow they untangled themselves and rose. He took her hand and they started walking, but somehow, it wasn't quick enough for the need pulling at her. Shooting him a half glance, she said, "Race you back?"

A boyish grin erupted on his face, his teeth white against his tanned skin. "And the prize is?"

It took her only a second to consider what she wanted and to answer. "Winner gets to be on top."

With that, she dropped his hand and took off down the beach.

Lizzy broke into a run, her long legs quickly eating up ground. He could have watched her run, the elegance and fluidity of it, but he was much too competitive to just let her win the challenge.

He dashed after her, trying to make up the ground that he had lost, although it did occur to him that even if he did lose it would still be a pleasurable experience. Lizzy on top, he thought, and stumbled for a moment.

Dashing that thought from his mind because it was too distracting and the blood was shifting to places that weren't conducive to speed, he slowly closed the gap between them as Lizzy kicked up the sand before him.

He reached the cottage just paces behind her. Heard Lizzy's delighted laughter at the door as she said, "I win."

"Why don't I feel like I lost?" he said, his voice tinged with humor and sex because all he could think about was making love with her.

Lizzy shot him a suddenly shy smile, but threw the door open and backpedaled into the room, all the time motioning to him that he should follow.

He did and plastered himself to her as they paused for just a moment in their headlong flight toward what he hoped was Lizzy's bedroom.

As she gazed up at him, there was a look in her eyes that said she truly cared for him.

Normally he would have banked money on knowing that look was real.

But lately, and particularly around Lizzy, he no longer could be certain. His gut, however, was telling him that nothing wrong was going on right now. That he should have no fear. No concern.

He hoped it was right.

Chapter 19

Great, Lucia thought as she flipped from one camera feed to the next and realized that someone was jamming the signal. And with Aidan deciding to go incommunicado, she had no idea whether or not he was in any kind of trouble.

Over and over she tried to restore the signal, but the cameras were unresponsive. Whatever was screwing up the transmission was pretty powerful. Which meant that she might be able to track its location and shut it down.

But first…

She rose from the table and snatched her binoculars from the tabletop. Hurrying to the windows, she searched the beach, but there was no sign of Aidan or Ms. Moore. Shifting downward, she noticed the lights were on in the cottage. Through the window, she was able to pick out Aidan and Lizzy as they…

Well. It sure didn't look like Aidan was in any kind of trouble. Well, at least not of the physical kind.

Emotionally… That was a whole 'nother issue. She had

sensed his indecision during this assignment. Realized that he was either unwilling or unable to get past his attraction to the Sparrow.

There was more going on than just the mission. That was not good. And as for what was about to happen in the cottage...

Lucia walked back to the table holding her laptop and the surveillance monitors. She needed to find what was jamming the cameras and how Elizabeth had managed to activate it with Aidan literally at her side the whole time.

She would give the Sparrow credit. She sure seemed to know her spy stuff.

Let's hope Aidan realizes that, Lucia thought.

Aidan wrapped his arms around Lizzy's waist and dragged her close. Her shirt accidentally rode up with the action and his forearm brushed along her bare back. It was slightly damp, probably from their mad dash up the beach.

It was happening so fast. Too fast, he thought, doubting he had the patience to finish this upstairs in her bedroom.

As she eased her hand beneath his jacket and under the hem of his T-shirt, he knew he couldn't wait.

He gripped her to him tightly and bending his head, he laid his forehead against hers, brushed a kiss there before moving lower to meet her lips in a kiss.

Opening his mouth against hers, he tasted her, savored the slick slide of her tongue along his. Imagined it sliding along...

He groaned and pulled away, his breathing rough. "Lizzy, I can't—"

She placed a finger on his mouth, a sexy smile on her face. "I won't let you run from me now, Aidan." She didn't wait for his answer, choosing instead to stand on tiptoe and run her tongue along his jaw and then down to the side of his neck, to the sensitive hollow close to his shoulder where she gave another lick before a bite.

He cradled the back of her head in his hand and she gave another quick bite before licking and sucking at the spot.

He hadn't gotten a hickey since high school. He had forgotten how good it felt. How wonderful it was to put the bite on her, he realized as he brought his face to the hollow between her neck and shoulder. Bit and sucked and licked until they were both moaning and clutching each other.

They finally eased away from one another. Breathing heavily. Bodies tense with need.

He was certain of one thing. It was going to be…

Wild, he thought as she hopped up and wrapped her legs around him, bringing herself hard against erection. "Lizzy?"

"Touch me, Aidan. Like you did before," she urged, her hands locked behind his head, drawing him close.

He kept one hand at her back while he jammed the other under the edge of her tank top, moved it upward until he was cupping her breast. Her nipple was a tight peak in the center of his palm. He gripped it between his thumb and forefinger, rotated the peak and she let out a little gasp of pleasure, tightened her legs around his waist.

In the back of his mind came the thought that this was wrong. That Lucia would be watching and hoped she knew the meaning of discretion and shut off the cameras because…

He wanted to hear more. Feel more. Taste more. Smell more: he wanted everything with her.

Somehow he bared that breast to his gaze. Her nipple was a sweet caramel color against the cream of her skin. As he brushed his lips against it, Lizzy let out another little gasp and his erection tightened painfully at that sound.

He needed to be inside her. Hearing her pleasure spill from her lips as he moved within.

But first, he had to taste her again.

He licked the tip of her. Sweet. Hard against his mouth as he closed his lips around her nipple and sucked.

She gripped his head to her with one hand. Eased the other one under his shirt. Her palm was soft against his skin. Warm.

He didn't know how it happened, but they were suddenly on the edge of the large sofa in the middle of the room. She was leaning back against the soft, welcoming cushions, her legs open. He was immediately there, drawing himself against her as he continued caressing her breast.

She held him close, and he moved his mouth on her. Sucking. Biting.

He wanted her to do the same. All over him. Which meant they had way too much clothing on.

Elizabeth must have felt the same way since she eagerly reached for the hem of her tank top and ripped it off, revealing herself.

It distracted him for a moment. He sat back on his heels and looked his fill. Placed his hands on her midsection and traced the indentations in her abs. Slowly shifted upward until he was holding her breasts in his hands. Rubbing his thumbs across the distended tips of her nipples.

She surged forward, slipped her hands beneath his jacket and eased it off.

His T-shirt followed quickly as he removed it and knelt before her again. She ran her palms all along his skin and he leaned close, shifted his hands to her back to bring her nearer.

She did the same, but encountered the hard ridges of scar as she did so.

He sensed her hesitation and immediately reminded, "Shrapnel. Army, remember?"

With an accepting bob of her head, she traced the edges of his scars with her fingers, as if to soothe, although the hurt was long gone, Aidan thought.

A shudder ripped through his body at her actions and he gripped her tight, buried his head against her neck.

Her comforting brought a change in what had been happening between them. A banking of the fires for the moment as they held one another, drawing succor from the embrace.

Finally he eased away, reached up and brushed a lock of her hair back from her face. "You're…beautiful."

She smiled. A slow, comfortable smile that did something funny to his insides. "Thank you."

He brought his hand down to her shoulder, where he traced the straight line of it. Moved down a little further and ran his thumb along the classically defined edge of her collarbone.

He bent his head, ran his lips along that strong line before urging her upward so that he could kiss her breasts again. Lick her nipples before sucking on them gently.

She cradled his head to her and kissed it. Urged him on with soft cries that told him how much she liked what he was doing. When she leaned back onto the cushions of the sofa, he took the moment once again to admire the strength in her, the lean muscles along her midsection that were impossible to resist.

He laid his hands there, running his finger along the ridges before replacing his hands with his mouth. He paused to kiss the tempting indentation of her navel before reaching the edge of her low-rise black jeans. She shifted her hips up then, and he smiled against her belly.

"Impatient, Lizzy. That's not a good—"

She silenced him with a kiss that rocked him with its intensity. When she pulled away and sat on the edge of her couch, her sherry-brown eyes were liquid heat. Warm as her gaze, her hands ran down his body while he kneeled before her. They felt even hotter as she eased her fingers beneath the waistband of his jeans before she undid the snap and dragged the zipper down the nearly painful length of his erection.

He was so hard, he immediately sprang out once she released the zipper. She wasted no time in wrapping her hand around him.

"Very impatient," she confessed.

Almost lightheaded from the surge of desire, he somehow managed to kick off his pants and tightie whities while leaving his wallet, with his condoms, within easy reach.

He was standing before her, ready to kneel again when she leaned forward and kissed the tip of his jutting erection. It trapped his breath somewhere in the middle of his chest, but then she took him into his mouth and his breath disappeared completely.

She was amazing, he thought as he held her head to him. Her mouth was hot and eager as she sucked on him and then withdrew to lick the tip. She bit around the head of his penis while with one hand, she cupped his balls.

His knees nearly buckled and it took all his control not to come right then. Somehow, he mustered his strength, reached for her and urged her to stand. He undid the zipper on her jeans, parted them and slipped his hand beneath to encounter nothing but sleek warm skin.

He was so on the edge, he couldn't waste the time to take off her pants. Easing his hand downward, he found the center of her. Applied pressure to the bud nestled between her damp lips. He stroked her until she was clinging to him, her breasts against his chest. Her hand stroking up and down the length of him, wet from her mouth.

He met her gaze again and saw her need. Saw her indecision, as well. At least he wasn't alone in what he was feeling.

She grabbed hold of his shoulders and he finally eased a finger inside her. That action dragged her eyes closed. He didn't know why, but he needed her to see him. He needed to see what she was experiencing through those amazingly expressive eyes.

"Open your eyes, Lizzy," he said in soft tones.

It was a battle to do what Aidan asked. It wasn't just the pleasure she was experiencing from the way he was moving his fingers inside her, or the way her breasts brushed against his smooth chest. Maybe it was that she might give up too much of herself if she did so. Too much of what she was feeling. Hoping for.

"Lizzy, please," he urged, and in his voice there was something that said she wasn't alone in her yearnings or her fears.

She did as he asked. Those gorgeous eyes of his were a fusion of lighter and darker blues, like the ocean during a storm, revealing to her as much she had feared.

Cradling the side of his face, she traced the line of his cheek and then shifted downward to the edge of his lips. She moved her thumb across them and he bit down on it, which created a tsunami of desire that swamped her senses.

"Lizzy?" he questioned, his gaze searching her face. Making it impossible for her to do anything other than tell him the truth.

"I want you to kiss me...there."

Aidan groaned, but hastily removed her jeans.

She sank onto the giving cushions of the sofa, opening her legs as he knelt before her. He rubbed his hands up and down her thighs nervously and his gaze as it skittered up to hers was equally tense.

"Aidan?" she asked and cradled the side of his face.

"You're like no one I've ever met," he confessed and dropped a kiss on the palm of her hand.

"I hope that's a good thing," she said, feeling exposed on too many levels.

"It is, only... I might not be able to stop after this."

She laid her hands over his to still the motion of his hands as he moved them on her thighs.

"Who said we had to stop?"

His hands trembled hands beneath hers.

He looked up, his gaze intense. Compelling. Troubled.

She suspected that she knew the reason why. Leaning forward, she cradled the back of his head and kissed him. A re-assuring kiss. One that said, no matter what happens, it's okay.

And it was.

When he finally parted her with a hesitant kiss and then licked the swollen bud of her clitoris, she nearly jumped out of her skin. It had been too long and Aidan...Aidan knew just what to do even before she thought it, much less gave voice to it. He slowly licked until shc was pressing toward him. Then he sucked and slipped first one finger inside, followed by a second.

She was writhing on the couch, holding his head to her when he bit down on that nub and sent her over the edge.

"Aidan."

She cried his name out and he rose, was suddenly poised

at her entrance. Somehow he'd managed to get a condom on. She couldn't recall when or how. Come to think of it, she couldn't remember anything other than how wonderful he was with his hands and mouth.

And although she had just had one of the most satisfying orgasms of her life—even if her experience was limited—she was suddenly on the edge again, wanting him to enter her and ride her to another.

She met his gaze, her breathing still shaky. Reaching for him so that he could join with her, she was surprised when he inched away a bit and shook his head. But when he grinned, she realized with relief that it wasn't about stopping.

"You won the race, remember?" he said, and, with that, he lay down on the floor and pillowed his head in his hands.

The race? Puzzlement turned to amusement. Ah, yes, the race. The win that guaranteed her position…at least for this time.

She eased off the couch and knelt beside him as he lay exposed to her. That long sculpted body within reach and absolutely impossible to ignore. Almost as impossible to ignore as the long, equally impressive state of his erection.

A pool of damp drenched her as she imagined what would happen soon.

But first, she had to touch.

Chapter 20

Lucia cursed as the signals from the cameras continued to be nothing more than static. She hadn't been able to end the jamming. But she had been able to pinpoint the general source of the transmission—a spot right behind the cottage where she had seen Aidan enter with the Sparrow.

She could head there, but by doing so, she risked compromising Aidan's assignment. Given what she had seen of what was going on...

Aidan was physically safe. His heart, however, was another matter. And the assignment...possibly already compromised if what she suspected was happening was actually happening.

Lucia had heard what he said about it being just about the job. But behind those tones, her women's intuition had picked up on his attraction to the Sparrow.

Glancing at her watch, she realized Aidan had been incommunicado for just over twenty minutes. That's all it took, she joked with herself, but realized she couldn't rush in just yet. She would get in gear, get prepared and give it just a little while longer before she went in search of the jamming device.

Alone. She knew that broke with procedure, but calling in Walker now was sure to cause problems and, as the lead, Aidan would not take it well.

They'd had enough problems without creating another.

Aidan lay watching Lizzy as, in turn, she looked at him. Her sherry-colored eyes had darkened to that cognac color he'd seen the other day. Her gaze was so rich with the heady promise of what was to come, that he nearly grew dizzy from it.

"Lizzy?" he questioned at her delay.

"Just…admiring," she answered and laid her hand in the middle of his chest. Shifted it over to caress his pec. Run it along the hard edge of his nipple.

He wanted to do the same, and he reached up, cupped her breast. Took her nipple between his fingers and gently twisted it.

Her eyes half closed for a moment and her breath hitched slightly. She liked that. A lot. But so did he.

He needed her closer, so he placed his hands on her hips, exerted gentle pressure so that she would straddle him, the center of her just above his erection, her soft hairs teasing the sensitive skin at the edge, just below the condom's reach. Then he reached up once more, cradled both her breasts and pleasured her as she slowly explored him.

She placed her hands on his chest and loitered for a moment before inching them down his body, investigating every hollow and plane. Her palms were smooth against his skin, warm and slightly damp.

When she met his gaze, her pupils were open wide. Her lips must have been dry because she licked them nervously.

And suddenly he wanted to lick them too.

He surged up, captured the back of her head in his hand and kissed her. Slipped his tongue into her mouth and sucked on it. When he pulled back a bit and their gazes collided, they both knew it was time.

He didn't lie back down. He needed to see her eyes. Be close to her as she took him in.

She shifted the final inch, raised her hips and hesitated for just a second, poised above him. Would she take him hard and fast or…

Slowly, Elizabeth thought.

The tip of him just breached her entrance. She lowered her hips, lingering over every inch of him as she moved downward. Her breath was held prisoner in her chest and his face filled her vision as he stretched her.

When she finally had taken all of him in, she paused as the sensation nearly overwhelmed her. "Aidan?" she said and licked her lips.

He picked up one hand and cupped the side of her face. The other was supporting him, allowing him to be close to her as she rode him. "Sweet Lizzy. This is…amazing."

She couldn't argue. His length tucked inside her was creating a jumble of sensations. Heat. Wet. A clenching of her insides that demanded she do more to satisfy the knot of need somewhere inside her. Was it down there and just sexual? Or was it in her heart? she wondered, but then she flexed her hips and moved upward, languidly.

The friction of it made her moan and close her eyes.

Aidan didn't press her then and she was glad for it. She wanted to focus on the pleasure of him next to her. In her. On the delicious sensations that came from moving on him, slowly at first, but then faster and faster as she sought her satisfaction.

He urged her on with soft encouraging words. With the lick of his tongue at the sensitive spot on her neck that he had sucked before. At her breasts as he caressed them with his hand.

At some point, he finally lay back down and brought his hands to her hips to help guide her.

With her hands leaning on his chest and her hips pumping against him, she was near the edge. Her breath was rough in her chest. Her body was trembling. It would only take a little more, she thought, aware that she was near release.

He must have sensed it, as well; for he exhorted her onward, and when she was poised at the edge, he leaned up just enough to suck at the tip of one breast, then bit it gently.

It pushed her over the edge.

She drove down on him hard, called out his name as her body shuddered and trembled with her climax. But he was still hard within her and even as he soothed her with his hands, she could feel her hunger coming back to life.

Aidan sensed her renewed need even as he marveled at it. She had pleasured herself with him, but the pleasure hadn't been all hers. The feel of her around him, of her breasts and legs and skin…of all of her, was so enticing that he didn't want it ever to end.

But already her renewed desire was dragging him toward his own climax. He was barely keeping control despite his wish to be with her.

Somehow he managed to get her on her back without breaking away from her. He would have rather died than lose that contact with her, he thought.

She looked up at him, wide-eyed and vulnerable. Almost disbelieving the passion sizzling between them. Afraid. "I'm feeling it too, Lizzy."

"It's…scary," she confessed, creating a spot in his heart for her he didn't want to have.

Leaning down, he brushed a kiss on her lips and said, "Don't be scared. I would never hurt you."

Although he knew he would, because there was no good way for this to end between them. If she wasn't the Sparrow, he'd still have to leave at the end of the day. He'd already warned her he wasn't a stay-at-home kind of guy.

And if she *was* the Sparrow…

He was doomed for sure, he thought, as he moved in her and brought them both to the edge again before they slipped over together.

Afterward, when they were finally breathing and their legs could hold them, they slowly walked upstairs to her bedroom and climbed into bed.

He held her cradled to his side, knowing they would make love again. It had been too amazing for them not to. But before then…

He had a mission. That was why he was here. Liar, the little voice in his head yelled, but he ignored it and pressed forward with his assignment.

"What was it like growing up here? Always being in one place?" he began, in part because he needed to discuss her family, but also because a part of him actually did wonder what such a life was like, having never had such stability during his younger years.

She ran her hand across his chest, the gesture soothing, one of connection rather than desire.

"Nice at times. Annoying at others. In a town as tiny as Leonia, everyone knows everyone. Everyone knows everything about you."

"Hmm," he said and rubbed his hand up and down her arm, but didn't say anything else. He didn't want to press too hard and arouse suspicions.

"And you? What was it like always moving around?"

Aidan's answer came quickly, too much so, he feared. "When I was younger, it was hard. I would just get used to the place and make friends and we would get our next assignment."

"And later? When you were older?" she asked and snuggled closer to him, her body plastered along his side, one thigh tossed over his legs beneath the sheets.

His arm was tucked under her and he eased his hand over the curve of her waist to hold her close. "When I was older? I stopped trying to make friends. It made it easier," he confessed.

She was quiet for a long time before she said, "I had my friends and family. And all the aunts and uncles and cousins, not to mention the neighbors and the milkman…" She stopped with a chuckle and he joined in her amusement.

"It must have been nice. I just had my family."

"And Mitch," she added.

Involuntarily, he stiffened at the mention of his friend's name. Especially coming from her. But she was right. He'd had Mitch. "Mitch was…like a brother."

"Did they ever find out—"

"Why he was killed. No," he answered tightly, since at the reference to his friend, the headache he'd had that morning had begun to return.

"I'm sorry. I didn't want to bring up anything painful." She sat up then and the sheet fell away, revealing all of her to him.

"Headache's back?" she added quickly. He must have been making a face of some sort for her to notice.

When he affirmed it, she straddled his legs so that she might have a better position and began a slow and careful massage along his temples. "Close your eyes," she said.

He did, not only because she asked, but because the sight and feel of her was arousing him again and he had other things that needed to get settled first.

"Was it hard for you? After your mom and dad—"

"I'd rather not talk about that time. It was…difficult."

He slowly opened his eyes, inspected her face. The hurt was there for the world to see. "Didn't your other family help out?"

Lizzy stopped her massage and dropped her hands to her sides. Of course there had been family to help out, she thought, but that hadn't made it any easier. Especially when the person closest to you, the one you knew you could always count on, had as good as lost it.

Dani had been inconsolable for days and then the grief had turned to anger. Anger at the police who couldn't find the killers and later, at all the bureaucrats who had seemed so intent on covering up anything to do with her parents' deaths. Maybe even anger at herself for not being there to stop it, Lizzy thought.

"Lizzy?" Aidan asked and placed his fist beneath her chin, applying gentle pressure so that he could read her face.

"Sometimes you're alone even when you're surrounded by people."

He cursed beneath his breath, slipped his hand to the nape of her neck to draw her close for a kiss. "I'm sorry," he whispered afterward. "For everything," he said and Lizzy got the weird sense he wasn't just talking about her parents.

Chapter 21

He didn't know how many times they made love that night. He had run out of condoms and Lizzy had supplied some more.

Enough times that he was sore. Dead tired. Exhausted.

Thoroughly satisfied. Totally confused.

Rolling onto his side, he propped his head up with one hand and glanced at her as she lay sprawled on her back beside him. A rumbly and all too regular noise came from her.

She was a snorer.

How long had it been since he'd spent enough time with a woman to know something like that?

Too long.

That had to be the explanation for his abandon. For the feelings he was having toward her. Walker could surely explain how it was transference or some other such psychological issue.

It certainly couldn't be love.

Her eyelids drifted open slowly and as she saw him there, a broad welcoming smile erupted on her face. "G'mornin'," she said, her voice husky.

He shifted over, dropped a quick kiss on her lips. "G'mornin'. Do you have any plans for today?"

A tired sigh escaped her. "Some errands to run in town before work. And you?"

"I'm supposed to meet a friend," he lied since he couldn't risk her going with him. Not when he had to report in and possibly go back to investigating her. Back to proving she was a killer.

She glanced at her wristwatch and grimaced. "I guess we should get going."

"I guess we should," he replied, but made no motion other than to shift closer, until he could lay his hand beneath the sheets on the indentation between her hip and waist.

"That's not going to get me moving."

"No? Then how about this?" He slipped his hand downward, parted her thighs and found the tender bud tucked between them.

"Oh. O-o-h. That might work," she answered and gripped his shoulders with her hands, urging him over her.

"I thought so."

Inside the hotel suite, Walker and Lucia were waiting for him.

He shot a quick look at his watch. Barely eight o'clock. "What's up?" he asked as he strolled in and then plopped himself on the couch next to Lucia.

"Besides you? All night?" Lucia teased and Aidan blushed as it occurred to him what Lucia might have seen during her surveillance.

Walker silenced her banter with a harsh glare and a sharp slash of his hand.

"Is this mission compromised, Spaulding?" Walker asked, clearly all about business this morning.

Aidan was not about to let the other man dictate to him as he seemed so fond of doing. He had always found Walker to be a fairly easygoing kind of guy, but he'd been anything but during this assignment. Not to mention that Walker chastising him for his arguably less than professional interest in Lizzy was kind of hypocritical to the max.

"Jealous? Not getting any from the doc?" Aidan shot back, referring to Walker's ongoing affair with the royal physician.

Walker was on his feet in a second, fists clenched at his sides. When he took a step toward him, Aidan rose, picked up his chin and stepped right up to him, spoiling for a fight.

They were of a like height and similar build. He knew he could hold his own, but this little show was accomplishing nothing. "I did what I had to for information," he said from behind gritted teeth, trying to defuse the situation.

"Was that the only reason?" Walker wondered aloud and arched a sandy-colored eyebrow to emphasize his point.

Lucia seemed to think it best to intervene, since she stepped between them and laid a hand on each of their chests. "Down boys. I'm overdosing on all the testosterone."

After a final exchange of glares, they all sat down again, an uneasy silence filling the room.

"Report, Spaulding. What did you learn during your midnight escapade that we can tell the duke? He is expecting us to find the *prince's* killer." Walker pressed and stared at him intently.

He had to give the other man credit. He had perfected the whole bushy-eyebrow, give-you-guilt look. And it worked. He was unable to meet his gaze as he said, "Nothing."

At least nothing that he would share. Like that Lizzy was an aggressively passionate lover. One who pleased as much as she liked being pleased. And that she snored...

He smiled at that last recollection. The seemingly perfect woman had at least one flaw.

Besides being an assassin? the voice in his head questioned snidely.

"The *Quiz* plans on going to press tomorrow with a story on the prince. It seems they've got more information than we do." After he spoke, Walker clasped his hands together and laid them across his midsection. It was a pose that seemed comfortable at first glance, but was anything but if you looked closely at the tight set of his jaw.

"We've got this," Lucia said and tossed something small, black and plastic on the coffee table before him.

Aidan picked up the object and examined it. He recognized it immediately. He had designed his share of jamming devices. This one was compact and well-made. Besides the on/off switch, there was a dial, he suspected for modulating the strength of the signal. It called to memory a similar device he had seen. "Where did you get this? It looks like MI6 issue."

"In the reeds behind Ms. Moore's cottage. It was on for the earlier part of the night until I was able to home in on its signal and retrieve it."

His relief that his time with Lizzy hadn't been monitored was short-lived. He inspected the device again and racked his brains for any moment he wasn't with Lizzy, trying to figure out when she could have planted the device. Nothing came to mind. "When did—"

"I don't know when she put it there. As far as I could tell, she was with you the whole time," Lucia admitted, but then pressed onward. "What I can tell you is that there were no prints, but there was DNA. She must have had it on a belt clip or something else that rode against her skin."

"And?" Walker asked, leaning forward intently now as he awaited her answer.

Lucia weakly motioned with her hands. "Xander is running the PCR tests as we speak. We'll have the results later today."

"We need more."

Aidan glanced at Walker after those words. "And how do you propose we get more?"

"As far as I'm concerned, you've jeopardized your position, Aidan. There's no sense in not coming clean with Ms. Moore."

He pictured telling her. If she was the Sparrow, he would be prepared to deal with the reaction. If she wasn't…

"I'm not sure—"

"Be sure," Walker jumped in. "The *Quiz* hits the streets tomorrow with whatever information they have. Real or imagined, we'd better have something to tell the duke so that he knows his money is being well-spent."

Risking a glance at Lucia, he realized she was as uncomfortable as he was. "What do you think, Lucia?"

"I don't like being rushed. If Ms. Moore is the Sparrow, I don't think she's going to give herself up just because you admit you're an agent for the Lazlo Group. She has no reason to fear us."

Walker confirmed his agreement with a quick nod. "You're right. But if she isn't the Sparrow—"

"She'll be afraid? I don't think you know Lizzy. She doesn't strike me as the type to be afraid."

"Lizzy, huh?" Walker said in low tones before shifting to the edge of his seat and leaning forward to emphasize his point.

"Be ready to deal with her if she's the Sparrow. Lucia and I will have your back."

He met Walker's gaze and surprisingly saw commiseration there. After all, the other man had fallen for the royal doctor during his assignment. He knew what it was like to mix pleasure and business. The difference was, Aidan could see no happy ending in his mission.

"Let me get cleaned up. Liz…Ms. Moore said she would be running some errands in town. If I can't find her there, I'll head for the restaurant."

Lucia rose and said, "We'll be there when you need us."

Aidan had no doubt they would be. Only, if Lizzy wasn't the Sparrow, the kind of support they could offer would do little to help the situation.

Less than half an hour later, he was back in the main part of the hotel suite, watching Lizzy in the monitors. Like him, she had showered. He wondered if, like him, she had thought of him as she'd run her hands over parts kissed during the night.

The reaction of his body was unwelcome right now given what he would shortly have to do. He muttered an explctive beneath his breath, drawing Lucia's attention at a nearby monitor.

"You ready?" she tossed over her shoulder as her hands flew over the keys on her laptop.

He wondered what she was working on so intently and approached. "What's up?"

"You got me thinking yesterday when you mentioned how our histories were altered. I've been trying to track down more info on Ms. Moore. Old info. Pre-alteration, if something like that occurred."

He leaned his hand on her shoulder and peered at the screen. It was a listing of past students from the Leonia High School Alumni Association. "Looks normal," he replied.

"It does, but I want to dig deeper. See if I can't hack into the server and check out their other files," she advised and chanced another glance at him. "You ready to go?"

He motioned with his head in Walker's direction. "What about him?"

She shrugged while typing. "Some kind of urgent call from Corbett. Said for you to go ahead and he would bc ready whenever you needed."

Which was fine by him. He didn't need Walker to watch his tail. He was perfectly capable of taking care of himself. Besides, first he had to meet up with Lizzy.

Returning to the far monitor, he realized she was no longer in her room. Flipping from one camera shot to the other, it became obvious that she was nowhere on the premises of either the restaurant or the cottage. Accessing the earlier images stored on the hard drive, he realized Lizzy had left the cottage. Picking up his binoculars, he scoped out the beach front and then tried to see if he could pick her out along the streets of Leonia.

Damn. Nothing. Time for him to hit the bricks.

"I'm out of here. The code word if I need assistance is…"

He stopped dead, wondering what they might be discussing in those moments after he made his revelation. Lucia turned to face him as he considered it. But it suddenly occurred to him there was one last thing he wanted the Sparrow to hear if that's how it played out. "The code word is *Mitch*."

She uneasily acknowledged it with a nod and he was out the door, hurrying down the stairs and onto the main street. Where might Lizzy be headed this morning? The docks and markets for food? One of her friends' places or the WAC?

He was closest to the latter and so he drifted by there, seemingly to check out what the WAC would be offering. The doors were closed as was the ticket office. Still, he lingered by the posted schedule, checking it out as any normal patron might. Anything to lessen attention.

After a few minutes, he ambled back in the direction of town, hands tucked into his jacket pockets. The reassuring weight of his HK Mark 23 dragged at one shoulder. At his ankle, the Glock 36 rubbed his pant leg.

He was ready for battle.

Once on the main street, he opted for Samantha's shop, which was closest. Inside the store, calm reigned, unlike the other day during the sale. Unfortunately, Samantha had taken the morning off, her sales clerk advised.

As he stepped out of the store, he wondered if Samantha had taken the time to be with Lizzy. If so, would Kate also be in on the outing?

Hurrying up the block to the next shop, he noticed a familiar figure up ahead on the opposite side of the street. Lizzy. Dressed in black jeans with a black leather jacket covering a figure-hugging white T-shirt. She looked stunning. Not at all tired. He called out to her, but she seemed not to hear.

Raising a hand and giving a wave, he once again yelled her name.

She finally noticed and looked his way, but acted as if she didn't even recognize him. Puzzled for a moment, his delay allowed her to turn down the side street before he could react.

Fixated on following her, he jumped into the street, but stopped short at the strident blare of a horn. He glared at the driver who had nearly hit him and who shook a fist at him angrily.

Aidan ignored the driver and continued across the street, past the traffic in the opposite lane and onward to the corner of the block onto which Lizzy had turned.

No Lizzy anywhere on the street. There were a number of shops, however, and so he walked down the block, pausing at the shop windows to peer within searching for her, but she was nowhere to be found. At the end of the street, which had turned out to be a dead end, he paused, wondering where she could have gone when Lucia came on over the wire.

"Blender Boy. The Sparrow's returned to her nest."

He examined the street, unable to determine how she had eluded him. "Confirm, Red Rover. Cottage or restaurant?"

"Cottage."

"I'm on it," he said, and foregoing any further exploration of the dead end, he rushed back to the main road and then to the restaurant. Once he was within sight of the low stone wall for the building, he said, "Red Rover. What's your ETA?"

"Walker and I are already in position about ten yards behind the cottage along the shore. Just say the word."

Mitch, he thought, a second before confirming Lucia's communication. Funny how after nearly two years of searching, his goal was within his grasp, but it gave him no satisfaction. No relief.

Entering through the gate to the restaurant, he cut across the front yard, straight to the back patio and the granite stepping stones that led to Lizzy's cottage. At the door, he hesitated and took a deep breath.

No matter the outcome of this confrontation, whatever was going on between him and Lizzy would never be the same.

Chapter 22

The knock at the door surprised her. She hadn't been expecting anyone, only possibly hoping for...

She smiled as she opened the door and her hope was fulfilled. A fierce and all too serious look marred his face. One that warned trouble was ahead. "You okay?"

"May I come in?" he asked and motioned to her front parlor. The parlor where, the night before, they had done wonderful things both to and with each other. She suspected that wouldn't be the case this morning.

"Sure," she said and extended her arm in invitation.

He walked in, but didn't sit. Just stood there, obviously awkward.

"You okay?" she asked again as she closed the door and went to stand before him.

He shrugged and the movement pulled the front of his jacket open slightly, revealing a quick glimpse of something at his side a moment before the black leather dropped down again, hiding it from sight.

"Saw you in town. Waved to you." A puzzled look crossed his features. "You were dressed differently."

Town? She'd been in and around the house and restaurant all morning. "I've been here," she said, but then it occurred to her what might have happened.

"Dani. She must have come home as a surprise." Joy swept over her at the prospect of seeing her sister.

"Dani? Who's Dani?" he asked, another quizzical look on his face.

"Dani's my twin sister. She must have—"

Aidan raised his hands and waved them while shaking his head vehemently. "You don't have a twin, Lizzy. Look, if you're having any kind of mental problems—"

Now it was her turn to silence him with a slash of her hand. "If anyone's gone mental, it's you. How the hell do you presume to know—"

She abruptly stopped when Aidan took out some official-looking badge from beneath his jacket and the movement also revealed the gun tucked into the holster. She realized then it was what she had spied before.

Barely glancing at the badge, her gaze snared by the weapon, she said in soft tones, "Who the hell are you?"

He hesitated, clearly troubled, before slipping the badge back into his pocket. "Aidan Spaulding. I work for the Lazlo Group. We've been hired to track down Prince Reginald's killer."

"You lied to me," she said and stepped close to him, wanting to see his eyes as he answered.

"I had to. I—"

She slapped him, hard enough to snap his head back. "You prick. You've been lying to me the whole time. You were lying to me when..."

She went for him again, but this time he snared her hand in midair. "Don't," he warned.

"Or what?" Anger drove her to taunt him.

"You have no twin. Nothing in the files supports that," he advised and released her.

She let out a harsh laugh. "Your files are wrong, Aidan. Danielle Elizabeth Moore is my twin sister. My older sister by half an hour."

Aidan examined her features carefully, but the lady was either an amazing liar, telling the truth, or totally demented. He didn't know which of the three possibilities he preferred. But two of them could be easily eliminated.

"Prove it," he said.

Lizzy immediately sprang into action. Striding to the bookcase at one side of the room, she knelt before it and rummaged through some of the books before saying, "It's gone."

He stood behind her and asked, "What's gone?"

She was shaking her head and flipping through the books once more. "Our high-school yearbook. Weird. But it doesn't matter. There's pictures in here."

She yanked a photo album from one of the shelves and flipped it open. As she balanced it on her thighs, she turned one page after another, her movements becoming more agitated as page after page failed to reveal anything other than pictures of her and her parents.

Her hands shook as she tossed that album aside and reached for another, repeated her search, her actions more frantic with each page of photos until finally she had gone through every album with no satisfaction. After she tossed aside the last one, she glanced up at him.

The look on her face had him leaning toward the demented possibility.

"I don't understand," she said, her tone uncertain, as if she was beginning to doubt her own sanity.

He bent down until he was face to face with her, reached out and cupped her cheek. "Lizzy—"

She batted away his hand. "Don't you dare ever call me that again."

He nodded, but pressed onward. "I can get help to cure this delusion."

"I'm not crazy." She enunciated each word carefully and with determination. It only worried him more.

A second later, she popped up and said, "I know where there's proof."

She hurried to the door and Aidan whispered into the wire, "Stay put, Red Rover. This isn't going the way I envisioned."

"I so totally copy that, Blender Boy," Lucia advised as he followed Lizzy to the restaurant and then down into the cellar. She purposefully strode to the safe, spun the lock and popped open the door.

He stepped beside her, recollecting the view he'd had of the safe just days earlier. It appeared the same except…

"There was a foot locker down at the bottom." He motioned to the glaring emptiness of the bottom shelf.

"Dani's foot locker. She must have come by to get it," Lizzy explained and grabbed a smaller box from another shelf. Working the lock on that box, she opened it and, as before, unsuccessfully rummaged through the papers there.

Every line of her body reflected her dejection. Her surprise. "I don't get it."

"Look, we have a doctor who can deal with this kind of thing," he said and laid a reassuring hand on her shoulder.

She shook off his touch. Her words were clipped, laced with anger. "I am *not* crazy."

With that she was in action again, heading back to the cottage and up the stairs to her bedroom, where she began tossing things out of the drawers at the desk in the corner of her room, clearly searching for something. Anything, apparently.

Aidan just stood watching until it became clear she would find nothing to justify her delusion. Turning his attention to the rest of the room, he examined it more carefully and something on the nightstand beside her bed caught his eye.

He walked over slowly, disbelievingly, until he got closer and closer and there was no denying what he was seeing.

Picking up the frame, he ran his fingers over the photo of the two women standing before the Spanish Steps in Rome.

Two identical women. No delusion could have fabricated this, he realized.

"Red Rover. Come in, Red Rover," he said and turned to face Lizzy.

She must have realized what he was holding, for her earlier anger and confusion fled from her face. She smiled, crossed her arms over her chest and said, "I told you I wasn't crazy."

He acknowledged it, but then Lucia finally responded.

"Come in. Walker wants to know if you have proof of the Sparrow's allegations?"

"I'm holding it, Lucia. I think you two need to get here so we can all discuss this."

As he spoke he looked at Elizabeth, who immediately said, "You're damn right that we'd better discuss this. My sister—"

"Is the Sparrow. She's a world-renowned assassin. We think she murdered the prince."

"And I should believe that because your information has been reliable so far?"

She didn't wait for his answer but turned on her heel and headed downstairs.

He watched her go and confessed to admiration at her spunk. He only hoped it would last past the interview with Walker and Lucia.

Elizabeth waited patiently for Aidan's colleagues to arrive. Or at least, she hoped she looked patient, since she was anything but. Her emotions were a jumble from the revelations that Aidan suspected her sister was a cold-blooded killer and that Aidan himself had been deceiving her. He had lied his way into her bed. Into her heart.

The former concerned her more since she knew he was wrong about Dani. Her sister could never do what he claimed. The latter…she couldn't begin to deal with the latter. With her poor judgment.

It took just five minutes or so after his call for a knock to come at the door. During those minutes, she and Aidan stared at one another awkwardly.

He looked guilty and upset. Good, the bastard deserved major angst after what he had done.

She picked up her chin and glared at him, conveying her rage as he walked to the door to allow his colleagues to enter.

Another man, one very similar in size and looks to Aidan, and an attractive coffee-color-skinned woman walked through the door. Aidan motioned them in the direction of the couch where she was sitting. "Elizabeth Moore," he offered in explanation.

Elizabeth rose slowly.

The tall sandy-haired man held out his hand. "Dr. Walker Shaw."

The woman was next. "Lucia Cordez."

She noticed that the woman had a laptop in her other hand and Elizabeth motioned to it. "Is that where you have your proof?"

"No sense delaying, is there?" Shaw said and held out his hand, inviting her to sit once more.

She did, and the woman and Shaw bracketed either side of her. Aidan took a seat across the way, obviously having no need to see the proof.

Lucia powered up the laptop and, once it was running, assisted Shaw as he detailed their evidence that Dani was the Sparrow.

Elizabeth listened. Looked. The dates and facts for certain times she could personally confirm. Dates like the one that fell during the week that she and Dani had met in Rome.

Thinking back on it now, Dani had been so happy for the first few days and had even hinted at a new man in her life. One with whom she could get serious. But then, something had happened. Dani wouldn't say what, but her sister had been a changed woman by the end of the week.

And then there was the weekend for the cooking expo in the town near Prince Reginald's estate.

Dani had been home that weekend. A surprise trip, she had

said. She had even gone by the expo to see Elizabeth, although she hadn't come home until very late that night.

The night the prince had been murdered.

As each fact seemed to point to the possibility that her sister was what they said, Elizabeth scrambled to find an explanation for why she wasn't. Why they were wrong.

The explanations were hard to find.

"She couldn't have done all these things that you say," she countered weakly.

"These things were murders, Ms. Moore. Cold-blooded, for-hire assassinations," Shaw said.

The woman was a little more sympathetic. She laid a well-manicured hand over hers and squeezed reassuringly. "Look, my sister… She got into trouble, too. But I was able to help her."

"Help her? Like maybe we can do an intervention? Or maybe there's an anti-assassin patch that'll curb her need to kill?" Anger laced her words, mostly because despite the proof before her, she couldn't believe her sister was what they said.

"Maybe there's a reason why she did this," Aidan offered from across the way.

She picked up her head and shot him a glare. "A reason? How about that maybe you're wrong?"

"Maybe what happened to your parents pushed her over the edge," Shaw piped in.

Out of the corner of her eye, she examined the man beside her. Attractive, if you liked the Nordic type, which she obviously did since she'd given it up to Aidan. But his eyes weren't as clear a blue and his hair not as blond. And she could sense the tension between him and Aidan.

Although right now he was trying to be sympathetic. Caring. Possibly open to her pleas about Dani. "When Ma and Da were killed, Dani lost it. She felt guilty that she hadn't gone with them that morning. We had both slept in after a school dance."

"Did you feel the guilt?" Shaw asked.

"Wouldn't you?" she shot back quickly.

"If you'd gone, maybe you'd both be dead right now," Aidan said.

She met his gaze. "Maybe. It didn't make it any easier then. Not even now. You always wonder about the what if."

"What if that's what made Dani do this?" Lucia said and once again, squeezed her hand.

She considered it for only a moment. "Afterward...Dani wasn't quite the same. She had always been a protector and after, it was even more extreme. She became everyone's champion. Always there to right a wrong."

"Maybe that's how she justified all these kills. Except for Mitch, every one of these men were involved in nasty things. Seemingly above the law—"

"But not beyond the Sparrow's own brand of justice," Aidan finished for Shaw.

Even with that explanation, Elizabeth still couldn't believe it and shook her head. "You're wrong," she reiterated.

"And if we're not?" Shaw pressed, but Elizabeth didn't get to answer as all three of their cell phones went off at the same time, creating a noisy cacophony in her front parlor.

Shaw was quickest on the draw and, as the other two waited, he listened quietly. His expression grew darker with each second that passed. When he hung up and slipped the phone back into its holder, he shot an uneasy glance between Aidan and Lucia.

"We've got major problems. Lord Southgate will brief us back at the hotel, Lucia. Aidan, I think it's wiser for you to stay here. If the Sparrow's back in town—"

"She's bound to turn up around here. Brief me once you know more," he said and rose, walked the other two to the door. Once they had left, he faced Elizabeth and said, "You're not telling us everything about Dani."

"What?" she said, uncertain of what information Aidan thought she might have. "I've told you everything I know."

He strode over and suddenly loomed before her, his arms on either side of her on the back of the couch, effectively trapping her. "No, you haven't."

She tried to bat his arms away, but he held firm. With a sigh, she said, "What else could I possibly tell you?"

He knelt before her until there was no way she could avoid looking at him. Finally he said, "You can start by telling me where Dani is."

Chapter 23

Dani hurried along the coast road, intent on reaching the cottage. She had to find out who the man was making moves on her sister.

She thought she had seen him today, after she had dropped by Kate's to get the scoop on what was up. Kate was always the one in the know and things hadn't changed. Their old friend had been able to tell Dani about Mr. Tall, Blond and Dangerous who had appeared in town right after Lizzy's bartender had deserted her. A man who had made his attraction to Lizzy clear.

An attraction that even Kate had noticed was reciprocated by her younger sister.

Dani knew that well from what she had seen the night before from outside Lizzie's cottage.

Now she had to figure out who he was and what he wanted. Even more importantly, for whom he worked. Not, she hoped, the man who had hired her to kill the prince. If that was the case, Lizzy might be in danger and Dani had to make sure her sister was safe.

She hurried up the central road until she was past the docks. Then she cut down a shallow footpath through the dunes and grasses. The tall grasses hid her at times, but could also camouflage someone else along the path. She moved along with caution, therefore.

The path dipped toward the beach, and, once there, she hastened her pace, breaking into a slow jog so that she could reach her grandparents' cottage and start searching for more information on Mr. Aidan Rawlings.

That was the name Kate had provided, although Dani had no doubt it was an alias. Still, there were ways to get around that and secure more information.

Didn't she know it. She'd gone from Danielle Elizabeth Moore to Elizabeth Cavanaugh and most traces of her existence had been blotted out from official papers and computer databases. She had even been excised from the high-school yearbook that the Leonia Public Library kept as a record of every graduating class.

She was a ghost now. Nonexistent except to those people who knew her personally, and of course, to her sister.

Her sister who might be in danger, she thought and hurried onward.

About half a mile up the shore, there was another footpath leading to the base of the bluffs where her maternal grandparents had a cottage—her safehouse. The climb up this path was more arduous as it inclined sharply from the rocks and beach below to the start of the bluffs.

She was slightly out of breath from the climb as she entered the cottage and flipped on the light.

"So good to see you again," she heard from behind her and whirled, reaching for her gun.

A blow like an iron fist struck her, powerful enough to send her reeling backward. Searing pain erupted through her midsection. Her legs failed to cooperate, buckling beneath her.

She fell back heavily onto the couch in the middle of the room.

The pain was like a white-hot poker driving deep into her. She could barely breathe. When she finally did, her breath was shallow. Almost inconsequential.

This wasn't possible, she thought as the man approached, his voice and shape familiar from the night he had hired her to kill the prince. From the night they had fought on the docks when he'd failed to provide her the promised information on her parents' killers.

"Such a shame," he said as he finally stood before her, his face protected by a black ski mask. A slimy smile slicked across his lips as he trained his gun on her. "The Sparrow won't elude this trap."

Dani tried to go for her weapon, but her body wasn't responding. Still, the man wasn't taking any chances. He reached under her jacket and removed her gun from its holster.

She had the Sigma tucked behind her. Could feel its presence against her spine, but knew she would be unable to draw that weapon.

He inspected the HK and smiled. "Nice piece. Seems a shame to waste it, don't you think?"

He tucked it into his belt with one hand and raised his gun with the other. Pointing the barrel at her head, he sighted the shot.

Dani met his cold eyes along the matte black of the barrel and stared him down. If she was going to die, it wasn't going to be like a coward, pleading and begging for her life.

His hand trembled for a moment and she mustered enough breath to say, "What's…matter? Not man enough to do it while…I watch?"

He laughed harshly, his dark eyes glittering through the slits of the black ski mask. "Actually, no. Just taking time to appreciate that you broke your own rules. You let yourself get distracted. A fatal mistake, wouldn't you say?"

Dani gritted her teeth against the pain and struggled for another breath. He was right. She had been so worried about

Lizzy, she hadn't noticed that the fine wire she had rigged on the door to the cottage had fallen off, as it should have if the area was compromised.

And he was also right about another thing—she was dying. She could tell from the way the warmth was fleeing from her fingers and toes. Trying to pull into the center of her as her body battled to hold onto life.

She risked a glance downward. So much blood. Oozing down the front of her shirt. Too much.

"That's right, my dear. You're dying. And of course, I could spare you the pain and end it now, only…" He laughed with malice once again. "You've caused me too many problems. Better you should suffer a little before you go."

"Bastard," she spat out with a rough breath.

"Payback's a bitch, isn't it, Sparrow? And guess what? Little sis is next. Never leave anyone behind who can come in your place."

She tried to speak, causing a swirl of blackness to cloud her sight before she blessedly passed out.

There was no way Elizabeth was going to help him find her sister. Using more force than before, she broke past one of his arms, rose and braced herself for action. "Even if I did know, there's no way that I'd—"

He was on her before she knew it, his hands gripping her arms tightly. She reacted out of anger and out of frustration. Freeing one arm, she turned, dropped a little before flexing with her hip and sending him flying over her shoulder.

He landed with a satisfying thud, but not before upending an end table by the sofa and sending a lamp and some knick-knacks flying. As he lay there, recapturing the breath driven out of him by the fall, he muttered, "Learn that from big sis?"

"Yes. After…she insisted we take self-defense classes. In case they came back for us."

"She protected you then. Don't you think it makes sense to protect her now?" he posed, and in her mind's eye it was unfortunately too easy to see a full-scale manhunt for her sister. One in which Dani could be injured or killed.

She glared at him, hands on her hips and asked, "Promise you'll give Dani a chance to explain?"

He leaned up on his elbows, considered her proposition and agreed to her request with a nod. "Promise. Do you know where she is?"

With a hesitant hunch of her shoulders, she admitted, "My grandparents had a seaside cottage about a mile and a half away. Dani always loved going there to think things through."

He did a little jump/flip she had to admire and was immediately on his feet before her. "Let's go get a car."

She shook her head. "It's faster on foot. The coast road makes too many turns near the bluffs."

Without waiting for his reply, she whirled and raced out the door, alternately eager to see her sister and worried that Dani would not have an explanation for Aidan's allegations. She didn't hesitate, however, for she was sure about one thing: better they find Dani and not someone else.

Her steps were quick, nearly a jog as she hurried through the garden and up the path to the main road. She never paused to look behind her, sensing he was near as a tingle of fear grew swiftly. Gripped her. Urged her to rush.

Something was wrong with her twin. She was certain of it now as surely as she suddenly knew Dani would be at the cottage.

Increasing her pace, she weaved in and out by the pedestrians at the docks. She was at the farthest end of the wharf when she first noticed the car bearing down on them, racing along the coast road. There was something familiar about…

Loud pops, like those from a large firecracker, peppered the air before Aidan tackled her from behind. She hit the ground hard, his weight covering her protectively for just a moment.

Then he was on his feet, more gunfire shattering the stillness of the afternoon air as he returned fire.

She rolled onto her side. The car—it was a big black Hummer—fishtailed as it sped away from them. "That's the same car from the other day."

Aidan held his free hand out to her to help her rise. "It sure is."

In his other hand was a large black gun which he holstered in order to grab his PDA. "Come in, Red Rover."

"Copy, Blender Boy. We heard the noise. What's up?" she asked over the walkie-talkie, making the conversation audible to Elizabeth.

"Same perp in the Hummer. Can you get the locals to put out an APB?"

"I'm on it. Do you need backup at the cottage?"

Aidan glanced at Elizabeth for a second, hesitated, but kept his earlier promise. "That's a negative, Lucia. I think we can handle it for now."

A long silence filled the air before Lucia came back on. "Aidan. You need to hurry. The shit's hit the fan here."

"Copy, Lucia." With that, he popped the PDA back onto his belt and looked at Elizabeth.

Her gaze skipped away from his knowing one since there was no denying it any longer. Whoever was in the van was likely after her sister and had mistaken her for Dani. There could be only one explanation for why so many people were after her.

Cold settled inside her. And the fear that something else was wrong returned, even stronger than before. Aidan was still holding her hand, and he must have sensed the change that came over her.

"Lizzy? Are you okay?"

She finally met his gaze. His concern for her was clear. Heartwrenching since they were on opposite sides right now. "We have to hurry. Something's wrong with Dani."

He didn't question her. Just inclined his head in the direction of the path down to the beach. "This way?"

She nodded and they raced down the path together, hands still joined.

Chapter 24

The cottage, its outline stark against the skyline at the top of the cliff, was not as large as Lizzy's. Tall grasses almost hid it from sight as they approached, but then it was there, a lonely dark silhouette in the fading light of dusk.

There were no signs of life. No movement besides those of the grasses as they approached the door.

Aidan pulled out his gun and, standing to one side, motioned Lizzy to the other.

"Call her name," he mouthed and Lizzy did so. "Dani? It's Lizzy Bee. Are you home?"

At the silence, Aidan reached out and threw open the door.

Nothing happened, but he wasn't about to risk either himself or Lizzy. And above all, he didn't want to trade fire with her sister. He crouched down and cautiously stepped inside the doorway, hit the switch.

Lights flared to life inside the cottage.

On a sofa in the middle of the room, Lizzy's twin lay

slumped. The front of her white T-shirt from her midsection down was soaked in blood. The T-shirt, jacket and jeans were those he had seen that morning on the woman he had called to. That had been Dani and not Lizzy, he realized as he lowered his gun.

Lizzy stepped inside and, seeing Dani, exploded from his side to that of her sister.

"Dani," she said as she took hold of her twin's limp, blood-stained hand and stroked a lock of hair back from Dani's ghostly face.

Dani's eyelids fluttered open. She smiled weakly. "Lizzy Bee. I didn't think…" She stopped and grimaced, but fought back the pain to finish. "I wanted to see you."

Lizzy stroked Dani's hair once more and smiled tearily. "I'm here, Dani. I'm here. You'll be okay, Dani. I know you will."

Dani nodded, but shot a look at Aidan as he approached and stood watching. A look that told him she knew she was dying. Not if he could help it. He picked up his PDA and called Lucia with the walkie-talkie. "We need EMTs, stat. A cottage on the coast road about a mile and a half up and off toward the bluffs."

"Got your location already with the GPS chip. I'm on it," she acknowledged, and with that, he sprang into action, pulling a tea towel from a nearby caddy. He kneeled beside the sofa, folded the towel and applied it to Dani's wound—a gunshot. Fairly large caliber and close range based on the damage done. He applied pressure to staunch the blood still pouring profusely from the wound. The blood was a dark color, causing him to suspect the shot had caught her liver. Not good. She might bleed out before help arrived.

Dani moaned, closed her eyes, and ground her teeth as he applied the pressure.

"Sorry, but—"

"S'okay," she said, her voice weaker than it had been just moments earlier.

"Why did you do it?" He needed to know not only to accomplish his mission, but to also to protect Lizzy from whoever had tried to kill her. From whoever had shot Dani.

Lizzy glared at him. "Shut up, Aidan."

"S'okay, Lizzy Bee. It's not what you think," Dani offered, each word more frail than the one before.

"You didn't kill the prince?" he pressed, hating that he might be ruining Lizzy's last moments with her sister, but having little choice.

"I dangled…" she began, but squeezed her eyes shut against the pain before continuing, each word expelled with a rough breath. "The bait. Left…coke on…table."

"And Mr. Party Boy swallowed the bait," he finished for her. "Who hired you?"

Dani's gaze fixed on her sister as she said, "Let…personal interfere with…job." Every word was a struggle.

"What job, Dani?" Lizzy asked and comforted Dani by stroking the side of her sister's face lovingly.

"My…job. Made a…mistake," her eyes rolled back in her head and she sagged against the cushions of the sofa.

"Dani," Lizzy said and shook Dani's hand, trying to revive her. When she didn't rouse, she repeated her name again, more urgently.

Aidan continued to apply pressure to the wound in Dani's midsection, but with his free hand, he felt for a pulse along her neck. Weak. Too weak. He didn't have much time left to get the complete story from the Sparrow.

"Dani," he urged and stroked the side of her face gently, a face so much like Lizzy's that it hurt.

Once more Dani's eyelids fluttered open, her gaze slightly unfocused for a moment while she struggled to regain consciousness.

When she was with them again, Aidan forged ahead, time too short for delay. "Who hired you?"

"Man named Donovan." Each word was laced with anguish and fear. Each breath more shallow. Less substantial. "Said Reginald…not…true prince."

Lizzy looked up at him, her gaze as confused as he was. As far as he knew, Reginald was the one and only heir to the throne, but that question was for another day.

"Is that why you did it?"

She shook her head with more force than he thought her capable of. "Donovan…pictures." She paused, fighting for a breath. Trying to hold onto consciousness.

Winning the battle for the moment, she continued. "Reginald with drug dealers… The ones who killed Ma…Da." As she finished, she stared at her sister and tears slipped unbidden down her cheeks. "Did it for them."

"I understand, Dani," Lizzy said and leaned forward, slipping an arm around her sister to hold her close. She kissed the side of Dani's face and in soft tones repeated, "I understand."

"What did Donovan look like?"

"Mask…didn't see. Nothing else…distinguishable."

Her eyelids drifted downward again as she battled for awareness.

Aidan checked her pulse once more. Thready and barely noticeable. He had to act fast. "Lizzy, give me your hand."

She released her sister's hand and he took hold of Lizzy's, placed it over the blood-soaked towel. "Keep pressure on here. Hard pressure. Understand?"

"Aidan?" she questioned and he stroked the side of her face.

"I'm going to check on that help."

Elizabeth watched as he stepped away, grabbed his PDA and once again called someone.

"Lizzy?" her sister said and her voice seemed stronger than before, giving her hope that Dani would be all right.

She bent close to her, stroked the side of her face with her free hand. "I'm here, Dani. I'll always be here for you no matter what."

Dani's eyes, a greener shade than her own, darkened with dismay. "The prince—"

"Chose his own poison. I know," she said and leaned her forehead against his sister's. "But the rest—"

"It's not what it seems…." Dani began, but immediately began to struggle for air.

"Dani?" She applied more pressure and wrapped her one arm around her sister's shoulders, trying to comfort her. "Hang on, Dani. Please. Just a little longer."

Dani bit her lip, drawing blood. She gulped in a breath, forced a rush of words out with her exhalation. "Doing a job… Not what they think… Didn't kill…"

Aidan stepped over then, crouched down so Dani could look into his face.

"Mitch? Why did you kill Mitch?" he asked, needing to understand why his friend had died by her hand.

Tears blurred Elizabeth's vision as she pulled away from her sister. She still held Dani in her arms while she was applying pressure, but beneath the palm of her hand, the warmth of her sister's blood was too real a reminder that these might be her last moments.

"Aidan, please," she pleaded, but Dani whispered, "Oh, God. Mitch."

Tears flowed harder from Dani then and her gaze was unfocused as she stared ahead, labored for another breath, a hesitant, almost nonexistent one, and yet she somehow managed to whisper, "Didn't…kill. Loved Mitch."

A breath came. Like the hiss of air escaping a balloon. A last breath. Her body went limp and her eyes lost their life before they closed.

Elizabeth continued to hold her as Aidan searched for a pulse.

"Shit," he cursed and called Lucia again. "Damn it. What's the ETA on those EMTs?"

"Two minutes."

"Shit," he cursed again. When his gaze met hers, she finally understood Dani was gone.

"No," she said softly, but then it grew into a wail as she repeated it over and over, and cradled Dani in her arms, rocking her lifeless body back and forth.

Aidan couldn't just stand there, watching Lizzy's heart

break. Knowing that with every second that passed, there was less and less possibility of bringing Dani back.

"Lizzy, please. Give me room."

He slipped his one arm between Lizzy and her sister, pried Lizzy away so he could pick up Dani and carry her over to a free spot on the floor. Laying her out, he knelt beside her and began to do CPR. Lizzy knelt opposite him and took hold of Dani's slack hand.

He kept up the CPR for what seemed like hours until the wail of a siren grew closer and closer.

The EMTs arrived barely a minute later and urged them to the side so they could immediately get to work on Dani. Walker was with them, but as he observed from afar, Aidan could see in the other man's eyes that Dani's condition was not improving.

The EMTs were still working on her as they wheeled the gurney from the room. Lizzy went to go with them, but Walker shot out his arm and blocked her way. "I'm sorry, but that won't be possible."

"What?" Aidan shouted and advanced on the other man, grabbed his arm and yanked it down, but Walker immediately blocked their way once more when Aidan would have led Lizzy to the ambulance.

"Get out of the way, Walker. Lizzy should be with her sister."

Walker shook his head and faced Lizzy. "I'm sorry, Ms. Moore. But given who your sister is—"

"The Sparrow," Lizzy said weakly, her arms wrapped around herself as she gazed beyond Walker to the ambulance outside as it pulled away from the cottage.

Walker nodded stiffly. "Yes, the Sparrow. She's being taken to a secure location where she can be treated. If she should survive—"

"You cold-hearted prick," Aidan said and forcefully shoved Walker out of the way. "Let's go, Lizzy."

She laid a hand on his arm. A hand that was cold and covered with her sister's blood. Despite that, she was calm.

Much calmer than he. He finally realized his anger on her behalf was only causing her even more grief. He reached out and dragged her into his arms. "I'm sorry, Lizzy. I really am."

"I'm...okay. Now."

He stepped away, but not before he caressed the side of her face and said, "She'll be okay."

Lizzy confronted Walker. "When can I see her?"

Walker seemed truly uncomfortable about his answer, which made Aidan only a little less angry. Maybe he wasn't as big a prick as he seemed. "I'm not sure, Ms. Moore. Things are a bit...unsettled right now. If we all return to our hotel, I'll be able to tell you more and we can wait for news on your sister's...condition."

With a gracious nod, Lizzy walked out the door, her arms wrapped around herself once again as if that grip was all that was keeping her from breaking into pieces.

Walker was about to follow her out, when Aidan snared his arm.

The other man stopped, looked down at Aidan's hold and then up to his face. "You've let this get way too personal."

"You bet I have. You get Corbett on the line. You tell him that this business about a secure location is a load of crap."

"I'll do one better, Spaulding. I'll get him on the line so you can tell him yourself."

Chapter 25

Elizabeth sat on the couch in the hotel room that Aidan's crew used as their base of operations. Not the Leonia Inn as Aidan had mentioned, but the more upscale Lion's Heart Lodge.

A series of tables lined one wall, their surfaces littered with monitors and other surveillance equipment, computers and assorted phones.

Aidan and Lucia were huddled over one computer, intently reviewing something that had been sent to them by Lord Southgate, the Duke of Carrington. The man who would be king now that Prince Reginald was dead. As Aidan bent over the monitor, the holster with his gun dangled between his body and outstretched arm.

A gun.

If she had one in her hands right now, she could see herself killing the man who had hurt Dani. She understood better how her sister had taken a dark path on her way to avenging their parents.

Her sister the assassin. Or so the Lazlo Group claimed.

It had been nearly an hour without word, but she could sense Dani still. It gave her hope that her twin was hanging on.

She rubbed her arms against the chill from the air conditioning in the room. It was set on high, probably to deal with all the equipment within. As she did so, she roused the smell of blood.

Holding her hands out in front of her, she realized her sister's blood still clung to one hand. Glancing downward, she noted it on her shirtfront, as well from when she had cradled Dani in her arms.

"Lizzy?" Aidan questioned and took hold of her bloodstained hand with his own. "I'm sorry. I should have thought to get us cleaned up."

His hand also bore the remnants of Dani's blood as did his shirt from when he had carried her to the floor. "Thank you," she said and raked back a lock of his hair with her clean hand.

A puzzled look came to his face. "For what?"

"For keeping your promise. For helping Dani."

His eyes hardened. "I'm sorry I couldn't stop whoever shot her, Lizzy. But I promise—"

"Don't. Not that I don't want him dead, but… It just brings more death. More violence, doesn't it?"

"Yes. It does," he said and she could see in his eyes that he was thinking about Mitch.

Mitch, who Dani had said she'd loved. The pieces of part of the puzzle fell into place. "When Dani and I were in Rome, she told me she had met someone special. She was so happy for the first few days."

"Mitch, as well," Aidan admitted as he knelt before her.

"Then she came home one night… She was crying. Almost as inconsolable as when our parents had died. I figured Mr. Wonderful had broken it off with her."

"Maybe he did, but not for the reasons she thought. Maybe he was dead," he said.

"She loved him," she said and Aidan inclined his head in agreement.

"I think he loved her, only… The kind of lives we lead don't hold out many promises for happily ever after, Lizzy."

She hadn't needed him to tell her. Maybe it was his way of reminding her that he, too, had that kind of life. That he was a wanderin' man in a dangerous job who would move on as soon as this assignment was over. A man who one day, might end up like Mitch.

She wouldn't say, like Dani. No, not like Dani. Dani was still alive. Still with her, Lizzy believed with all her heart.

The door opened then and Walker Shaw stepped in, the planes of his face like granite. His blue eyes shuttered until he looked her way and said, "I'm sorry, Ms. Moore."

They were the last words she heard as Aidan caught her in his arms.

A tender touch skimmed the skin along her cheek, rousing her.

She opened her eyes and Aidan was there. "I'm sorry," he said and once again stroked his finger across her cheek.

Shaking her head, she said, "Dani's not dead."

"Lizzy—"

"She's not," she insisted and popped up. She realized someone had changed her shirt and cleaned her hands. It defused the situation immediately. "Did you do this?"

He nodded and took hold of her hand. "Are you okay?"

She would be better if she could see Dani. See for herself that Dani was dead since her twin instinct was telling her otherwise. "I want to see Dani. Say goodbye."

He rose and held out his hand to help her up. "I'm told that's not possible."

"Make it possible," she insisted as she went to his side.

With a nod, he said, "We can talk to Walker about it."

"Walker? I get the sense the two of you don't get along," she remarked, recalling the men's earlier confrontations.

Aidan shrugged away her concern. "That's what happens

when you put two alpha males to work on the same assignment. He's actually not such a bad guy."

"Let's hope so."

She walked out of the bedroom, Aidan following behind her, his hand riding at the small of her back. In the suite outside, Lucia and Walker sat at the monitors once more, but at her approach, they rose.

"Ms. Moore. I'm sorry for your loss," Walker offered and Lucia echoed his sentiments.

Elizabeth picked her head up a notch. "I want to see Dani. I want to say goodbye to my sister."

Walker's gaze skittered from her back to Aidan. "Didn't you tell her?"

"I did, but I can't agree with the decision. Elizabeth should be able to see her sister," Aidan replied.

"It's not possible," Lucia jumped in and came to stand before Lizzy. "I know this must be hard—"

"What do you know about how hard this is for me?" Elizabeth snapped. "You tell me my sister's dead, but you won't let me see her body. Won't let me say goodbye."

Walker also took a step toward her. "Ms. Moore—"

"Save it, Dr. Shaw. If you can't make it happen, get someone on the phone who can."

Walker looked back toward Aidan, as if to ask him to intercede. But as she risked a glance over her shoulder, Aidan just shrugged at the other man. "She's right on this. We all know it. It's what we'd all want if…"

An uneasy silence followed his words. A silence shattered by the ringing of the phone. Walker was the one who hurried over to pick it up. A one-sided conversation ensued, occasionally punctuated by Walker's yes sirs and no sirs. Finally there appeared to be a break and Walker said, "Mr. Lazlo. Ms. Moore has a request for you."

There was the static of a reply and then Walker moved to the table holding a speakerphone and hit a button. "Mr. Lazlo?" he said.

A crackle rent the air before a man's resonant voice said, "Ms. Moore. My sympathies are with you at your loss."

She walked closer to the speaker, leaned toward it so she would be clearly heard. "If you truly meant those words, Mr. Lazlo, you would let me see my sister."

"Unfortunately, the body—"

"My sister, Mr. Lazlo. Not just a body," she emphasized, her hands clenched on the surface of the table.

"Of course, Ms. Moore. Your sister. Unfortunately—"

"You're sounding like a broken record, Mr. Lazlo. And so far, I haven't heard a single reason why I can't see Dani one last time."

Aidan came up behind her and placed a hand on her shoulder. Leaning past her, he spoke into the speakerphone. "Corbett, it's not an unreasonable request."

"Mr. Spaulding. There are some things over which even I have no control," Lazlo responded, his tone bordering on sympathetic.

"Please, Mr. Lazlo. I'm sure a man with your connections can make the arrangements," Elizabeth added.

Lazlo stammered for a moment. "Yes, well. Of course, Ms. Moore. I shall endeavor to see about a last visit."

A last visit. The words made her knees go weak again, but luckily Aidan was behind her. He eased an arm around her waist and steadied her. "Thank you, Mr. Lazlo."

The sound of the dial tone filled the room for a second before Walker reached over and cut the connection. As she glanced over at him, he saluted. "Ms. Moore, you've just played one of the world's greatest players. My hat's off to you."

She was about to respond when a machine on another of the tables began to beep and spit out paper.

Lucia reacted immediately, heading over to pick up the sheet the machine spewed out. Her hands trembled for a moment as she read the document. When she finished she faced them and offered the fax to Walker, who also perused it quickly.

"What is it?" Elizabeth asked, seeing the look on the psychiatrist's face go hard once again.

"It's an advance copy of the *Quiz,* courtesy of Lord Southgate." He picked up the piece of paper and held it up for them to see.

The headline read: The Prince of Fake: Reginald's False Claim to Throne Revealed.

Chapter 26

The Lazlo Group clearly had a problem on their hands. A problem that needed their coordination with the royal family as soon as possible.

But she had her own problems, as well.

The restaurant would be in full swing by now, even if it was midweek. Natalie would be crazed, wondering where Elizabeth was, since she had never missed a day without notice. Calls had to be made.

After Aidan had instructed Lucia to print out the entire article and also the materials Lord Southgate had sent over earlier for their review, he turned to her. "I need to deal with this," he said, his tones apologetic.

"There are things I need to address, as well, Aidan. Arrangements for Dani—"

"Once Corbett tells us we can."

Anger boiled up inside of her and she moved close. So close her nose brushed the edge of his jaw. "No one decides what to do about Dani except me."

"Lizzy—"

"No one, Aidan." Her tone conveyed her emotions quite clearly.

"I understand. I'll do what I can. In the meantime—"

"I need to call Nat. She's probably frantic by now."

Aidan gave a resigned nod. "You'll need to stay here until we know more about Dani's assailant. For now, we should keep any information regarding Dani's death to ourselves."

She walked over to a phone and dialed the restaurant. When the hostess answered, she asked for Natalie.

"Lizzy Bee! Thank God. We were so worried about you," Natalie immediately said as she answered.

"I'm okay, Nat, but Dani… She's been hurt. Bad. I'll need to stay with her for a little while so please close the restaurant for a few days," she explained, all the time looking at Aidan to make sure she didn't give out any more information than was necessary.

"Will she be okay?" Natalie asked and tears came to Lizzy's eyes.

She bit back the tears, but her voice was tight as she answered. "I'm not sure, Nat. I'll keep you posted."

"Lizzy. If you need anything, absolutely anything—"

"I know, Nat. Please tell Kate and Samantha. I'll keep you posted, okay?" she said, but didn't wait for an answer as the tears came more furiously.

Aidan reached out and pulled her into his embrace. "You need to get some rest, Lizzy."

"I'm not sure I can," she mumbled against his chest.

He tightened his hold and rubbed one hand up and down her back in a soothing gesture. As he did so, he called out, "Guys, I just need some time."

"Aidan," she protested, but he silenced her by gently placing a finger against her lips.

"Don't argue on this, Lizzy. The next few days may be rough. You need to be ready to deal with them."

With that, he slipped his hands to her shoulders and applied light pressure, guiding her in the direction of the room she had been in earlier. Once inside, he led her to the bed and made her climb in. As he tucked the sheets in around her, she laid her head on the pillow and smelled his scent.

"Is this your room?"

He confirmed it with a shrug. "Is that a problem?"

"No. Thank you."

It was so awkward between them when just last night…

"Was any of it true? The army? The moving around?" she asked, peering up at him as he stood by the side of the bed.

He stroked her hair. "It was all true, Lizzy."

She looked away to the edge of the sheet, afraid to ask about the rest. About his feelings for her. Despite that, he must have known what she was thinking.

"Lizzy. What happened…it was real. I never meant to hurt you. Believe that, please."

If she'd had any doubts, they vanished in that moment. The sincerity in his voice quashed any qualms about his true feelings. "I believe you, Aidan. But it doesn't change anything does it?"

His lips thinned into a harsh line. "No. It doesn't. I'll go and let you rest now."

He pushed away from the bed. She didn't look up until she heard the solid thunk of the door closing.

Then and only then did she give in to the tears she had been holding back. Tears for her sister and the man she'd loved. Tears for herself, selfish as they were.

Aidan heard her sobs even through the thick wood of the door. It made him want to return to the room and comfort her, only that would be a bad move all around.

Lizzy was strong. She would deal with whatever came in the days ahead. Without him.

He forced his attentions to the mission that still needed to be completed. Lucia and Walker were sitting around the coffee table in the middle of the suite, reviewing the assorted papers sent to them today.

When he approached, Lucia handed him a set to peruse and he plopped down on the sofa and got to work.

The news article from the *Quiz* detailed how Prince Reginald was not the biological son of King Weston and the queen. But other than going into detail about the DNA tests that had proven it, the story was basically a rehash of past speculation about the prince's recreational habits and the possible suspects in his killing. The *Quiz* even went so far as to bring up the months-old speculation that it was quite convenient that Lord Southgate, the next in line, had immediately stepped in and married the prince's betrothed.

Aidan tossed it aside, finding nothing of interest in the article other than the claims regarding Reginald's paternity. Dani had mentioned the same assertion.

He tossed that out for consideration by his colleagues. "The Sparrow indicated that the man who had hired her claimed to be doing it so that the true prince might inherit the throne."

"Who hired her?" Lucia asked.

"He said his name was Donovan," he advised, earning the interest of both his colleagues. "Yeah, I thought the same thing. Nikolas Donovan and his Union for Democracy are making trouble and the Sparrow's employer has the same name."

"Could be someone wants to cause trouble for Donovan, as well," Walker tossed out.

"Could be. If you discredit Donovan and the Union for Democracy, the royals get a free pass to choose whomever they want to be king," Lucia hypothesized.

"The royals being Lord Southgate." Aidan picked up the faxed copy of the *Quiz* article. "Pretty much says the same in this tabloid."

"So far they've gotten more information than we have," Walker said irately before flipping through the other papers that had been sent over earlier. "Not to mention that after weeks of trying to open this vault—"

"All you get is a fingerprint and a lock of hair once you break in. Is Xander working on it already?" Aidan asked.

Lucia nodded. "He thinks he'll have an answer for us in the morning."

Tired and frustrated, Aidan tossed the papers onto the coffee table. "I'm calling it a night, then. We'll pick up where we left off in the morning?"

Walker rose and stretched his long frame. "Let's all get some rest. I think that when this story hits the stands tomorrow, we'll need all the energy we've got."

With a wave at his two colleagues, Aidan walked to the door to his room, but hesitated at the entrance. Pressing his ear to the wood, he listened intently.

Silence.

He breathed a cowardly sigh of relief. He didn't think he had the strength to deal with her tears. But he couldn't leave her alone, either.

Entering, he trod softly so as not to wake her. She was asleep on her back and snoring. It yanked a smile to his face as it brought a recollection of their one and only night together.

He pictured himself sleeping with her again. Making love with her.

She stirred and caught him spying on her. He hoped his emotions weren't obvious.

"Did Mr. Lazlo call about Dani?" she asked and sat up.

He walked over to the bed and settled himself beside her. "Not yet."

With a slow nod, she leaned back against the wooden headboard and crossed her arms. "I can feel her still. I know that you say she's dead, but…she's still here with me."

He pointed to a spot right above his heart. "It's because Dani will always be with you. In here."

Lizzy peered at him. She wondered who stayed in his heart. Whether she might be there. "Is Mitch there with you?"

"Sometimes," he admitted immediately.

"That's good," she said.

A furrow appeared between his brows as he mused about her statement. "Why?"

"Because I don't like to think of you being alone," she confessed.

He closed his eyes, shook his head and expelled a harsh breath. When he opened them, the look in his eyes was intense. Devouring. There was no denying what he wanted any more than she could deny she wanted the same.

"If we do this tonight—"

"It will be for all the wrong reasons, wouldn't it?" she finished for him.

"I think I should leave, Lizzy," he said and rose from the bed, but she reached out and grabbed hold of his arm.

"I don't want to be alone tonight, Aidan. I just want you to… Just hold me."

He obviously couldn't resist her plea. He toed off his sneakers, slipped onto the bed beside her and wrapped an arm around her shoulders.

She went willingly, settling into his side, one hand laid over his heart. He placed his hand over hers, rubbed it as if to warm it. Not that he could. A deep chill had established its hold over her core earlier—when she had heard Walker say Dani was dead.

"I feel…cold inside. Numb," she admitted.

"It'll go away," he replied and rubbed a little harder.

"When?" she wondered aloud and snuggled closer, the warmth of his body calling to her.

He sighed heavily. "When Mitch was killed… It took a while."

Nodding, she eased back a bit so she could examine his face. There was a closed look about it. His jaw was set tightly and his eyes were hard. Frigid. Like the ice of an arctic glacier. She knew then that the cold…the pain it represented…never really went away.

"I won't believe she's dead until I see her, Aidan. Until I can hold her hand one last time. Kiss her goodbye so she knows someone cared."

He cursed before gripping her arms tightly, so tightly she

suspected she would have bruises in the morning. "She knows you cared, Lizzy. You were with her when... She knows, damn it."

Somehow she knew his anger was about more. She reached up and caressed his cheek. Ran her finger along his lips before inching up slowly and brushing a kiss there. "Mitch knew it also, Aidan."

He expelled a harsh breath and cursed again. "Close your eyes, Lizzy. Try to get some rest."

She inclined her head in agreement, but kissed him again lightly before relaxing against him and shutting her eyes.

He moved his hand to the small of her back, slipped it beneath the hem of her shirt, as if needing the contact with her skin.

She welcomed it, craving his touch. Wanting to feel anything besides the numbness inside.

"Aidan?" she said and glanced up at him.

"What is it, Lizzy?" he asked and cupped her cheek with his free hand.

"I don't care that it's for all the wrong reasons."

Chapter 27

A shudder ripped through him at her words.

He didn't care, either.

Bending his head, he kissed her. Gently at first, wanting to push away the thoughts of what had happened today. Wanting to ease her pain, if only for the night, since in the morning…

He opened his mouth, invited her to join him and she did, easing her tongue inside his mouth. Tasting him.

He cradled her face as if it was a precious work of art. Tracing the lines and shape of it with his hands as he kissed her, he remembered that somewhere on an ice-cold slab, a woman with an identical face lay dead.

It tempered his passion, turned it into something…deeper. More intense.

She must have sensed the change in him. She withdrew from him so she could see his face. Running her hands over it so as to soothe what she saw, she whispered, "It's okay, Aidan. I understand this doesn't change anything."

It already had, he thought, bending his head to kiss her again. He might be unable to voice his thoughts since the emotion was too strong, but he could show her. Let her feel it as he made love to her.

He kissed her over and over while he moved his hands down, and then cupped her breasts. A little hitch in her breath told him she liked it. Wanted him to continue.

He did, barely brushing his fingers over the tips until they hardened into tight peaks. Taking those peaks between his fingers, he kneaded them until her breath came uneven against his lips and her hands gripped his shoulders, pulling him close.

He slid his hands beneath the hem of her borrowed shirt, moved it up and over her head to reveal her to him. The cream-colored bra she wore was trimmed with lace. A front clasp. He undid it and her breasts spilled free.

Bending, he replaced his hands with his mouth, skimming his lips against the tips until she was straining toward him. Finally taking one hard peak into his mouth, he sucked as she cradled his head to her.

Elizabeth sighed at the heat of his mouth on her nipple. She took a hesitant breath when he sucked and then circled it with his tongue.

She held his head to her, urged him on. The feelings he roused…they chased away the chill. The deadness inside of her, but not Dani.

No matter what anyone said, Dani was still there.

As Aidan would be even after he was long gone.

And that made her need more of him. She needed it to remember a bit longer what it was like to be loved so much.

She urged him up and kissed him. Deeply, never wavering as she told him with her lips and mouth how much she needed him. Never hesitating as she pulled on his shirt and dragged it over his head. She reached down and undid the zipper on his jeans, freed him.

He groaned when she held him and broke away from her

kiss. Leaning his forehead against hers, he whispered, "I want you so badly, but…not so fast."

"Not fast," she repeated. "Only, I want you next to me. Making me warm."

He smiled and cradled her face. "I want it, too."

With those words and a smile, they both quickly undressed and then slipped beneath the sheets together. Bodies naked, warm, as skin met skin.

"That feels…good," she said and ran a hand along the muscles of his chest.

"Really good?" he teased and ran his hand along her breasts, rousing her again.

She savored it. The light caress of the back of his hand, hardly touching her.

Easing her thigh between his legs, she shifted so they were closer. At her belly, his erection nestled contentedly, which was perfect. She wanted so much more right now.

She laid her hands on his shoulders and kissed him, made love to him with her mouth. Opening his mouth with her tongue to slip inside, she danced it beside his tongue before withdrawing it to trace the edges of his lips, eager to memorize the shape of them, the feel, so that once he was gone, she could still remember them.

When that memory was imprinted on her brain, she shifted her mouth to his jaw, kissed along the line of it. Moved up to the shell of his ear and his lobe, which she bit gently, sending a shudder through his body.

He moved his hands to her back and pulled her close until their bodies were pressed together. Her breasts against the hardness of chest. His hardness jutting into her belly.

He moved his mouth to her ear and then lower, to the juncture of her neck and shoulder and the spot that was still sensitive from the night before. When he brushed his lips there, it awakened her within and her insides clenched.

She butted her hips against him, but he whispered, "I feel it, too, Lizzy. Touch me."

She did, reaching between their bodies to wrap her hand around him while she moved her mouth to the side of his neck. There was a purple spot she'd put there. Her love bite. She covered that same spot, sucked gently and he moaned. His erection jumped in her hand.

But she still took it slowly, sucking on his neck while gently caressing him with her hand.

He lowered his head, kissed her breasts over and over before moving one hand downward and parting her. He eased his hand over the center of her, already damp and hot from his caresses. "You feel so warm," he whispered.

She wanted another part of him to feel it and eased her thigh over his, shifted her hips and guided him with her hand until he was nestled between her thighs. His erection pressed along the length of her.

He groaned, rubbed himself along her while she held him to her with her hand. He was breathing hard, gripping her shoulders to control himself. "I wish I could be inside you. Feel the heat. The wet, but…"

She wanted it, too, but knew they couldn't do it without the protection that was just a few feet away in the nightstand. "Just feel this for now," she urged, moving her hips to rub along his shaft. She dampened him with her desire, warmed him with the heat of her.

He was breathing roughly, barely in control when he finally reached for a condom from the nightstand. His hands were shaking so badly, he couldn't open the foil packet, and so she reached up, did it for him. Took out the condom and gently unrolled it over his erection.

He groaned again as she did so, and then he was between her legs and pressing into her. The width of him stretching her. Slowly, he eased in until she no longer could focus on anything other than the way him being inside rocked her. Hot and so hard.

When he flexed his hips, she brought her hand to the small of his back and stilled his motion.

He met her gaze and seemed to know what she wanted, for he pressed forward just a bit more, causing her breath to leave her sharply. After, he met her lips in a kiss and for the longest time, that was all they did.

Just kiss with him buried inside her.

When that was no longer enough, he bent and sucked her nipples. Teethed the tips until her insides clenched around him. She knew he felt it because he groaned against her breasts.

"Do you like that?" she asked, and he looked up from her breasts.

"Yes," he said, but then immediately bit the tip of her breast, yanking a mew of pleasure from her. "Like you like this," he teased and did it again.

She held his head to her and tightened on him. It seemed as though he grew even larger within her, grew hotter, and she continued moving her muscles on him that way while enjoying his mouth on her breasts until it too wasn't enough.

With the flex of her hips, she rolled him onto his back and straddled him. Drove him even deeper, which she hadn't thought possible. She stilled for a moment, savoring the sensation. Relishing the warmth of him that was finally beginning to dispel the chill within.

And as temporary a feeling as that was, she strove for it. Shifted her hips and rode him to build the heat until her body was shaking and, beneath her, he was likewise trembling.

She met his gaze, joined her hands with his as the passion built even more as she pumped away on him faster and faster until, finally, her body clenched around him tightly. He pushed up into her to send her over the edge and he called out his own completion.

She dropped down onto him, breathing roughly, her body damp with sweat.

He pulled the sheet up to keep her warm and wrapped his arms around her. She snuggled against him and laid her head on his chest. The strong, if somewhat erratic, beat of his heart reminded her they were still alive.

It was that beat and the warmth of him that finally lulled her to sleep.

Chapter 28

Lucia had been kind enough to retrieve some of Elizabeth's own clothes while she showered. So now she sat, refreshed and clean, waiting for a call from Corbett Lazlo.

Despite that, she jumped when the phone rang.

Someone had run a longer cord so that the phone now sat on the coffee table in front of the couch where she and Aidan were seated. Opposite them, Walker and Lucia waited in matching wing chairs.

It was Lucia who caught her gaze for a moment before reaching over and picking up the phone. "Lucia Cordez," she answered and a second later, she said, "Yes, of course, Mr. Lazlo."

She reached over again, this time to engage the speaker. "Can you hear us, Mr. Lazlo?"

"Yes, thank you, Lucia. Ms. Moore, are you there?"

As if she'd be somewhere else, she thought, but didn't voice. "Yes, I am. Do you have any news for me?"

"I'm sorry, Ms. Moore. I spoke to the various authorities, but you must understand—"

"All I understand is that you say my sister is dead, Mr. Lazlo, but you refuse to let me see her," she interjected, pain and annoyance coloring the tones of her voice.

"That won't be possible, Ms. Moore. I have the CIA, MI6, even Interpol who all want their time with the bod…with your sister. They all want their experts to gather the evidence they need to close their cases."

The cold returned full force. She swallowed, her throat tight with emotion. Struggling for control, she nevertheless managed to say, "I don't want Dani's body butchered, Mr. Lazlo."

Aidan reached over then, grabbed hold of her hand to offer support. She latched onto him, needing the stability.

"I assure you she'll be treated with the utmost respect."

His promise did little to calm her fears. "I want to bury her here. With our parents. When can I…"

She couldn't finish. Couldn't picture laying Dani in the ground alongside her Ma and Da. She was too young to be dead. Her presence still too alive with Lizzy for her to believe it possible.

"I'm sorry, Ms. Moore, but that may take some time. You must understand that the Sparrow… Well, there's a lot of work that needs to be done," Lazlo blustered uneasily.

It was Aidan who jumped in on her behalf. "She needs closure, Corbett. Let her see Dani and then let the experts do what they need to. It's the humane thing to do, damn it."

"Mr. Spaulding. I would have thought that you more than anyone would appreciate how important it is to get the evidence we need. You do want to confirm who killed Agent Lama, don't you."

Aidan was about to protest again, but she squeezed his hand. An unlikely defender rose up, however. "I imagine that by now you already have the Sparrow's fingerprints and DNA. What more could you need?" Walker challenged.

A sigh that was part annoyance, part fatigue came across

the speakerphone. "Dr. Shaw, et tu? This discussion is concluded. When the various agencies are done, I promise you, Ms. Moore, that the Lazlo Group will make the finest of arrangements for your sister."

"Thank you, Mr. Lazlo," she replied, but had no sooner finished when Lazlo continued.

"As for DNA, it's time we got to business. Lord Southgate is on his way and I'm afraid we have some rather disturbing news for him."

Elizabeth shot a look at Aidan to question whether she should leave, but he shook his head and leaned over. "Stay and I'll walk you back to your cottage."

She nodded, sat back and prepared herself for the report that was to follow, fearing yet more negative things about Dani.

"Xander, here. We've matched the Sparrow's DNA to that at the scene, but that's not the news for the day," he reported in a too-cheerful tone.

"Mr. Forrest. Decorum, please. What news do you have?" Lazlo admonished.

"Lord Southgate provided the fingerprints and DNA retrieved from the vault located by Doctors Shaw and Smith. I got a match on the fingerprints from the Silvershire police archives."

Lucia inched to the edge of her chair and shifted toward the speaker. "Xander, please make this long story short."

"The fingerprints belong to Nikolas Donovan and the DNA from the hair links its donor to King Weston. Short enough?" His loud guffaw followed the bluntly worded report.

"Donovan?" Elizabeth said aloud. "As in the same man who hired Dani?"

"And if the prints belong to him, what are the odds that the DNA doesn't?" Walker added and shook his head.

"Lord Southgate—"

"Isn't going to like this one bit," came from the doorway. Everyone jumped to their feet and stood awkwardly, except for Elizabeth. She immediately dipped into a curtsy. "Your Grace."

Lord Russell Southgate, Duke of Carrington and soon to

be king, waved off her display, clearly uncomfortable. "Please, Ms. Moore. Rise, and also accept my sympathies for your recent loss."

"Thank you, Your Grace," she responded and watched as the duke sauntered in and stood before the group.

"Mr. Lazlo, are you there?" he asked the speakerphone.

"I am, Your Grace, and I apologize about the manner in which this information came to you," Corbett Lazlo replied, obviously annoyed.

"That's fine, but…Mr. Xander. Are you sure about the results?"

Xander hesitated and in the background, the sound of rustling papers came across the line before the young agent finally responded. "Yes, sir. No doubt about the match on the prints or the DNA. If we find the donor of the hair, you've found Weston's real son."

"And you believe that would be Nikolas Donovan?" the duke pressed.

"Yes. It's only logical that since the prints and hair were the only things in the vault, there's a connection," Lazlo offered up for his technician.

"And easy enough to confirm if you can get a sample. Some more hair, preferably with the root or some skin. Saliva or some other body fluid," Xander said calmly.

Elizabeth had been listening intently and almost failed to notice that the duke had now turned his attention to her and Aidan. When he spoke, it was directed to them.

"I understand that the Sparrow identified a man named Donovan as the one who hired her to eliminate Reginald."

Aidan quickly added, "We also suspect that Donovan was the one who shot the Sparrow."

Lord Southgate paced back and forth for a second before advising, "Although Nikolas served in the military, I find it hard to believe that he could locate and kill someone that various international agencies have been unsuccessfully chasing for years."

"He had information the Sparrow wanted. That might have made her vulnerable," Aidan offered and Elizabeth chimed in with, "Donovan told my sister that he possessed information on who murdered our parents."

Again Southgate paused to digest that statement. Finally he asked, "And Reginald was somehow connected to their murder?

"Apparently, Reginald was using cocaine he purchased from the men responsible for the murders. I know killing him was wrong, but Reginald and those men should have been punished for what they did," she urged.

The duke shocked her by agreeing. "Punishment delayed is punishment denied. Nevertheless, Donovan's reasons for Reginald's murder would seem to be for personal gain. Highly unlike the Nikolas Donovan I know."

"I would suggest that we track him down and get not only the sample, but question him about his whereabouts the last few days. We could also do a GSR test to confirm whether he's fired a weapon recently," Aidan suggested.

"Sounds like a plan, but… Nikolas and I know each other. Quite well, actually."

"We can provide backup, Your Grace, if I understand that what you'd like to do is approach him first," Lazlo offered.

Lord Southgate ratified that was his intent with a regal motion of his head. "That's exactly what I'd like to do."

"Lucia and I will go along, Mr. Lazlo. Agent Spaulding needs to keep an eye on Ms. Moore until we ascertain whether she's still in danger," Walker indicated and rose from his chair.

After a flurry of goodbyes, only Aidan and Elizabeth remained, standing before each other awkwardly. "I guess I should walk you back to the cottage. Make sure the surveillance and other things are still intact so I can keep an eye on you."

"You know that's really not necessary. The watching. Once Lord Southgate talks to Donovan—"

"I understand, Lizzy. I don't have to be the one watching." With those words, he stepped away and made a call. He was speaking too low for her to hear. When he returned, however, he said, "I've arranged for a detail to watch your grounds. This way you can try and get things back to normal."

Elizabeth couldn't imagine things being normal. At least not for awhile. First she had to call family and friends, tell them about Dani's death. After that, she'd arrange for a memorial until the Lazlo Group released her body and after that…maybe after that…

Who was she kidding? Even after that things wouldn't be normal. Her sister was dead and Aidan…

Aidan would be gone. "I need to go. I've got a lot to handle," she said.

He walked with her all the way back to her cottage. As they neared her home, the door opened and Nat, Kate and Samantha stepped out.

"I called them earlier," he said. "Figured you could use the support."

Tears came to her eyes at this thoughtfulness. "Thank you."

She faced him and swiped at the tears. "I guess this is…goodbye."

Aidan stuffed his fingertips into his jeans pockets. A familiar pose. One which dragged a smile to her face despite the sadness of the moment.

He rocked back and forth on his heels for a second and then finally said, "I'll be around for a little while. If you need me."

"Right. Take care of yourself, Aidan," she said and whirled, hurried from him and toward the women anxiously waiting at the door to the cottage.

They circled her and herded her inside, but not before looking his way and shooting him looks that warned him to go away and stay away. He couldn't blame them in a way. He'd hurt her. Nothing was going to change that.

But in time, she would forget him.

In time, he was certain he would forget her, as well.

It was part of who he was. What he was. What he had done since he was a child and become used to a wandering life.

Nothing was going to change that, especially not a woman like Elizabeth who needed stability and a place to call home. Those things were not in his game plan. Ever.

Chapter 29

Nikolas Donovan had disappeared.

Lord Southgate had tried every location he knew. Called every friend they had in common. None had any idea where Donovan had gone.

Donovan had run like the guilty man he might be, Aidan thought as he reviewed the report Lazlo had e-mailed that morning about Donovan's disappearance.

From the looks of it, Donovan had left some time close to when Dani had been shot. Now, days later, the only clue they had was a report that he had been spotted in France.

Which meant that for the moment, Lizzy was safe.

The cell phone on his PDA rang and he pulled it off his belt, answered. "Spaulding here."

"Mr. Spaulding. Lazlo here."

As if he wouldn't recognize his boss's voice after seven years. "Mr. Lazlo. I was just getting ready to call. It would appear it's time to give Ms. Moore back her privacy."

"Do it then, Aidan. Remove the surveillance equipment and the detail guarding her, but after…Lord Southgate has asked us to track down Nikolas Donovan."

Donovan. He wanted him found and punished almost as much as he had wanted vengeance on the Sparrow. Maybe even more. "What will it entail?"

"I've called in Rhia de Hayes to track down Donovan."

Aidan couldn't hold back his disbelief. "Rhia? Doesn't she normally specialize in more…youthful targets?"

Lazlo also allowed himself a chuckle. "Yes, she does. In fact, Rhia is rather amused by this assignment. She's currently finishing up a case and will be available in a few days to get on Donovan's trail."

Aidan appreciated being kept in the loop, but wondered about it since it wasn't standard operating procedure. Which could only mean one thing… "Do you need something else from me, Corbett? Or do you have my next assignment already?"

"How badly do you want Donovan?"

He should have known he couldn't fool Corbett. "Badly. He killed Liz…Ms. Moore's sister."

"Then I guess you wouldn't mind being backup for Rhia. It would mean leaving in a few days to meet her in Paris," Lazlo advised.

Leaving Leonia. Leaving Lizzy.

"I understand, Corbett. Let me finish up here. Clean up everything. Get things settled." It would give him a few more days of seeing Lizzy. A few more days to work up the courage to say a proper goodbye. Not the hurried and angered one they had shared days earlier.

"You sound…hesitant, Mr. Spaulding."

He wondered how the man could be so intuitive across a telephone line. "I just need to straighten out a few things here before I go."

"Get it done quickly, Mr. Spaulding. Rhia could use your help."

With that, Aidan hung up, but immediately contacted the

four agents who he had assigned to keep an eye on Lizzy while he…

While he kept an eye on her, his PDA tuned into the various channels as he watched her with friends and family when they came by to pay their condolences. Worried as she stood by the window at night, staring out at the ocean. So alone. So wounded.

He wished her relief from her pain. Hungered to see her back at what she did best—tending to her gardens, her hands skimming over the flowers and herbs as she selected what she would need for one of her fabulous dishes.

Only, it was too soon since Dani's death. The restaurant had been closed for days and would remain closed until Dani's memorial service. It was scheduled for tomorrow and he, along with Lucia and Walker, planned on attending.

After that, Lucia would pack up and head back to New York to await another assignment. Walker had resigned his position with the Lazlo Group to stay with Dr. Zara Smith, the royal physician. As for him…

The assignment with Rhia seemed the right thing to do. Not that he normally cared, but Silvershire was in an uproar and finding Donovan would help calm things down. On a personal level, Lazlo had been right that finding and dealing with Donovan would give him great satisfaction.

And possibly bring some closure for Lizzy to know that her sister's killer had been apprehended.

The lead agent on the detail watching Lizzy called to confirm that all four men were returning to the hotel. Now it was up to him to remove the surveillance equipment only…

Lizzy was likely preparing for Dani's memorial service. He didn't want to intrude in that fashion at such a difficult time.

Removing the cameras could wait another day…or two.

Lizzy smoothed her fingers over the photo she had chosen for the service later that day. It was the one of Dani and her taken in Rome two years earlier. Both of them were smiling brilliantly, the happiness apparent to anyone who viewed the picture.

It was the way she wanted to remember Dani. Full of life. Full of love for her and for Mitch.

Inside the restaurant, Nat, Kate and Samantha were setting up chairs for those coming to the memorial service. On the mantel above the fireplace was an enlargement of the Rome photo.

Out back, she'd had her staff set up tables and chairs for a cold buffet she planned on serving her guests. A simple meal, mostly prepared by Nat. She couldn't face going into the kitchen or out into the gardens.

Guilt swamped her that she was alive when Dani was dead.

And in the back of her mind, she kept on hoping it was all a mistake. That Dani would walk through her door at any moment, because inside her, Dani's presence niggled at her, begging to be acknowledged.

A knock came at the door and her heart sped up. She'd seen the agents leaving earlier. Could that mean Dani's killer had been caught? Could it be Aidan coming by with news?

She hurried to the door, but it was only a boy from a few houses down with an armful of flowers for her. "Mum says you might want some for the service."

"Thank you, Billy. Thank your mother, as well." she said to the ten-year-old as she took the flowers from him and cradled them to her chest.

Billy seemed satisfied with her response since he gave her a spontaneous hug and dashed off.

She buried her nose in the large bouquet of flowers and inhaled deeply. Their fragrance was heavenly. Billy's mum always had the nicest garden in town and was quite particular about her blooms. That she would cut so many flowers from it for Dani...

Her throat tightened and she decided to walk the bouquet over to the restaurant, complete the preparations for the memorial.

Inside the restaurant, Samantha and Kate had finished setting up the chairs and were now placing the hostess's podium at the front of the room for those who wanted to speak. Elizabeth hadn't wanted anything too formal or religious. Dani had sworn off religion after their parents had died.

As she walked through the door with the flowers, her friends rushed over to take them from her.

"These are lovely," Kate said and smelled them.

"Mrs. Sanders?" Samantha asked.

"Yes and yes. Can I help with anything?"

Kate placed her hands on her hips and looked around. "We're pretty much done. Maybe Nat needs some help in the kitchen?"

"Subtle, Kate. Really subtle," Samantha chided and elbowed Kate in the side.

"I'm not…" Elizabeth was going to say she wasn't ready, but stopped short. When had she ever not wanted to cook? In the months after her parents had died, cooking for her and Dani had helped numb the pain. Later, working at the health food restaurant had done more than just provide money for the assorted things she and Dani needed. The joy of creating something tasty had driven away her sadness. Brought happiness back into her life.

Meeting her friends' gazes, she nodded and said, "I'll go see if Nat needs my help."

She was in the kitchen, cooking. Flitting from the prep table to the stove where she hovered by one of the chef's assistants as they worked on something. From the stove back to the prep table where another of the assistants was busy assembling a large salad.

Finally, she walked over to the ovens where Natalie was checking on a large pastry of some kind. Lizzy stood next to Nat and the two women seemed to confer about the pastry before easing it back into the oven. After, Lizzy turned to Nat and embraced the younger woman tightly, the emotion clear on the faces of the two women.

Emotion that he had no right to be spying on.

He shut down his PDA and looked at his watch. Another hour until the memorial service. Another hour until he saw her, up close and personal.

What would he say? That he was sorry about Dani? He was, but that sorrow was tempered by the anger surrounding Mitch's death and a sense of incompleteness when he thought that maybe, just maybe, Dani hadn't been the one responsible.

And of course, Dani's death had just created another wrong to be righted. He considered whether he would be the one to take up that wrong and see it avenged, whether leaving here and going on that quest would bring him peace. Or was it just another windmill he was tilting at?

Nagging doubt chased him as he showered and dressed for the service. He met Lucia and Walker down in the lobby and they paused at a flower shop on the way to purchase a mixed bouquet, one filled with the colors and flowers he recalled from Lizzy's garden.

Funny how vividly the memory was of those things Lizzy. The flowers. The food. The way she looked jogging along the shore and how she could pound the hell out of the heavy bag down in her cellar. The slight, but noticeable aroma of plumeria that clung to her at night, after she had finished in the kitchen and indulged in the luxury of moisturizing her hands with the lotion from Kate's shop.

It was crazy to be here, he thought as he reached the entry to the restaurant grounds. He hesitated at the stone wall, wondering if it was wise to come here, to invade her space at such a personal time.

"Aidan?" Lucia asked and laid a hand on the arm of his dark charcoal-gray suit, the one he had worn to convince Lizzy to hire him. The one that had unfortunately already seen another funeral. "What's the matter?"

"I'm not sure I—"

"She would want you here," Walker added and grasped his shoulder in a reassuring gesture.

"It's the right thing to do," he said out loud, almost as if to convince himself. It *was* the right thing, but also the painful thing. The thing that would add yet another memory that he could dredge up whenever…

He missed her.

With a deep sigh, he pushed forward, walked through the open door of the restaurant and to the back of the room so as to not call attention to himself.

Lizzy was at the front, bending down and talking to two blue-haired ladies in the first row. She was dressed all in black, in a simple dress that hung loose on her body. She seemed to have lost weight in just a few days.

Dark smudges beneath her eyes were a stark contrast to the paleness of her face. Her rich brown hair, shot through with auburn and blond highlights, was pulled back from her face with a black scarf. Her smile when it came, was forced. A toothless slash of her lips into a thin line. A brittle smile that looked ready to shatter.

He winced for her, knowing how hard it must be.

A few more people straggled in and a priest sitting in the front row rose and motioned for everyone to take their seats. He was young, barely older than Lizzy. A fact that was confirmed when he began his speech.

"I want to thank you all for coming to celebrate Dani's life. Lizzy asked me to speak first since, at one time, I fancied myself marrying Dani before I got an offer from someone else," he said, prompting a round of chuckles.

He went on to describe the Dani he knew. A vibrant, loving woman who was quick to anger, but equally as quick to apologize. A woman who stood up for what she believed to be right and wasn't afraid to take action when necessary.

After he finished, he asked others to share their memories and one by one, a myriad of people came up to the podium. The one common element was that Dani had been their friend and their champion. The one everyone could speak to. The one they turned to when a wrong needed to be righted, when someone needed protection.

It matched what Lizzy had told him about her sister. Lizzy, who sat there flanked by Kate and Samantha on either side and Natalie behind her, but sitting on the edge of her chair with her hand on Lizzy's shoulder. As he examined the crowd, he noted other familiar faces—Addy and others from the hedge veg adventure. Some people he recalled serving drinks to at the restaurant.

He had no doubt she would be well taken care of by her friends, family and the assorted neighbors and townspeople who had filled the restaurant to capacity. As he looked toward the door, he realized there was a crowd of people there, as well, and that the back wall and sides of the dining area were standing room only.

Dani had apparently been well-liked and respected. It made him wonder about Lizzy's sister and what she really was—a champion or a cold-blooded killer?

Finally it was Lizzy's turn. As she rose, he thought she wavered for a moment. Kate reached out and offered a steadying hand and Lizzy took it, let Kate help her up to the podium.

Once there, she hesitated and even from this far, the glint of tears was visible as she took note of everyone who was in attendance. "Thank you all for coming. I appreciate it. I know Dani does, as well."

She struggled for composure and he wanted to rush up there, found himself beginning to rise when Walker laid a hand on his arm. "What can you offer, Aidan? You'll be long gone in a few days," he whispered.

He hated that Walker was right. He dejectedly dropped back down into his seat and waited for Lizzy to go on.

"After my parents died, it was hard for Dani. She missed them terribly. She wanted justice for them." Again she paused, as if reconsidering where she was going, but then she charged onward. "Dani always stood up for what she believed in.

Always was there to help if someone asked. She was every-one's champion. She was *my* champion. My best friend. A sister who I will miss every day of my life, but who will always be alive in here," she said and motioned to a spot above her heart.

"I know Dani is okay and in a better place. One where she's with her loved ones. One where she's happy. Because of that, I can't grieve for long."

The tears finally came, spilling over to run down her cheeks, but she didn't wipe them away. Instead, she took a shuddering breath and said, "Thank you all for your kind words and support. For those of you who wish to stay a bit longer, please step into the back garden for some refreshments."

Moving from behind the podium, she stepped into the crowd of well-wishers, moving from one to the next to give her personal thanks. Embrace one person or the other and motion them in the direction of the side door that led to the back patio.

Aidan waited alongside his colleagues until the room was almost empty and they were some of the last people standing there. Lizzy finally seemed to notice them. A guarded smile came to her face.

She walked over, embraced Lucia and shook Walker's hand. They both offered their condolences and then with a sidelong glance at him, excused themselves.

Lizzy stood before him, her hands clasped together. Her body language sending the clear signal that she was uncom-fortable. That whatever he did, he shouldn't touch.

He broke the ice first by holding out the bouquet. "I came to say how sorry I am. I know how hard this is for you."

"Thank you. I really do appreciate all you've done on behalf of Dani," she said, but made no motion to embrace him or even shake his hand as she had with Walker. She seemed too fragile to do so. When she took the flowers, she cradled them tightly to her body. So tightly that a petal fell off one stem and fluttered to the ground.

"Well, I'll be going soon. In the meantime, I was going to drop by tomorrow and remove our surveillance equipment," he explained and motioned to the room around them.

A stain of color came to her cheeks at his words. "You bugged my restaurant? What about my house? Did people see what—?"

"No, they didn't. Dani jammed the signal. I'm sorry. It was what we had to do to catch—"

She silenced him with a tense wave of her hand. "Don't. Dani said it wasn't what we thought. That's what I want to believe."

Given what he had heard from person after person during the memorial service, he could understand why she wanted to hold onto that belief. So many people couldn't be wrong. It made him wonder yet again what Dani had meant when she had said she'd been doing a job. That it hadn't been what it seemed.

"I understand, and again, I'm sorry. About everything."

She said nothing and for a moment, he thought the rigor might leave her body, but it didn't. Despite that, he embraced her awkwardly, needing that last touch since he had decided that tomorrow he would send the men from the guard detail to remove the equipment.

It would be better that way, he thought as he stepped away and raced out the door, eager to put some distance between them.

Lizzy roused too many feelings, some of them threatening to the way he lived his life—carefree, exciting and without any attachments.

It was the way it had been all his life.

He wasn't about to allow one woman to change it all.

Chapter 30

Days had passed since the Lazlo Group technicians had come to retrieve their equipment, removing cameras from every room in the restaurant, the gardens and even her front parlor.

She assumed Aidan was long gone, as well, moving onto his next assignment. Did he ever look back? she wondered. Did he think about the job he had just finished and the people he had met?

The people he'd slept with and lied to? People whose lives he had irrevocably changed?

Rubbing her temples to quell her growing headache, she stared out her bedroom window. The ocean was calm tonight. Totally unlike the way she was feeling. Restless. Angry. Lonely.

Even though Dani had been gone often, there had always been the prospect of seeing her. That would never happen again. Ever.

Just as she would never see Aidan again. Ever. He and Dani had had so much in common. They were both warriors and wanderers. She only hoped that Aidan's life didn't end like Dani's. Or like his friend Mitch's.

If there was any consolation in either of their deaths, it was that neither had died alone. She and Aidan had been at Dani's side. Aidan had been with his friend.

And one day, Aidan would…

She shook her head and drove that thought away.

She wanted to wedge any remnants of him from her mind. Best to forget what had happened between them. It would only bring continued pain since, like Dani, Aidan was gone from her life forever.

Unable to stay in her room for another second since it brought too many reminders of what she had shared with him, she rushed from the cottage and out onto the beachfront.

A breeze, strong and brisk, washed over her. As she walked along the shore, she wished for it to wash away memories of him. To cleanse her spirit and bring peace to her heart, a heart battered by the loss of two people she had loved.

Dani and Aidan. Both lost to her. One never to return. The other…

He had given them the location of every camera except one. He'd known it was wrong, but convinced himself that he'd done it for her sake. So that he might keep an eye on her just in case Donovan returned. Just in case she needed him.

Her image filled his laptop screen. The smallish picture on the PDA didn't quite satisfy his need.

Lizzy was at the window facing the ocean. A familiar stance for her lately. She had been at the window every night since he had brought her home after Dani's death.

Unlike those other nights when he had watched her in silence, his observation was interrupted by the shrill ring of his cell phone. "Spaulding."

"Aidan. Ms. de Hayes has advised that she should be arriving in Paris in two days. Are you prepared to meet her?"

Was he? he wondered. When Corbett had mentioned continuing with the next part of this assignment, he'd been eager. After all, it entailed tracking down Dani's killer and someone who might be a possible threat to Lizzy.

A good reason to leave Leonia and Lizzy. Or so he'd thought.

But faced with the prospect of it now…

"Aidan? You have terminated your surveillance of Ms. Moore, haven't you?" Corbett asked and Aidan sensed that the other man somehow knew about the remaining camera.

He didn't have it in him to lie. "No, sir. But…"

He could have said that he'd remove it immediately, but he couldn't. He needed that connection to her. Hell, he needed her.

For days he had been telling himself otherwise. Trying to convince himself that staying in Leonia would be as boring as shit. That there was nothing there to keep his interest.

Except Lizzy. And some really nice people. Her crazy friends. Some fine fishing and surfing areas. Beautiful gardens and cute little homes along the road and the stunning coast and beachfront.

"Aidan?" Corbett prompted again and this time, Aidan knew exactly what to say.

"While working with Rhia would be quite an experience, I've decided that it's time I resigned my position with the Lazlo Group."

"Are you sure about this?" Corbett asked, and Aidan shot another peek at his laptop.

Was he?

The answer came immediately.

"I'm sure, Corbett."

The other man chuckled, surprising him. "This is getting to be a costly operation for my group. First Walker resigns and now you."

"I'm sorry if this leaves you in a lurch."

"Not to worry, Aidan. Rhia can probably handle this job on her own for the moment. Despite the Sparrow's deathbed information, I can't see Nikolas Donovan as her killer," Corbett advised, confusing Aidan with the statement.

"What? Donovan's Union for Democracy has splintered into two factions, one of them violent. What makes you believe Donovan isn't responsible for that violent bent and Dani's death?" Aidan questioned.

"Lord Southgate is quite familiar with Nikolas Donovan. He believes him innocent in Reginald's death and also in that of the Sparrow."

Aidan wasn't quite as convinced. "If Rhia needs backup, I'm there," he said, guilt driving him. He liked the woman, who had an adventurous streak and could be a refreshing smart ass at times.

"I appreciate the offer, but if I'm right, we won't be needing your muscle on this one," Corbett advised and then quickly added, "And you, Mr. Spaulding, have a lady to contact."

He peeked at the laptop and cursed beneath his breath when he saw her room was empty. But he knew where she would go. Where she always went when she was troubled. "Goodbye, Corbett. It's been a pleasure."

"Not goodbye, Aidan. I do expect an invitation to the wedding."

He chuckled at the other man's audacity. "You'll get it," he said, not that Corbett Lazlo would show. In the seven years that he had worked for the man, he had never met him.

But that was for another day. First he had to get the lady in question to agree to marry him.

Grabbing his jacket, he raced out of the hotel and down the public-access ramp to the beach. Much as he had expected, she was walking down the beach, headed in his direction. When she noticed him, she paused and wrapped her arms around herself, waited there for a moment before continuing toward him.

No coward, his Lizzy.

He didn't wait. He hopped down onto the sand and raced in her direction. When they finally stood facing one another, barely a foot apart, he said, "Lizzy."

Duh. Totally stupid. Inane.

"Aidan. I would have thought that you'd be gone by now." Her arms remained wrapped around herself and she rubbed her hands up and down in a telling gesture.

He reached out, laid his hands over hers to still that motion. "I would have thought so, too, only…I couldn't imagine leaving you, Lizzy."

Elizabeth's breath caught in her throat with his words. Was she imagining this? She shook her head in disbelief. "I don't understand, Aidan."

He smiled and his blue eyes glittered with joy as he said, "I don't understand, either. Maybe it's because I've found an adventure more compelling than any other."

"An adventure," she repeated, unsure of what he meant.

"Yes. You. And if you'll have me, I can't imagine a more interesting and challenging way to spend my life," he said and took hold of her hands, dropped to one knee.

"Marry me, Lizzy."

This was insane. Totally outrageous. And yes, possibly an adventure. One she was willing to risk with the man kneeling before her. "On one condition."

"Just one? As I recall, you had quite a few that night," he teased, raising one sandy brow playfully.

She laughed and embraced him, urged him to rise. "Do you think you could be happy here in little ol' Leonia?"

"I can be happy anywhere you are, Lizzy," he answered and as she searched his features, she recognized the truth of his statement.

She trailed her hands down and twined her fingers with his. "Can you be happy being my bartender?"

Aidan grimaced. "That may take a little … No, make that a long while. Unless I can develop something," he said and pulled out his PDA, began explaining to her how he had managed to survive behind the bar.

"So let me get this," she began as he sketched his idea for a new bar area filled with electronic gadgets with the stylus of his PDA. "You're ex-military. An MIT grad in electronics. Anything else I should know?"

"That I love you. Totally and completely love you. All the rest, you can learn in the years to come," he said and, grabbing hold of her hand, gave it a playful shake. "So, will you marry me?"

"When you put it that way, how can a girl refuse?"

Epilogue

The stone-and-bronze marker matched the one laid over a decade earlier for her parents.

Elizabeth knelt and ran her hands over the words engraved in the bronze.

Danielle Elizabeth Moore. September 10, 1980—August 22, 2006. She was everyone's champion.

She wondered who had decided to add the last. Corbett Lazlo possibly?

"Lizzy, you okay?" Aidan asked and kneeled beside her. In his hand he held a bouquet of flowers she had cut from the garden earlier that morning.

"I'm okay."

"There's a big 'except' there, Lizzy. What is it?" he asked and laid his free hand over hers as it rested on Dani's grave marker. The sun caught the gold band on his ring finger. It glinted brightly against the darker color of the bronze and the even deeper brown of the freshly turned earth.

"I've been waiting for months for Dani to come home. I thought it would bring closure."

"But?" he pressed.

"I can feel her, Aidan. As if she was still alive. Still with me," she urged; for in the many months since Dani had been carried away in the ambulance, her sister's presence remained strong.

"Lizzy, I can't begin to understand this twin thing. But I do understand you. If you believe this, I won't argue with you."

She smiled, leaned close and kissed the side of his face. "How like a husband, you sound. Indulging me in this even if you don't believe."

Aidan laid the bouquet of flowers along the top of the grave marker and then cradled her face in his hands. "I will always be at your side. Stand by whatever you believe, Lizzy. Believe that."

The amazing thing was that she did. She trusted Aidan as she had no else before, except for Dani. But unlike Dani, Aidan had shown her he was here to stay.

It might have started off as just another mission for him, but now it was more. He was her champion. She was his home. It couldn't be any more perfect than that.

* * * * *

Turn the page for a sneak peek at
THE REBEL KING,
Kathleen Creighton's breathtaking conclusion to
CAPTURING THE CROWN!
Available September 2006

He'd always been a little in love with Paris. She was the village eccentric, that mysterious lady down the street reputed to possess a past both lurid and glorious. And while she may have been mistrusted and reviled—and secretly envied—by her more conventional neighbors, one knew she was always ready to welcome a lad in need of refuge with open arms.

And there had never been a lad more in need of a refuge than Nikolas Donovan. His life had recently gone careening out of control with the dizzying speed of a sports car traveling down a steep and winding mountain road without brakes. It seemed to him a ride that could end only one way: with a calamitous plunge off a cliff.

In the past several months, Silvershire, the island country of his birth and of his heart, had experienced more than its share of violence—murder, blackmail, attempted murder, conspiracy, terrorist bombings and assassination plots against the ruling family—and he had been suspected of connections

to that violence. Now the country seemed poised on the brink
of outright rebellion—a rebellion Nikolas was assuredly
guilty, at least in part, of fomenting.

He hadn't wanted rebellion.

Change, yes. He'd worked all his life for change. But not
through violence. Never through violence.

But now change had come, and with a vengeance. Catas-
trophic change. Just not quite the way he'd expected.

Feeling more alienated and alone than ever, Nikolas quickened his steps toward home.

On a quiet tree-lined street not far from the Eiffel Tower
he paused to look up at the third-floor windows of the
borrowed flat that was his temporary refuge now. He wasn't
sure what made him do that—perhaps a habit of caution
learned from his life as a rebel with a cause, accustomed to
watching his own back. Whatever the reason for that quick,
casual glance, the move that followed it was launched by
pure instinct, and it was not in the least casual: He slipped into
the shadows between trees and parked cars and became
utterly and completely still while he studied the window of
his supposedly empty apartment where, a moment before, he
was absolutely certain he'd seen something move.

The movement didn't come again, but never for a moment
did he believe it had been a trick of the eye, or the reflection
of a passing bird. Unlikely as it seemed, someone or something had just entered his flat through the balcony window.

All his senses were on full alert as he quickly crossed the
street and let himself into the building using his key. Inside
he paused again to listen, but it was quiet as a mausoleum;
most Parisians would still be out and about this early on such
an evening, at least until the forecast rain arrived.

He mounted the last flight of stairs on tiptoe and moved
soundlessly down the hallway, footsteps swallowed by the
carpet runner. At the door to his flat he paused one last time
to consider the situation. Which was, the way he saw it, as
follows: Someone had entered the flat through the balcony

window. That someone either was or was not still in the flat. If not, he'd have a little mystery to solve at his leisure. On the other hand, if someone *was* in the flat, odds seemed against whoever it was being there for friendly purposes.

It had been a good eight years since his military service and commando training, but he was gratified to feel his mind and body shifting gears, settling into that particular state of quiet readiness he thought he'd forgotten. He could almost hear the hum of his heightened senses as he took hold of the doorknob and silently turned it.

The flat was in shadows, the darkness not yet complete. He'd left no light burning, but everything seemed as he'd left it. Aware that the slightly brighter backdrop of the hallway must cast him in silhouette, he stepped quickly into the room and closed the door behind him, checking as he did so for a body that might have been flattened against the wall behind it. Then he paused again, the old-fashioned metal key gripped in his hand like a weapon, and sniffed the air like a wild animal.

The room was empty now, he could feel it. But moments ago *someone* had been here, someone who had left traces, a faint aura...a scent too delicate and ephemeral to be after-shave or perfume.

Something about that scent jolted him with an untimely sense of déjà vu. But before the feeling could coalesce into thought, he received a different kind of jolt entirely—a shock-wave of pure adrenaline.

There—a movement. Swift and furtive, just on the edges of his field of vision. The window curtain, stirring where no breezes blew.

Nikolas was naturally athletic and very quick for a big man. Moving swiftly and soundlessly, like a creature of the night himself, he crossed the room and slipped through the open casement window onto the balcony. In the fast-fading twilight he could see a figure dressed in black standing frozen beside the balcony railing. He heard a sound...saw a hand come up and extend toward him...and before the sound could become speech or the hand activate whatever death-dealing object it may have been holding, he launched himself toward the intruder, going in low, aiming for the knees.

He was a little surprised at how easy it was. There was no resistance at all, in fact, just a soft gasp when he drove his shoulder into a surprisingly slim midsection, then a somewhat louder *"Oof!"* as his momentum carried both him and the intruder to the balcony's plaster floor. With that slender body pinned half under him, Nikolas caught both wrists and jerked them roughly to the small of the intruder's back.

It was over just that quickly—so quickly, in fact, that it took another second or two for Nikolas's senses to catch up with his reactions, and for him to realize first that his would-be assailant carried no weapon, and second that he wasn't a "he" at all.

Wrists that slender, a bottom so nicely rounded and fitting so sweetly against his belly, that elusive scent…those could only belong to a woman.

The revelation didn't induce him to relax his vigilance or ease his grip, however. If there was anything he'd learned from the recent events in his homeland, it was that assassins came in all sizes and both genders. And that no one—*no one*—could be trusted.

"I expected someone with a bit more in the way of fighting skills," he said through gritted teeth, his face half buried in the woman's warm, humid nape. Her warmth, the smell of her hair made his head swim.

That scent…I know it…from somewhere.

"I have skills…you can't even imagine," his prisoner replied in a breathless, constricted voice. "Just didn't think…it'd be smart…to kick a future king…where it'd hurt the most. Not exactly…a brilliant career move, you know? Plus…there's that little matter…of you being required to produce an heir…"

That remark, as well as the fact that the woman's accent was distinctly of the American South, barely registered.

"Who are you? Who sent you? Was it Weston? Carrington? *Who,* damn you?"

"Neither. Well…sort of— Look, if you'll get off me and let me up so I can get to my ID…"

"Not a chance." An ingrained habit of courtesy under similar physical circumstances did induce him to take some of his weight off the woman—a concession he made sure to compensate for by tightening his grip on her wrists. She wasn't showing much inclination to resist, but he wasn't ready to take anything for granted. "I'll get it. Where is it?"

She gave an irritable-sounding snort. "Oh for God's sake. It's in my jacket—inside pocket. Left side. Just don't—"

He was already in the process of shifting both himself and his prisoner onto their sides so he could slip his hand inside her jacket, which was leather and as far as he could tell, fit her like her own skin. It closed with a zipper, which was pulled all the way up, almost to her chin. "Don't…what?" He found the tab and jerked it down, impatient with it and with his own senses for noticing and passing on to him at such an inopportune moment how supple and buttery-soft the leather was, almost indistinguishable from her skin, in fact…and how warm and fragrant her hair…*and what was that damn scent, anyway?*

He thrust his hand inside the jacket opening…and froze.

"Never mind." A rich chuckle—hers—seemed to ripple down the length of his body as his hand closed—entirely of its own volition, he'd swear—over a breast of unanticipated voluptuousness. Furthermore, the only barrier between his hand and that seductive bounty was something silky, lacy and, he felt certain, incredibly thin. A chemise? It seemed to him an unlikely choice of attire for an assassin.

And the nipple nested in his palm was already hardening, nudging the nerve-rich hollow of his hand with each of her quickened breaths in a way that seemed almost playful. As if, he thought, she were deliberately taunting him. Testing his self-control.

A growl of desperation and fury vibrated deep in his throat.

He tried again to shift his weight to give his hand more room to maneuver inside the jacket and only succeeded in bringing her bottom into even closer contact with the part of his own anatomy least subject to his will.

"You're not going to have much luck finding it where you're looking," she remarked, her voice bumpy with what he was sure must be suppressed laughter.

"I'm so glad you're finding this entertaining," he said in his stuffiest, British old-school tone, feeling more sweaty and flustered than he had since his own schoolboy years. "Forgive me if I don't share your amusement… These days I don't consider— *Ah!*" With a sense of profound relief, he withdrew his hand from its enticing prison with a thin leather folder captured triumphantly between two fingers. "Yes—*here* we are."

"How are you going to look at it? It's dark out here." The woman pinned beneath him now seemed as overheated and winded as he, and her body heat was merging with his in steamy intimacy that should have been unwelcome between two strangers—or, he thought, at the very least, unsettling. Exotic. Instead there was that odd familiarity, as if he'd been in this exact same place with this same woman before.

The situation was becoming intolerable. Nikolas levered himself to his feet, hauling his unwelcome visitor with him. "Come on—inside. Now." His natural bent toward gallantry deserted him as he hauled her none too gently through the casement window.

"This really isn't necessary," she panted, and he was grimly pleased to note there was no laughter, suppressed or otherwise, in her voice now. "If I'd wanted to leave we wouldn't be having this conversation."

"Yes, and then the question becomes, why are you here at all, doesn't it?" He quick-marched her across the shadowy room to the light switch beside the front door, and flipped it on, filling the room with the soft light from an art-deco chandelier. "Now then, let's see who… Ah—the Lazlo Group. I say—I'm impressed. And you are—" And he halted, the ID in his hand forgotten…or irrelevant.

That face.

The face he'd half convinced himself must have been a fantasy.

The impossibly beautiful woman who had come from out of nowhere to land—almost literally—in his lap…and had proceeded to make passionate love to him, and then…vanished without a trace.

* * * * *

*Experience the anticipation, the thrill of the
chase and the sheer rush of falling in love!
Turn the page for a sneak preview of
a new book from Harlequin Romance
THE REBEL PRINCE
by Raye Morgan
On sale August 29th
wherever books are sold*

"OH, NO!"

The reaction slipped out before Emma Valentine could stop it, for there stood the very man she most wanted to avoid seeing again.

He didn't look any happier to see her.

"Well, come on, get on board," he said gruffly. "I won't bite." One eyebrow rose. "Though I might nibble a little," he added, mostly to amuse himself.

But she wasn't paying any attention to what he was saying. She was staring at him, taking in the royal blue uniform he was wearing, with gold braid and glistening badges decorating the sleeves, epaulettes and an upright collar. Ribbons and medals covered the breast of the short, fitted jacket. A gold-encrusted sabre hung at his side. And suddenly it was clear to her who this man really was.

She gulped wordlessly. Reaching out, he took her elbow and pulled her aboard. The doors slid closed. And finally she found her tongue.

"You...you're the prince."

He nodded, barely glancing at her. "Yes. Of course."

She raised a hand and covered her mouth for a moment. "I should have known."

"Of course you should have. I don't know why you didn't." He punched the ground-floor button to get the elevator moving again, then turned to look down at her. "A relatively bright five-year-old child would have tumbled to the truth right away."

Her shock faded as her indignation at his tone asserted itself. He might be the prince, but he was still just as annoying as he had been earlier that day.

"A relatively bright five-year-old child without a bump on the head from a badly thrown water polo ball, maybe," she said defensively. She wasn't feeling woozy any longer and she wasn't about to let him bully her, no matter how royal he was. "I was unconscious half the time."

"And just clueless the other half, I guess," he said, looking bemused.

The arrogance of the man was really galling.

"I suppose you think your 'royalness' is so obvious it sort of shimmers around you for all to see?" she challenged. "Or better yet, oozes from your pores like...like sweat on a hot day?"

"Something like that," he acknowledged calmly. "Most people tumble to it pretty quickly. In fact, it's hard to hide even when I want to avoid dealing with it."

"Poor baby," she said, still resenting his manner. "I guess that works better with injured people who are half asleep." Looking at him, she felt a strange emotion she couldn't identify. It was as though she wanted to prove something to him, but she wasn't sure what. "And anyway, you know you did your best to fool me," she added.

His brows knit together as though he really didn't know what she was talking about. "I didn't do a thing."

"You told me your name was Monty."

"It is." He shrugged. "I have a lot of names. Some of them are too rude to be spoken to my face, I'm sure." He glanced at her sideways, his hand on the hilt of his sabre. "Perhaps you're contemplating one of those right now."

You bet I am.

That was what she would like to say. But it suddenly occurred to her that she was supposed to be working for this man. If she wanted to keep the job of coronation chef, maybe she'd better keep her opinions to herself. So she clamped her mouth shut, took a deep breath and looked away, trying hard to calm down.

The elevator ground to a halt and the doors slid open laboriously. She moved to step forward, hoping to make her escape, but his hand shot out again and caught her elbow.

"Wait a minute. *You're* a woman," he said, as though that thought had just presented itself to him.

"That's a rare ability for insight you have there, Your Highness," she snapped before she could stop herself. And then she winced. She was going to have to do better than that if she was going to keep this relationship on an even keel.

But he was ignoring her dig. Nodding, he stared at her with a speculative gleam in his golden eyes. "I've been looking for a woman, but you'll do."

She blanched, stiffening. "I'll do for what?"

He made a head gesture in a direction she knew was opposite of where she was going and his grip tightened on her elbow.

"Come with me," he said abruptly, making it an order.

She dug in her heels, thinking fast. She didn't much like orders. "Wait! I can't. I have to get to the kitchen."

"Not yet. I need you."

"You what?" Her breathless gasp of surprise was soft, but she knew he'd heard it.

"I need you," he said firmly. "Oh, don't look so shocked. I'm not planning to throw you into the hay and have my way with you. I need you for something a bit more mundane than that."

She felt color rushing into her cheeks and she silently

begged it to stop. Here she was, formless and stodgy in her chef's whites. No makeup, no stiletto heels. Hardly the picture of the femmes fatales he was undoubtedly used to. The likelihood that he would have any carnal interest in her was remote at best. To have him think she was hysterically defending her virtue was humiliating.

"Well, what if I don't want to go with you?" she said in hopes of deflecting his attention from her blush.

"Too bad."

"What?"

Amusement sparkled in his eyes. He was certainly enjoying this. And that only made her more determined to resist him.

"I'm the prince, remember? And we're in the castle. My orders take precedence. It's that old pesky divine rights thing."

Her jaw jutted out. Despite her embarrassment, she couldn't let that pass.

"Over my free will? Never!"

Exasperation filled his face.

"Hey, call out the historians. Someone will write a book about you and your courageous principles." His eyes glittered sardonically. "But in the meantime, Emma Valentine, you're coming with me."

* * * * *

SAVE UP TO $30! SIGN UP TODAY!

INSIDE *Romance*

The complete guide to your favorite
Harlequin®, Silhouette® and Love Inspired® books.

✓ Newsletter ABSOLUTELY FREE! No purchase necessary.

✓ Valuable coupons for future purchases of Harlequin,
  Silhouette and Love Inspired books in every issue!

✓ Special excerpts & previews in each issue. Learn about all
  the hottest titles before they arrive in stores.

✓ No hassle—mailed directly to your door!

✓ Comes complete with a handy shopping checklist
  so you won't miss out on any titles.

- -

SIGN ME UP TO RECEIVE INSIDE ROMANCE
ABSOLUTELY FREE

(Please print clearly)

_____

Name

_____

Address

_____

City/Town   State/Province   Zip/Postal Code

(098 KKM EJL9)

Please mail this form to:
In the U.S.A.: Inside Romance, P.O. Box 9057, Buffalo, NY 14269-9057
In Canada: Inside Romance, P.O. Box 622, Fort Erie, ON L2A 5X3
OR visit http://www.eHarlequin.com/insideromance

IRNBPA06R   ® and ™ are trademarks owned and used by the trademark owner and/or its licensee.

Silhouette Desire

**Introducing an exciting appearance
by legendary
New York Times bestselling author**

DIANA PALMER
HEARTBREAKER

He's the ultimate bachelor...
but he may have just met
the one woman to change his ways!

Join the drama in the story of a confirmed
bachelor, an amnesiac beauty and their
unexpected passionate romance.

"Diana Palmer is a mesmerizing storyteller
who captures the essence of what
a romance should be."—*Affaire de Coeur*

**Heartbreaker *is available from Silhouette Desire
in September 2006.***

Visit Silhouette Books at www.eHarlequin.com   SDDPIBC

HARLEQUIN® *Blaze*

"Super-steamy!"
—*Cosmopolitan* magazine

New York Times bestselling author
Elizabeth Bevarly
delivers another sexy adventure!

As a former vice cop, small-town police chief
Sam Maguire knows when things don't add up.
And there's definitely something suspicious happen-
ing behind the scenes at Rosie Bliss's flower shop.
Rumor has it she's not selling just flowers.
But once he gets close and gets his hands on her,
uh, goods, he's in big trouble…of the sensual kind!

Pick up your copy of
MY ONLY VICE
by Elizabeth Bevarly

*Available this September,
wherever series romances are sold.*

www.eHarlequin.com

HBEB0906

If you enjoyed what you just read,
then we've got an offer you can't resist!

Take 2 bestselling love stories FREE!

Plus get a FREE surprise gift!

Clip this page and mail it to Silhouette Reader Service™

IN U.S.A.	IN CANADA
3010 Walden Ave.	P.O. Box 609
P.O. Box 1867	Fort Erie, Ontario
Buffalo, N.Y. 14240-1867	L2A 5X3

YES! Please send me 2 free Silhouette Intimate Moments® novels and my free surprise gift. After receiving them, if I don't wish to receive anymore, I can return the shipping statement marked cancel. If I don't cancel, I will receive 6 brand-new novels every month, before they're available in stores! In the U.S.A., bill me at the bargain price of $4.24 plus 25¢ shipping and handling per book and applicable sales tax, if any*. In Canada, bill me at the bargain price of $4.99 plus 25¢ shipping and handling per book and applicable taxes**. That's the complete price and a savings of at least 10% off the cover prices—what a great deal! I understand that accepting the 2 free books and gift places me under no obligation ever to buy any books. I can always return a shipment and cancel at any time. Even if I never buy another book from Silhouette, the 2 free books and gift are mine to keep forever.

245 SDN DZ9A
345 SDN DZ9C

Name _____ (PLEASE PRINT)

Address _____ Apt.# _____

City _____ State/Prov. _____ Zip/Postal Code _____

Not valid to current Silhouette Intimate Moments® subscribers.

Want to try two free books from another series?
Call 1-800-873-8635 or visit www.morefreebooks.com.

 * Terms and prices subject to change without notice. Sales tax applicable in N.Y.
** Canadian residents will be charged applicable provincial taxes and GST.
   All orders subject to approval. Offer limited to one per household].
   ® are registered trademarks owned and used by the trademark owner and or its licensee.

INMOM04R   ©2004 Harlequin Enterprises Limited

HARLEQUIN® *Romance*®

The family saga continues…

The Brides of Bella Lucia

THE REBEL PRINCE by Raye Morgan

Just an ordinary girl and…a jet-setting playboy of a prince who is about to be crowned king!

Prince Sebastian has one last act of rebellion in store, and it involves giving chef Emma Valentine a brand-new title!

ON SALE SEPTEMBER 2006.

From the Heart. For the Heart.

www.eHarlequin.com

HRIBC0806BW

HARLEQUIN®

Super Romance

ANGELS OF THE BIG SKY
by Roz Denny Fox

(#1368)

Widow Marlee Stein returns to Montana with her
young daughter, ready to help out with Cloud Chasers,
the flying service owned by her brother. When Marlee
takes over piloting duties, she finds herself in conflict
with a client, ranger Wylie Ames. Too bad Marlee's
attracted to a man she doesn't even want to like!

On sale September 2006!

THE CLOUD CHASERS—
Life is looking up.

Watch for the second story in Roz Denny Fox's two-
book series THE CLOUD CHASERS, available in
December 2006.

*Available wherever books are sold, including most
bookstores, supermarkets, discount stores and drugstores.*

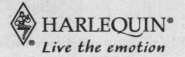

HARLEQUIN®
Live the emotion

www.eHarlequin.com   HSRTCC0906